KIM FIELDING

STAGED

BELONGING 'VERSE

ANGLERFISH
PRESS

Anglerfish Press
PO Box 1537
Burnsville, NC 28714
www.AnglerFishPress.com
Anglerfish Press is an imprint of Riptide Publishing.
www.RiptidePublishing.com

Staged

Cover art: Tami Santarossa, lillilolita.deviantart.com
Editor: Rachel Haimowitz
Layout: L.C. Chase, lcchase.com/design.htm

ISBN: 978-1-62649-466-4

First edition
July, 2016

Also available in ebook:
ISBN: 978-1-62649-465-7

KIM
FIELDING

STAGED

BELONGING

'VERSE

ANGLERFISH
PRESS

CHAPTER ONE

As the clapping ended, Sky smiled at the meager audience and tried to ignore the stone-faced man at the table in front of the stage. "Thank you, ladies and gentlemen. We're going to take a quick break, and then we'll be back with more." Sky turned and ducked behind the curtains to join the members of the band, who were already sprawled in the ratty backstage chairs, scarfing leftovers from the kitchen.

"Here," said his handler, putting a towel in one hand and a mug in the other.

Sky blotted his face—careful not to smear his makeup—and gave the towel back, then sniffed the steaming mug. "Thanks, Bill." It was a special concoction Bill brewed just for him: hot tea with lemon, honey, and ginger. It wouldn't heal the damage inflicted by too many hours of singing, but it would help soothe Sky's sore vocal cords.

He took a careful sip, then turned to the guitar player, who was sitting close to him. "That was a good set," Sky said.

The guitarist shrugged and stuffed half a dinner roll into his mouth.

Sky didn't know the band well. The club manager had leased them only a week earlier in what Sky assumed was an attempt to save money. This group was less skilled than the last band, and smaller—just a guitar player, a keyboardist, and a drummer. But Sky preferred to get on their good side, because if they wanted to, a band could make the singer look really bad. These guys weren't easily warming up to him, though.

"Is there anything you'd really like to play?" Sky asked. "Something different from what we did last night, maybe?"

The guitarist shook his head. "We'll do whatever we're supposed to."

Sky wanted to say that their musicianship would never progress beyond mediocre if they didn't find some passion in their work, but what was the point? They were slaves, just like him. They played whatever their owners told them to. This particular gig had benefits, though—decent food, a reasonably comfortable dorm, and a handler who was willing to learn his charges' needs and cater to them as much as possible. Sky hoped those advantages would encourage this band to at least try to perform decently.

"Five more minutes," Bill said. The band mumbled, "Thank you, five," as Sky drained the mug. Bill took it from him, then ran a hand through his thinning hair and grimaced, looking as unhappy as he had all evening. "Ms. Avery wants you to report to her office after this set."

Dread weighted Sky's stomach, making him glad he'd eaten a light dinner. "I'm doing my best. If I could sing one fewer set each day—maybe for just a week—my voice would recover, and—"

"I don't think she intends to punish you."

That assurance should have calmed Sky, but Bill's frown made him feel ill. "Then what does she want?"

Bill just shook his head before walking over to say something to the drummer.

Sky took a few deep breaths and tried another smile at the guitarist. "If you could do a couple long solos, I'd really appreciate it." He tapped his throat. "Give me a little break?"

The guitarist seemed to consider this for a moment, then gave a curt nod.

For a few minutes, Sky leaned back against a thick support beam and closed his eyes. He tried not think of why Ms. Avery might be angry with him. He'd given good shows tonight, belting out the tunes even when his throat was raw, swiveling his hips and shaking his ass, flirting with the microphone as if it were a lover. Yeah, the place was half-empty tonight—as it had been for months—but that wasn't his fault. Club Paradiso was passé. The menu was tired, the décor years out-of-date, and the entire concept out of vogue. People didn't want live music with their dinners anymore; they wanted to get drunk and dance under flashing lights to music that was all rhythm and no melody.

"It's time," Bill said with a gentle nudge to Sky's arm.

The crowd had further thinned during the break. But even through the glare of the stage lights, Sky saw that the man at the front center table remained. Middle-aged, dressed in a suit, expressionless. He was alone, which was odd enough, but he also hadn't eaten anything. Instead he'd sipped his beer so slowly that, after nearly two hours, the glass still wasn't empty. Throughout the previous sets, his gaze had never once left Sky.

As Sky reached for the mic, a realization turned his spine to ice. *That's why Ms. Avery wants me.* The management didn't rent him out often because too little rest made his performance suffer. But business had been so bad that maybe they needed the money more than a good show. Besides, tomorrow was Sunday and the club was closed.

Sky pasted on a fake smile and tried to keep his voice from shaking. "And we're back, ladies and gentleman. I hope you're still in the mood to rock!" He turned his head and nodded at the band, which began a familiar tune. Good. "Hotel California." Everyone liked that one, plus it had a nice long guitar solo.

He closed his eyes. *Pull yourself together!* He wasn't sure which was worse: anger that his one day to rest would now be ruined, or fear over what that man would do to him. People who rented him for the night weren't supposed to damage him—most folks didn't think it was worth the penalty fees—but they could still inflict a lot of temporary pain. The kind that didn't leave marks. Sky had a feeling this man, with his cold stare, knew a lot of ways to do that.

His cue came, and Sky began to sing.

Usually Sky had to help the servers clean up after the club closed. He didn't mind. Although he was always exhausted by then, at least that task didn't require him to use his voice. And despite the servers being free men and women, they treated him as if he were one of them, joking and good-naturedly complaining with him.

Tonight, though, Bill collected him as soon as the front doors were locked. The band retired immediately to the crowded dorm, where they'd soon be joined by the two members of the kitchen staff who, aside from Sky, were the only slaves the club owned. They would shower, chat for a while, and maybe even sneak a few handjobs once the lights were out. But Sky had to report to Ms. Avery.

"Bill, that man—" Sky whispered as they trudged to the office. His throat felt as if it were lined with barbed wire.

"C'mon, Sky. You know it's no use arguing."

"I'm not arguing. I'm . . ." Sky swallowed. "I'm scared."

Bill stopped and grasped Sky's arm. He looked pale, the lines on his face deeper than usual. "I'm sorry about this. It wasn't my idea; I need you to know that. I tried to talk them out of it."

Sky just looked at him. Bill was a good guy, but Sky couldn't feel pity for him. Not when Bill got to go home to his apartment and his girlfriend and his day off. Not when Bill had the power to say *no* when he didn't want to do something.

Bill's expression hardened. "The club's failing. You know that. We need a total remodel, a whole new concept . . . and that costs money. Aside from the building itself, you're the club's only real asset. You may not like it, but you're a slave."

As if Sky needed to be reminded of that.

The door to Ms. Avery's office was closed. Bill knocked once before opening it. He gestured Sky inside first, perhaps afraid that otherwise he would run. Jaw clenched, Sky entered.

Ms. Avery was sitting on the edge of her desk with her legs crossed. Maybe someone else in that pose would have looked casual and relaxed, but Ms. Avery *never* looked casual or relaxed. Sometimes Sky was surprised she could move without cracking.

The man in the suit was sitting on one of the plush chairs opposite Ms. Avery's desk, holding a coffee cup. He'd turned to look as soon as Sky came in, and now he continued the same blank-faced stare he'd been giving Sky all evening.

Ms. Avery glanced at Bill and waved him back against the wall, leaving Sky alone in the center of the room. He smelled his own sweat, sour and acrid.

"Strip," Ms. Avery said.

Sky's hands shook as he undid the buttons of his paisley silk shirt. Nobody moved to take the shirt from him, and he knew Ms. Avery would be angry if he put it on one of her nice upholstered chairs, so he simply let it drop to the floor. He unzipped his tall black boots and pulled them off, grateful he didn't lose his balance in the process, then peeled off his socks. Finally, he unfastened his fly and worked his way out of the skintight faux-leather pants. Once finished, he stood with his hands at his sides and his head bowed, wearing nothing but the shiny steel slave bracelets welded around his wrists.

For a long moment, nobody moved or spoke. Sky kept his gaze fixed on the wood floor. It needed refinishing. Finally he heard the quiet thud of a mug being placed on a hard surface, and the man stood and approached him. His shoes were well polished.

The man grasped Sky's chin and lifted his head. This close, Sky smelled the beer and coffee on his breath, along with a woodsy tang of cologne or aftershave. The man was probably in his late forties and, although still muscular, had developed a paunch that his suit didn't quite hide. He towered over Sky's rather average height, and he would have been almost handsome if his brown eyes held any kindness or humanity. With one broad thumb, he lifted each of Sky's eyelids in turn. Then he let go of Sky's chin. "Open," he barked.

Sky had to force himself to unlock his jaw, and then not to bite down when the man inspected the inside of his mouth.

After that, the man ran his palms down Sky's arms, squeezing now and then to feel the muscles. He did the same across Sky's chest and belly, grunting at the sparse blond hairs that grew there—Sky couldn't tell whether the man approved or not. It came as no surprise when the man grabbed Sky's dick and gave it a few hard tugs, then squeezed his balls almost hard enough to make him yelp. It took all of Sky's willpower not to pull away, but he couldn't stop his hands from balling into fists. When the man finally let go, a burst of air escaped Sky's lungs.

"Turn around," the man ordered.

Sky obeyed. That left him facing Bill while the man prodded Sky's shoulders, back, and ass cheeks. Bill leaned against the wall with his arms crossed, the corners of his mouth turned down, and did not meet Sky's gaze.

The men and women who rented Sky didn't normally examine him like this, although some spent their time admiring him once they had him in private. They'd already seen enough of him on stage to decide he was worth fucking. But this man was thorough, poking his thighs and digging hard fingers into his hips.

"Bend over and spread."

Sky's face flushed with heat and his eyes prickled, but he spread his legs, folded at the waist, and pulled his ass cheeks apart. The man touched a finger to Sky's clenched hole without, thank heavens, pushing inside, and then gave Sky's flank a stinging slap. "All right."

Sky assumed that meant he could stand upright again. He stared at a framed photo hanging to the left of Bill: a bunch of people in 1980s clothes, grinning during Club Paradiso's grand opening. It would be easier, Sky thought, if what people said about the slave gene were true, if he really didn't feel things like freemen did. He tried to imagine himself as an animated piece of furniture with nothing but emptiness where a man's soul ought to be. It didn't help.

"Well?" Ms. Avery asked, her voice especially tight.

"He'll do."

"He's worth—"

"I *know* how much he's worth, Gwendolyn."

Gwendolyn? It had somehow never occurred to Sky that Ms. Avery had a first name. He was certain she'd never been a child, either, but had instead burst forth—fully grown and wearing heels that clacked on the hard floors—from Club Paradiso itself. It had also never occurred to him that someone could interrupt her, especially in that tone of voice, and survive the experience. Not even the free employees of the club would dare such a thing.

But behind him, Sky heard her sigh. "Fine. Here's the paperwork."

A pen scratched.

Then the man stepped close, settled a hand in the center of Sky's back, and shoved him toward the door. "Let's go."

Sky stumbled a bit, then regained his balance. His heart hammered, and he felt light-headed. "Please," he begged Bill.

Bill pursed his mouth and shook his head. "I'm sorry," he said quietly before looking away.

The man grabbed Sky's arm in an iron grip and jerked him. "I said, let's go," he growled.

"M-my clothes, sir."

"Don't need 'em."

Sky tried to keep his dignity as he was dragged naked through the club and past the gawking servers, but it was a lost cause. Ms. Avery unlocked the door to let them out, and the chilly early-autumn air wasn't the only reason Sky began to shiver. At least at this very early morning hour, nobody was on the sidewalk to see him. Nobody except the driver of the dark van idling at the curb. The man from the club opened the van's rear doors and let go of Sky's arm, only to swat the back of his head. "Get in."

Sky scrambled inside. The back of the van was bare—no carpet or seats, no windows, nothing but a metal wall between the cargo area and the cab. After the man slammed the doors closed and locked them with a noisy clunk, Sky was left alone in complete darkness. The van smelled of bleach and, more faintly, urine and vomit.

The van accelerated abruptly, bouncing Sky against the rear doors. Disoriented, terrified, and cold, he curled into a ball on his side and pressed back into a corner.

He didn't know how long the trip lasted. It seemed like forever, but maybe that was because nerves and the rough ride made him nauseated. He thought of his narrow cot in the dorm, the sounds of snoring slaves and the guard's quiet radio, the promise of Sunday—the one day a week when he could relax. Small pleasures, but those were the only kind a slave could have.

Eventually the van stopped and the engine shut down. After a brief pause, the lock clunked and the doors squealed open. Sky carefully unwound himself and peered out, but all he could discern was the silhouette of the man who'd rented him. "Come on," the man said, sounding weary and impatient.

Sky climbed out of the van and looked around. They were in a large parking lot, dimly lit with a few overhead lights and empty except for a half-dozen vans and a small assortment of cars and SUVs. At the opposite end of the lot, a large building hulked in the darkness, looking a lot like a warehouse.

"Wh-what?" The man wasn't just bringing Sky to his apartment for a quick fuck; he clearly had something grander in mind.

The man grunted loudly and grabbed Sky's arm. "Come *on*, slave."

In his fear, Sky did the unthinkable: he disobeyed. Instead of docilely following along, he wrenched his arm free and pressed himself back against the van. "No, no, please . . ."

The man swore, pulled something from inside his suit jacket, and pressed it to Sky's hip. Sky realized what it was, but not in enough time to jerk away. The electric shock ran through his body like a flame, making him yelp and fall sideways onto the concrete. The man swore again. Then he tucked the prod away and hauled Sky upright. "Next time it's your balls. They might have indulged your spoiled diva shit at that lousy club, but that ends now."

With the man's grip on his arm hard enough to bruise, Sky staggered across the parking lot. Loose bits of gravel dug painfully into his feet, and he was having a difficult time breathing.

But true panic didn't come until the man opened the warehouse door and shoved Sky hard enough to send him to his knees. When he looked up, he saw the chains hanging from the walls and ceiling, the rows of iron cages. That was when he understood that the man hadn't just rented him for the night.

The man had bought him.

CHAPTER TWO

The doctor removed his gloved finger from Sky's ass and nodded at Mr. Burgess. "Anal sphincter has good tone, and there are no problems with the prostate."

Sky remained bent over the metal table. After three days in the warehouse, he had emphatically learned that slaves were to obey instantly and precisely, and that Mr. Burgess and employees did not approve of slaves who took action of their own accord. The metal was cold against Sky's chest, but then, he hadn't been truly warm since Mr. Burgess had dragged him out of Club Paradiso. He hadn't left the main room of the warehouse, either, not even for this exam, which was taking place in a well-lit corner not far from the rows of cages.

Mr. Burgess looked grudgingly pleased. "So no problems, then."

The doctor peeled off the glove and tossed it into a trash can. "He's healthy. A little on the thin side, and I wouldn't recommend him for strong physical labor. But most of your clients aren't looking for that anyway."

"No, I'm hoping he'll go to a high bidder. He better, considering what I paid for him."

As Sky watched, the doctor took a clipboard from Mr. Burgess, pulled a pen from his shirt pocket, and signed. "There," the doctor said, handing the clipboard back. "You've got your health certificate. Now let me see the one with the limp."

Mr. Burgess gestured to one of the hulking guards, who stomped forward, pulled Sky up by the hair, and shoved a wad of fabric against Sky's chest. "Put it on."

So they weren't even going to allow him to wipe the sticky lube from his ass. Biting his lip to keep from complaining, Sky pulled on the tunic. It was all he'd been given to wear since he'd arrived, and it hung only to midthigh. He showed his ass every time he bent over, and he flashed his junk if he didn't sit and lie with his legs together. The coarse fabric was scratchy and the color of mud, but it did insulate him a bit from the chill.

The guard didn't need to tell Sky where to go—the man just settled one hand on the shock prod at his waist and gestured with his other toward the cages. Sky walked back to his little cell, entered obediently, and flinched when the guard slammed the heavy door closed.

As far as Sky could tell, all of the cells were identical: about eight feet square, with heavy iron bars on four sides and overhead, and a smooth concrete floor. A thin rubber mat served as a mattress, and there was no bedding. Each cage had a toilet with a sink built into the top. No privacy, and the fluorescent lights hanging from the high ceiling were never all turned off at once. Sounds echoed: the heavy tread of the guards' boots, the tinny speakers of the television in the corner where the guards took their breaks, the muffled sobs of his fellow slaves. Sky had cried too, off and on for the first day, but now the tears were gone and he felt desiccated inside.

The constant fear was terrible, as was the raging uncertainty about his future. But the boredom and loneliness were bad too. At the club, he'd been able to talk to the band, the servers, even to Bill. Here, guards advanced with their shock sticks drawn if slaves so much as whispered to each other. Besides, the cages nearest Sky were empty; in fact, only about one-tenth of the many cages were occupied.

Sky sat on the mat with his knees drawn up and his back propped by the corner of the cage. He wished he knew how to pray. Everyone said God wouldn't listen to slaves since they had no souls, but maybe he'd take pity on one nonetheless. The problem was that even if Sky had known the words, he didn't know what to pray for. A kind master? Experience had taught him that no such thing existed. The best a slave could hope for was an owner who was consistent and . . . indifferent, like Ms. Avery and the rest of the club management. They had cared very little about Sky as long as he sang well, brought in paying customers, and didn't cause problems. They'd never gone out of their way to harm him.

He missed music. During the second day in the warehouse, he'd tried humming one of his favorite songs, but a guard had thundered over and told him to shut the fuck up. Now Sky closed his eyes and wished himself gone.

An hour or two later—he'd dozed and wasn't sure how much time had passed—he heard the clatter of a wheeled cart. His stomach growled, and he stood and paced impatiently. Unless you counted the doctor's rectal exam and the guards demanding blowjobs, mealtime was the only interesting event in the warehouse.

It took a long time for the slave with the cart to get to him. She was a permanent worker there, Sky guessed, and not intended for sale, probably because she was too old to fetch a decent price. While most of the slaves in cages were white or at least very light-skinned blacks, this woman's skin was a deep reddish-brown. As always, she wore loose gray sweats. She didn't say anything when she unlocked a hatch on Sky's cage, opened a little swinging door, and passed his tray through the opening. But she smiled warmly, which was nice. Sky smiled back.

The three daily meals were all the same: a bowl of lukewarm mush, a slab of something that looked like gray foam and tasted like wet wool, a pile of soggy unidentifiable vegetables, and a piece of fruit. At least the fruit varied slightly. Usually it was a small apple, but this time it was orange segments. Sky had little appetite, but the guards punished him if he didn't eat. Besides, it gave him something to do. So he sat back on his mat and nibbled at the food.

After he finished, he stood and walked to the toilet-sink fixture, carrying the empty bowl from the mush. Although it was possible to drink directly from the sink faucet, he always managed to splash cold water down his neck and chest. So before the tray and bowl were taken away, he rinsed the last of the mush from the bowl, filled it with water, and drank.

The woman returned soon after and collected the items with another warm smile. He sat back on his mat and wondered whether she had ever had children, and if so, if they'd been allowed to stay with her for a time.

Sky had been eight when he'd been sold away from the brothel that owned his mother. A man had walked in one evening, and instead of inspecting the men and women he could rent by the hour, he'd called for Sky, who was carrying drinks to customers waiting in the lounge. Sky had been terrified. Not long before then, his mother, grim-faced, had explained to him that soon customers would want to use him the same way they used the brothel's other slaves. She had described ways to please men and women and warned him that what the customers did to him would often hurt—but that he must submit anyway.

When Sky, fighting back tears, approached the man, he'd been surprised that the man only examined his face and then ordered him to sing. After listening to three songs, the man nodded and left to speak with the brothel owner. Twenty minutes later, Sky had a new master. He did not get to say good-bye to his mother, and he never saw her again. If he cried when he was supposed to be practicing, his new master beat him, so Sky soon forced himself to stop thinking about her.

Now, though, as he watched the woman slowly pushing her cart away, he wondered if his mother was still alive and where she might be. Did she ever think of him, or had she hardened her heart against loss, the way slaves had to do? Maybe she was a *good* slave, and losing Sky had the same effect on her as a stone tossed into a pond—a few small ripples, then nothing.

"—wait two more weeks, we'll be holding an auction, and our stock won't be nearly as bare. We'll have the slaves cleaned up much better, and you'll find the auction house much more comfortable than the warehouse."

Sky awoke from a light doze to the strange sound of Mr. Burgess attempting to be ingratiating. But the man accompanying Mr. Burgess didn't seem impressed. "I don't want to wait two weeks. Either you have what I need, or I'll go elsewhere. You're not the only slave trader in New York."

"No, no, Mr. Wallace. I'm sure we have *something* that will meet your needs."

Mr. Wallace was the most interesting thing Sky had seen in days, a distraction from the daily drudgery but also a potential cause for concern. He was as tall as Mr. Burgess and equally broad in the shoulders, but unlike Sky's master, Mr. Wallace's muscular physique included a trim stomach. He was dressed casually in jeans, a formfitting black T-shirt, and a leather jacket, but Sky was willing to bet that those jeans cost more than a night with a pretty slave. Mr. Wallace was in his midthirties, had an expensive haircut and artful stubble, and was maybe just slightly too strong-featured to be truly handsome, with a nose that curved slightly to one side. He walked with the confidence of a man used to getting his way, but Sky couldn't tell if cruelty accompanied that self-confidence.

Mr. Burgess led him to a cage in the same row as Sky's, but closer to the front of the warehouse. The slave inside the cage—a boy in his late teens—stared at the freemen's chins with wide eyes. "Stand up," Mr. Burgess barked at the slave. "Let him see you."

The boy stood, and even down the long row, Sky saw his legs shaking. But the boy gathered the hem of his tunic and lifted it to his neck, baring himself for inspection.

"See?" Mr. Burgess said, gesturing. "Very pretty. And still young enough that if you castrate him—"

The boy whimpered, and Mr. Wallace shook his head. "I don't want a child, and I do *not* want a eunuch. I told you. I want a man."

Frowning, Mr. Burgess waved at the boy, who lowered his tunic and collapsed into the corner of his cage with a sob. Ordinarily, the boy might have been beaten for crying, but Mr. Burgess was already walking away, piloting Mr. Wallace to a cage several rows over. Sky couldn't see that slave, but he heard the disapproval of the slave's delicacy. Mr. Wallace didn't like the next one because *that* slave wasn't handsome enough, and by the time he rejected a fourth slave—again too young—it sounded as if Mr. Burgess's forced good humor was failing.

Sky indulged in a secret smile at his owner's discomposure—until both men stopped in front of his cage. Although he was filled with dread, Sky stood without being told and rucked up his tunic. He supposed this master would be as good—or bad—as any, and at least knowing his fate was better than sitting in the warehouse with nothing to do but worry.

Mr. Wallace looked Sky up and down, and when he didn't immediately object, Mr. Burgess appeared heartened. "He needs some scrubbing up for you to see his potential, but this one's very attractive. And he's certainly not a child. He's thirty-two, but looks younger."

"Is he trained as a companion?" Mr. Wallace's voice was a little rougher than his carefully polished looks would suggest.

"No, none of the in-stock males are. But his previous owners rented him out, so he's experienced enough."

Sky kept his jaw firm, his raised hands steady, and his gaze fixed on Mr. Wallace's chest. Mr. Burgess was right about him not looking his best. He hadn't been allowed to bathe thoroughly since he'd arrived at the warehouse; the guards had hosed him down perfunctorily, so he was dirty, his shoulder-length hair falling in lank, greasy tangles.

"What *is* he trained in?" Mr. Wallace asked.

"Singing. He came in second on *My Slave's Got Talent*." Mr. Burgess didn't mention that had been over ten years ago.

Mr. Wallace snorted. "I don't watch that show."

"He was also in a musical group that had a few hits. Uh, 2Nyte. One of those boy bands."

"Never heard of them." Mr. Wallace paused for a moment, then asked, "Were you any good?"

Surprised to be addressed directly, Sky glanced up at his face, then quickly down again. "We were okay, sir. We looked better than we sounded."

For some reason, that answer made Mr. Wallace bark a laugh. "And what have you been doing since your boy-band days?"

"I sang at Club Paradiso, sir." Actually, there had been another club before that—glitzier by far—as well as some chorus work in a few shows. But Sky didn't think Mr. Wallace would care about that much detail.

For a minute or two, Mr. Wallace seemed to be considering. Then Mr. Burgess stepped closer to him. "If you'd like to inspect him more closely, we have a private room. I'll have him cleaned better first." He leered, making his meaning clear, and Sky tried not to shudder.

But Mr. Wallace shook his head. "Not necessary. Let's go talk terms." He marched away with Mr. Burgess practically skipping beside him.

Sky took a few shaky breaths and let the hem of his tunic fall. Then he waited.

It wasn't Mr. Burgess or Mr. Wallace who arrived next, but two of the guards. One of them unlocked Sky's cage, and they led him silently to a dark area in the far corner of the warehouse. One of the guards flipped on a light, and Sky nearly balked when he saw what waited for him: a waist-high bench mounted with wooden stocks to immobilize his arms. But he didn't put up a fight when one of the guards lifted the hinged top of the stocks, pushed Sky forward, and placed his arms in the openings before slamming the top closed. "Stay put," the guard growled.

It wasn't painful, actually. The guards slipped protective cuffs between Sky's steel bracelets and his wrists, then used a whirring rotary blade to cut the bracelets off. Sky winced at the flying sparks. For a minute or two, he wore no bracelets, just like a freeman. It sent shivers up his spine, even though he knew he was still, and always, a slave. Even if he magically broke free that very moment and somehow managed to run away, he'd be tracked down quickly via the GPS chip embedded in his collarbone.

In any case, he didn't remain without bracelets for long. His eyes widened when he saw the new ones—instead of steel, these were braided silver with gold accents. They looked more like nice jewelry than the marks of slavery. Sky watched as one of the guards welded them onto his wrists.

Once Sky was freed from the bench, the guards took him to the front door. They were both scowling as if they disapproved, maybe because his new bracelets would have cost them a week's salary. One of them shoved Sky hard enough to make him fall. Both guards laughed as he scrambled to his feet.

They waited near the door for about five minutes before Mr. Wallace and Mr. Burgess emerged from the nearby office. Mr. Wallace looked at Sky and nodded when he saw the new bracelets.

"Want us to hose him down?" Mr. Burgess asked.

Mr. Wallace frowned. "No. I'll give him a good scrub later. Where's his stuff?"

Mr. Burgess looked amused. "He's a slave. He doesn't have any stuff."

"Not even any— Never mind." Mr. Wallace jerked his head toward the door. "C'mon." He didn't pause to shake Mr. Burgess's hand or even to make sure Sky was following. Which of course Sky was.

Due to the constant artificial light and lack of windows in the warehouse, Sky hadn't known what time of day it was. When he stepped outside, the sun proved it was close to noon. The vast parking lot was still nearly empty, but a sleek limo idled not far away; Sky was grateful he didn't have to walk far in bare feet. The driver was a tall black slave who held the door open for Mr. Wallace but sent a slight scowl in Sky's direction. Sky didn't blame him—he was bound to get the car upholstery dirty.

In the back of the limo, Sky scrunched against the door, his hands knotted in his lap. It was nice and warm inside, but he wrinkled his nose at his own stink. Mr. Wallace waited for the limo to pull out of the lot, then leaned forward to open a drink cabinet. He poured himself a shot of whiskey, downed it quickly, then poured another. He closed the cabinet and sat back with a sigh. "What's your name, anyway?"

"Sky, sir. Uh, Master." He'd have to be careful about that—it had been a long time since he'd answered directly to his owner.

"What kind of name is that?"

"The one my owner gave me, Master. My stage name was Sky Blue." It hadn't been his original name, although sometimes he forgot that. The owner of the brothel—his first owner—had called him Thursday because that was the day he was born. It was his second owner who came up with Sky Blue.

"I guess we'll just go with Sky, then," said Mr. Wallace. "I'm *not* calling you Blue."

"Yes, Master."

The conversation died after that. Master took out his phone and appeared to be surfing the internet or reading his email. Sky looked out the window as they rolled through the city. No one could see him through the tinted windows, which was slightly comforting.

Sky didn't know the city well, and it wasn't until they passed through a tunnel that he realized the warehouse was in Queens. Now they were heading into Manhattan. Like a tourist, Sky gawked at the Empire State Building—he'd heard that several hundred slaves had died during construction—and then at the Chrysler Building, which he thought was more elegant. The limo stopped in front of Hotel 234, a tall and narrow building of decorative brick next to an ugly glass-and-steel skyscraper.

A uniformed man opened the door for Master and did a double-take when he caught sight of Sky. Of course, Master didn't have to explain his slave to this man, whose own polished steel bracelets peeked out from beneath the cuffs of his fancy jacket. "Welcome back, sir," the doorman said.

Master climbed out, then gestured for Sky to follow. They were in a small portico, but passersby gawked at Sky nonetheless. "Have housekeeping bring extra towels," Master said to the doorman.

"Of course, sir. Right away."

The small lobby gleamed with marble and polished wood. Master ignored the greeting from the woman behind the reception desk and marched straight to the bank of elevators. Their car arrived as soon as he pushed the button; inside, he swiped a card before pushing the button for the top floor. He texted as they quickly ascended.

Sky was somewhat surprised by Master's room, which wasn't as grand as some of the fancy suites he'd seen while rented out. It was a fairly spacious room with a king-sized bed, a tall bureau, a large desk with a wheeled chair, and a lounge area with a couch and comfy chairs. The big windows offered nice views, and the cream-colored carpet felt plush under his bare feet.

Master pointed at a closed door. "Take a shower or bath or whatever it's going to take to get clean. I need to— Shit. What size do you wear?" He seemed to measure Sky with his eyes. "My stuff won't fit you." When Sky blinked at him in confusion, Master sighed. "I'll just get you some sweats or something. Buy you something better when we hit the West Coast."

Sky's jaw dropped. The West Coast? But then Master frowned, and Sky hurried into the bathroom. He wasn't sure what to do about the door—was he to leave it open or closed?—but Master answered that by slamming it shut.

Alone in the bathroom, Sky looked around. It wasn't huge, but it was much nicer than what he'd shared in the dorm at Club Paradiso, and of course it was a far cry from the sink/toilet combination he'd endured at the warehouse. He winced when he caught sight of himself in the mirror. After a moment's consideration, he decided that the best course of action would be a quick shower to wash away the surface grime, followed by a soak in the tub to get rid of the rest. Besides, he very rarely had access to a bathtub, and immersing himself in warm water sounded like a precious treat.

The shower felt wonderful—infinitely better than the lukewarm trickle from the tap at the club dorm. But as soon as he became accustomed to the hot spray, he faced a dilemma. Was he supposed to use the cake of soap and the little bottles of shampoo and conditioner that the hotel provided? There was nothing else to use, and he doubted water alone would do the trick. But they were Master's. Sky weighed the likelihood of being punished for using them versus being punished for not getting completely clean, and decided to risk their use. Master could always ask housekeeping for more. Besides, if Master was in the mood to punish a slave, he was going to do so regardless of what Sky did.

Relieved at reaching a decision, Sky opened the shampoo.

Master didn't come into the bathroom even after Sky had soaked long enough for his skin to wrinkle and the water to cool. The bath felt so decadently wonderful that he was tempted to refill it with hot water, but that might try Master's patience. With a sigh, Sky used a soapy finger to clean around and slightly inside his anus. Then he rinsed, pulled the plug, and stepped out of the tub. The towels were thick and oversized, but he wasn't brave enough to use one of the plush hotel robes.

Sky looked in the mirror again. He needed to shave and to brush his hair and teeth, but he was much improved over the pathetic creature Master had dragged from the warehouse.

After picking up his tunic, Sky timidly opened the bathroom door and discovered that the main room was empty. He couldn't remember ever having been left alone like this.

Run! said a voice in his head. A very stupid voice, because where would he go, naked except for his new bracelets? He'd be caught at once, even without the chip.

But he didn't know what to do with himself—Master hadn't given him any orders—so he spent a long time standing near the bathroom doorway. Eventually he built up enough nerve to walk to a window and look out. Unwilling to cover his clean body in dirty fabric, he kept the tunic wadded in his hand.

He didn't know how much time had passed before the door to the hallway clicked open, making him jump. Master entered with several shopping bags in hand. He frowned at Sky but didn't chastise him for gazing outside. "Here," Master said as he marched over. He thrust one of the bags at Sky. "Razor and stuff."

"Thank you, Master."

They both stood there until Master huffed. "Go *use* them. And throw that filthy rag away."

"Yes, Master." Sky hurried into the bathroom, nerves jangling as Master watched him brush his hair and teeth.

When Sky started to drag the disposable razor over his cheek, Master spoke up. "Don't bother shaving anything but your face. I'll get you waxed later."

Successfully avoiding a wince, Sky said, "Yes, Master." When he'd been in 2Nyte, the company that owned the band insisted on regular waxing for all the members. Hairless bodies looked better on stage and in photos, apparently.

After Sky finished grooming, Master continued to stare at him. Sky tried not to fidget, but he didn't know how to be obedient when he hadn't yet been told what to do. He was relieved when Master nodded. "All right. You could stand to gain a couple of pounds and some muscle. We'll work on that later too. What kind of exercises do you usually do?"

"Um, running?"

"You don't sound very sure about that."

"There was a treadmill at the club." It was an ancient, rickety thing tucked into a corner of the dorm, and Sky was the only one who used it. Mostly at Bill's insistence: *So you don't waste away into nothing but a pale wraith.* Not that the treadmill did anything to darken Sky's milk-white complexion, the result of his rare time outdoors.

Mr. Wallace frowned. "We'll do better than that. I need you in top shape." He didn't say for what.

He followed Master back into the main room, where Master handed him another bag. "Put these on. They ought to fit."

The bag contained a silky white T-shirt, a pair of gray fleece joggers, and a matching hoodie. Sky gaped when he saw the designer labels and the hefty price tags; Master certainly hadn't gone the inexpensive route. There was even a package of pricey boxer briefs. No socks, though, and just a pair of cheap flip-flops for shoes. "Wasn't sure of your shoe size," Master said, sounding oddly apologetic.

Sky got dressed quickly and disposed of the bags and tags in a nearby wastebasket. By then, Master had settled at the desk with an open laptop. Again uncertain of what he was supposed to do, Sky . . . stood.

After a few minutes, Master glared at Sky over his shoulder. "What the hell are you doing?"

"N-nothing."

"Stop hovering! You're driving me nuts."

It would be a lot easier on both of them, Sky thought, if Master would just tell him what to do. But of course Sky couldn't come out and suggest such a logical course of action, at least not so plainly. "How may I serve you, Master?" he asked meekly.

Master narrowed his eyes and opened his mouth, but then stopped and huffed out a breath. "I don't need anything right now. Just . . . I don't know. Watch TV or something. Quietly." He turned back to his laptop.

Sky practically tiptoed over to retrieve the remote from the nightstand. He ended up sitting on the floor as he watched a movie with a lot of car chases. He didn't understand what the movie was about, mainly because he kept the sound turned all the way down, but that was all right. It was a nice diversion. After the movie, a news show with a handsome slave anchorman came on.

Shortly after the news ended, Master stood and stretched, groaning loudly. "Christ, I'm wiped."

Sky tried not to goggle at the blasphemy. Rich men like Master were generally pretty pious—it was hard for freemen to get ahead if they weren't church-on-Sunday types. One of the very few benefits of being a slave in showbiz was that nobody thought it worth forcing you to be prayed at.

Master picked up the hotel phone, punched some buttons, and ordered what sounded like a delectable meal. Sky hoped some of it was for him; he hadn't eaten since that morning and his stomach was complaining. After hanging up the phone, Master puttered around a little, folding some clothes and stuffing them into a suitcase, poking at his phone, frowning out a window at whatever he saw below. Still sitting in front of the television, Sky watched him out of the corner of his eye.

Room service arrived quickly. Master had the waiter set the trays on the table, and sweet heavens, whatever was under those metal covers smelled amazing. Sky's stomach gurgled.

"Come here," Master called after the waiter left.

Sky scrambled to his feet. He was pleasantly surprised that Master expected him to sit across the table, and he was even happier when Master lifted the lid to reveal a large steak and a pile of buttery green beans. "No potato," Master said unhappily. "I'm cutting back on carbs."

Potato or not, the shared meal was delicious. But Sky would have enjoyed it more if Master hadn't been scrutinizing him. Finally Master washed down a mouthful of food with a swallow of the wine he'd ordered for himself. "So you know how to sing and fuck. Anything else?"

"I'm not sure—"

"Do you have any other skills? I was told you can read."

Sky nodded eagerly. "Yes, Master." Most slaves weren't taught to read, but a previous master wanted him to learn song lyrics more easily.

"Okay. That's something, I guess. Anything else?"

"I . . . Sometimes when the club was really busy, the band would play some songs without me and I'd help the servers." Club Paradiso hadn't been that busy in ages.

"You brought people their food and drinks?"

"Yes, Master."

"Hmm. That might come in handy, actually."

As Sky puzzled over that statement, it occurred to him that maybe Master wasn't his new owner after all. Perhaps he was merely an agent acting on behalf of someone else. But then he might have given a correction when Sky had first addressed him as Master.

"Are you queer?" Master asked.

"Master?"

Master huffed. He did that often. "Are. You. Queer? You know that word, right? Do you like to fuck men?"

"I . . . I know how to please men and women."

"Yeah, yeah. But that's not what I'm asking. What I want to know is whether men turn you on. Do you get hard thinking of dick?"

It was a very strange question. Nobody ever asked—or cared—about a slave's sexual preferences. It didn't usually matter to freemen if the slave they were using was enjoying the experience. Yes, occasionally women had rented Sky, but even they didn't seem to mind whether or not he got an erection as long as he was capable with his tongue and fingers. Even during the rare times when Sky had chosen to engage in a sexual encounter—a quick fumble in the shower when the guard wasn't looking, perhaps—his partner had merely been a matter of convenience: the nearest willing slave. Preference had nothing to do with it.

"I'm queer," Sky said. Because in his dreams, and when he imagined that the hand on his cock wasn't his own, all his lovers were male.

Master seemed pleased. "Well, that makes things easier, I guess."

What sorts of things, he didn't say.

They watched TV together after dinner, Master reclining on the bed and Sky on the floor, leaning back against the mattress. The sound was on now. Master first settled on a drama about policemen, then snorted and changed the channel to a documentary about the Red Death, the plague that had once spread from America to the Old World and wiped out half of Europe. After the program ended, he clicked off the TV. "We're getting an early start tomorrow. Time to hit the hay."

He spent a long while in the bathroom, and when he came out, he was wearing nothing but a pair of boxer briefs very much like the ones he'd bought Sky. The hair on his chest was thick and dark, like the hair on his head, but it didn't hide his sharply defined abs and trim belly. His furry thighs were well muscled too. He looked capable of breaking Sky in half.

"You're going to have to wear those clothes in the morning, so you may as well take them off now," he said.

Sky complied, carefully folding everything and setting the neat pile on a chair. While he did that, Master got into bed. Then he lifted the blankets and looked at Sky expectantly. "It's better than the floor. Turn off the lights and climb in."

Sky followed those orders too, even though his hands shook. *Maybe he won't hurt you*, he told himself. *Just because he can doesn't mean he will.* But his inner pep talk didn't help much. He lay stiffly on his back beside Master, hands curled into fists at his side, and waited.

Master rolled away from him, yawned, and within minutes began to snore.

CHAPTER THREE

Perhaps Master was a nervous flyer. He paced during their wait in the first-class lounge at the airport, and when he and Sky took their seats on the jet, Master jiggled his legs, fiddled with his phone, and ordered a shot of whiskey right away. He was on his second drink as the aircraft took to the sky. Meanwhile, the flight attendants and other passengers cast dirty looks Sky's way, obviously upset over a non-companion slave flying first class. One flight attendant had even tried to object before they took off, but Master narrowed his eyes at the woman and growled, "I paid for two first-class tickets, and *this* is where he's going to sit." Master was scary when he got like that; she'd backed off.

Sky wasn't nervous about flying, although he'd been in a plane only once before, when a previous master took him to New York to compete on *My Slave's Got Talent*. That time, Sky had sat in the back of the plane, in a center seat between two other slaves. First class was much more comfortable, and Master had told him to take the window seat, which meant Sky got to look out in wonder at the landscape below.

Master had a third drink, then sat and glared at the seat in front of him. Finally he turned to Sky. "You make noise in your sleep."

Appalled, Sky felt his stomach clench. "I'm sorry, Master. I—"

"It wasn't a complaint. Sometimes I don't sleep too well either. I was just wondering—nightmares or memories?"

Sky hesitated. "Memories, mostly," he said quietly.

"Yeah. Me too." Master turned his gaze away, leaving Sky to wonder what haunted him.

When mealtime came around, Master insisted that Sky get the same food he did, and then ordered Sky to clean his plate even though Master only picked at his own. He drank some more and dozed afterward. Sky would have liked to play with the entertainment console built into the seat back, but he didn't know if he was allowed to, and he certainly wasn't going to wake Master to ask. Eventually the roar of the engines lulled him to sleep too.

Sky found it strange that once they landed in San Francisco, Master insisted on dragging his own carry-on through the airport, rather than having Sky do it. Sky admired the confident way his master waded through the heavy crowds, moving so quickly that Sky had a little trouble keeping up. Master had placed a call as soon as they landed, and a driver was waiting for them when they reached a spot outside. A hired car, Sky presumed, because the driver and Mr. Wallace didn't seem to know each other.

Traffic was terribly slow, leaving Master fidgeting and tapping angrily at his phone, but Sky enjoyed the opportunity to goggle. There wasn't much to see near the airport, but as they got close to the city, he was treated to a view of the bay with the day's last sunlight gleaming on the water. A tangle of freeways followed, then a quick view of the skyline's glittering glass before they exited onto the surface streets.

Master had been paying little attention to their surroundings, but now he took notice, tucking his phone away and peering out the window. When the driver stopped in front of a squat brick structure that looked like an old warehouse, Sky swallowed bitter bile and began to shiver. Had Master flown him all the way across the country just to throw him into another cage?

"Are you sure this is the right place?" Master barked at the driver, apparently unaware of Sky's distress.

"Yes, sir. This is the address they gave me."

Instead of getting out of the car, Master poked angrily at his phone for a moment, then craned his neck to see the front of the building better. Whatever he saw made him growl, throw his door open, and jump out onto the curb. After a brief uncertainty, Sky followed. Master took his suitcase from the driver without a word before marching toward the building's entrance. He almost collided with several pedestrians and a young guy on a skateboard, but he didn't seem to care. Sky followed more carefully.

Master had a key for the front door, which led into a wide, shallow vestibule with a low ceiling. A bank of metal mailboxes lined the left wall, a stairway rose on the right, and glass doors in the rear led to a courtyard. All the surfaces were very shiny. Grumbling under his breath, Master stomped up the stairs, which took them to a long brick-walled corridor.

Sky's anxiety was somewhat relieved by this point. There was no indication that this place was a slave warehouse, and while the building may once have had other uses, it had pretty clearly been converted to apartments. But he didn't understand . . . well, anything about his situation. And the uncertainty was terrifying.

After a bit of fumbling with the locks, Master opened the door marked 212. He abandoned Sky and the suitcase while he clomped around on the wooden floors, exploring the open loft space. Judging by his expression, he wasn't happy. Sky could see most of the apartment from where he stood. Soaring ceiling, brick walls with large windows, a spacious kitchen area with a breakfast bar and pendant lights. The rest of the space was divided into various living areas marked by a dining set, a desk and shelves, a couch and oversized chairs, and a corner of gleaming weights and exercise machines. A set of open-riser stairs led to a platform area, which Sky guessed served as the bedroom, and through the doorway to his right was a bathroom. The only space he couldn't see was the far corner, hidden behind two eight-foot-high walls.

Although the apartment was expensively furnished, and a few abstract paintings hung on the walls, there were no personal details.

Master loped up the stairs, stomped around for a few moments, and then thundered back down. He banged a few cabinet doors open and closed before heading to the walled-off area. For a few seconds, there was silence.

"What the fuck is this?"

Sky jumped at the anger in Master's voice, then settled a bit when he realized Master was talking on the phone, not to him. And whoever was on the other end was getting an earful.

"This is not going to work. It's not what we talked about . . . Yeah, I *know* rental prices in this city are insane. But surely you can . . . It's not my fault we're working on such short notice. If Delancey had gotten his act together sooner . . . Yeah, well, Delancey *always* has his head up his ass." Master's voice lowered, and he sounded as if he were conceding. "No, no second thoughts. It has to be done and nobody else can do it right. Just . . . Christ. This isn't how it's supposed to be, you know? . . . Yeah, right. Since when have you known me to do that? Bye, Trish."

When Master returned to the apartment entrance, he looked more resigned than furious. But he scowled at Sky. "Why are you just standing there? At least you could have shut the damned door." He kicked it closed with a bang.

"Sorry, Master."

"You say that a lot. Come on. We have shit to do."

Sky was right about the bedroom. The platform upstairs housed an enormous bed and an equally enormous TV, along with a dresser, a small sitting area, and a closet and bathroom separated from the rest with opaque glass sliding doors. While Master seemed to be inventorying the expensive-looking clothes in the dresser and closet, Sky unpacked the few items in Master's suitcase, including his own meager collection of grooming supplies. Then, back on the main floor, he stood in the kitchen and wrote on hotel notepaper while Master poked around and dictated a grocery list.

"I hate shopping," Master complained when he was through. He leaned on the kitchen island for a moment, his face buried in his hands. Then he groaned and looked up at Sky. "That's what I really need a slave for—to do all those crappy jobs I hate like shopping and paying bills and going to the dentist."

"I . . . I don't think I can . . ."

"I know," Master said with a sigh. He looked exhausted and somehow weighed down. But when he gazed at Sky, his eyes were surprisingly warm.

Maybe that was what gave Sky the courage to ask a question. "Master? Please. What *do* you want me for?"

At first Master didn't respond, but then he seemed to reach a decision. He started walking and gestured for Sky to follow. They crossed to the corner of the apartment, pausing just inside the opening between the partial walls.

When Sky saw what was hidden behind them, his mouth went dry and, conversely, his bowels felt watery.

He supposed that if the space hadn't been in a second-floor apartment, it would have been called a dungeon. It contained several wooden and metal devices with padding, straps, and shackles, each clearly meant to confine a person in various positions. Hooks jutted from the walls, hung with chains, ropes, and floggers, while wooden shelves held gags, dildos, paddles, and things Sky couldn't identify— and didn't want to.

He couldn't face this. He couldn't— No. He had a choice: to fall apart or to wear a cloak of bravery. He took a deep breath, unzipped his hoodie, and pulled it off. As he started to take off his T-shirt, though, Master caught his arm. "No," Master said. "Not now."

It was stupid to feel relief over only a temporary reprieve, but Sky gave a shaky nod and let his arms drop to his sides, his hoodie clutched in one fist. Master faced him, standing so close their chests nearly touched. He cradled Sky's chin gently in his palm, drawing his head up so Sky looked him in the eyes. They were pretty eyes, coffee brown near the pupils and fading to golden near the rims.

"This isn't how I want it," Master said softly. "I'm not supposed to be the bad guy. But sometimes we have to do things . . . Ends justify the means, right?" He laughed without humor.

The terrible thing was that Sky found himself wanting to lean forward just a little more, to feel Master's warmth seep into his body. He craved scraps of tenderness and affection so badly that he'd beg them from the man who planned to torture him.

Master released Sky's chin and stepped backward a bit, perhaps regretting what he'd just said and done. He hadn't yet been cruel to Sky—had even been kind at times—but compassion toward a slave was a step too far. He kept *staring*, though. That was his right; Sky was his property to do with as he wished. But his gaze was so heavy that Sky suddenly broke.

"What do you want from me?" he shouted. And since he was damned already, he continued to yell. "You say you're going to use these things on me, but you say you don't want to. You give me good food and fancy clothing, but don't give me any work to do. You have me sleep in your bed, but you don't touch me. I want to be a good slave, but I'm just a singer and I don't understand!"

Sky didn't know which of them was more shocked by his outburst.

He stood, panting, reflecting wryly that at least he'd chosen a convenient place to erupt, seeing as Master had dozens of implements of punishment near at hand. Maybe Master would kill him. Sky couldn't even care any longer—he was far too tired and used up.

Master stopped gaping and began to laugh. It wasn't cruel laughter, but something warmer. Showing surprise, certainly, and . . . satisfaction? "I knew it! I knew there was a real man inside that pretty package." He came close enough to grasp Sky's shoulders, yet his grip was gentle. "It's why I chose you. I need someone who's not just ornamental. I need a slave who's *strong*. Here and here." He lightly tapped Sky's head and chest.

"I'm not," Sky whispered.

"Bullshit. You just yelled at your master when I've got thousands of dollars' worth of BDSM gear within arm's reach."

"That's not strength—it's disobedience."

Master laughed again. "Sometimes they're the same thing. And here you are, still arguing with me."

"You . . . you *want* me to argue with you?"

"Not really." Master's expression sobered. "In fact, I need you to comply with everything I tell you, and right away. If I tell you to do things that scare you, hurt you, humiliate you . . . whatever . . . I need you to do them anyway, and then I need you to keep on going. To not fall apart on me. I think you can do this."

Unable to fully process this bizarre declaration of confidence, Sky merely blinked.

"Look, Sky. Things are going to be ugly for a while. But with a little luck, not for long. A few weeks maybe. I want this over with as badly as you do. And no, I can't tell you what the hell's going on or why. I'm sorry for that. But I can promise that when it's over, you'll end up somewhere . . . safe. Find a nice little club that needs a singer, something like that."

Promises to a slave were like raindrops in the ocean—insignificant and meaningless. But Sky nodded anyway. False hope was better than none.

Master declared the corner of the loft—he called it the playroom—temporarily off-limits to both of them. He ordered a pizza, and when it arrived, he told Sky to grab a couple of plates and meet him at the couch. They watched TV together again, this time with Sky sitting on the furniture instead of the floor, and they munched pizza until they were both full.

"That was *not* on the diet," Master said, rubbing his stomach. "But totally worth it. Tomorrow, though, we get real. With the right food and some regular exercise, I think you'll have a real nice physique."

Sky stole a quick glance at Master's impressive body, and he must have looked skeptical, because Master chuckled. "Nah, not like me. I've always been big. Played football in high school. You're built leaner, more compact. Like a swimmer."

"I don't know how to swim," Sky replied, hazarding a small smile.

Master grinned back at him. "Water's way too cold around here for that anyway. And I think there's sharks. We'll stick to running. But I guess first thing tomorrow"—he grimaced—"we have to shop. And then I have some work to do, stuff I have to set up. Right now, let's get some rest."

Sky followed him upstairs, and again they took turns in the bathroom, Master first and then Sky. When Sky emerged, Master was standing at the bedside, plugging his phone into a charger. He was naked. It was the first time Sky had seen him completely unclothed, and although he felt a tingle of fear, it was a small one. All the whips and paddles were downstairs. Master had nothing to hurt Sky with up here except for his hands and his body. And while those things were certainly enough to cause damage, Sky would survive it.

Besides, another emotion had also hit him upon seeing Master nude, this one unexpected: lust. Master was a beautiful man. He had a muscular ass, nicely rounded, and when he turned to look at Sky, he revealed a long cock amid a neatly trimmed thatch of dark curls.

"I prefer sleeping in the buff," Master said with a shrug. "And anyway, you better get used to this." He waved his hands to indicate his entire body.

After only a brief hesitation, Sky nodded. "Yes, Master." Then he shed his own underwear, leaving himself as bare as Master—except for his slave bracelets, of course. Master smiled broadly and got into bed.

Sky turned off the light and climbed in too.

This bed was even nicer than the one at Hotel 234, and it felt heavenly to stretch out on his back after a long day of travel and emotional upheaval. The sheets smelled nice too, a little like salt spray and flowers, and when he looked up, he saw a skylight directly over the bed, with a view of the crescent moon.

This time, Master didn't go to sleep right away. He shifted around a little on the mattress, making the sheets rustle softly, then sighed and touched Sky's arm. Sky flinched, but all Master did was whisper his fingers against Sky's skin.

"I just realized something," Master said. He paused a moment as if expecting a response, but when Sky remained silent, Master continued. "I told you what I need from you. But I didn't ask what you need from me in order to make this work."

"I don't understand."

"What made you finally lose it earlier today, when you yelled? I don't think it was just jet lag."

"I didn't know what you wanted from me, and I was . . ." Scared. Frustrated. Angry. But slaves weren't allowed to be angry.

"I think I got it. So how do we avoid another meltdown, especially when things get hairy?" His soothing strokes somehow negated the dread those last words should have caused.

"Give me rules, Master." Sky almost left it at that, but Master seemed to welcome candor, so Sky continued. "I want to be a good slave. So please, tell me what I can and can't do. Otherwise I don't know, and I can't—"

"Got it. You can't follow directions if nobody gives them to you. I'm sorry I've been so shitty about it."

Master was apologizing to a slave? Sky was nearly speechless, but since Master seemed to expect a response, he finally managed a whisper. "Thank you, Master."

"I've never done this before. Owned a slave, I mean. Hell, I never even had a dog. It's . . . weird. But I guess if you do your best, I can do the same." He patted Sky's arm and then turned away.

But still Master remained awake, and Sky was very aware of the bulk of him lying inches away, the heat from their bare bodies mingling under the duvet. Master was such a confusing man, and nothing about him made sense. Like just now, when he said he'd never owned a slave before. Yet he was obviously rich, and like expensive houses and fancy cars, slaves were part of the trappings of wealth.

Maybe it was Master's mysteries that drew Sky to him, even as Sky remained frightened and insecure about what would come next.

When Sky had sung with 2Nyte, the band's manager had once arranged a photo shoot in a zoo. The singers had worn low-slung zebra-striped pants and had posed shirtless in front of the enclosures containing the great cats. But none of them had ever visited a zoo before—who took a slave to the zoo?—and they'd been so distracted by the animals that the shoot was difficult, and they'd all been beaten afterward as punishment. The beating had been worth it, though. Sky was especially fascinated with the tiger. He'd longed to touch the beautiful animal, even though he knew the cat would kill him if he got too close.

That was how he felt about Master.

"What are you laughing about?"

Startled, Sky turned, but couldn't make out Master's face in the dark. "I'm sorry, Master."

"For laughing?"

"For disturbing you."

"You didn't. I was just wondering what was going through your head."

Sky hesitated. "I was just . . . thinking about tigers."

It was Master's turn to chuckle. "You're definitely an interesting person, Sky Blue."

CHAPTER FOUR

Sky was not in good shape. Even though their running pace was clearly much slower than Master was used to, Sky was huffing and puffing within a few blocks. The fact that he was wearing flip-flops didn't help his athletic prowess. Master was surprisingly patient with him, though, urging him to go just a little bit farther and then jogging in place as Sky rested for a few minutes and gasped for air. When they got to the waterfront, Master told Sky to sit on a bench near the Ferry Building. "I forgot to bring water," he said apologetically. "Remind me next time."

Sky was still too winded to speak, so he just nodded. The sleeves of his hoodie hid his bracelets, so none of the passing commuters or tourists cast him scornful looks for daring to take up space on a public bench. Passing as free was a privilege granted by virtue of his white skin. As far as he knew, there were no black or native freemen—not in this country, anyway.

He was grateful to discover that Master wasn't in any particular hurry to resume exercising. For perhaps twenty minutes, they watched the ferries churning back and forth across the gray water and the cars soaring over to Oakland on the Bay Bridge. Sky liked the salty tang of the air, the faint smell of grilling fish from a nearby restaurant, the clang and clatter of the streetcars behind him.

"It's a pretty city," Master said, as if he'd been reading Sky's thoughts. "Have you been here before?"

"We did a concert here once. But I didn't get to see anything but the inside of the concert hall." Several bands had traveled together—all of them owned by the same company—and they'd crossed the country crammed together in a semitrailer. They'd been allowed to watch videos and listen to music, and although the seats weren't too uncomfortable, there hadn't been any windows. Once they arrived, each venue was pretty much like the others.

"I've only been here once before too. It's so different from where I grew up."

Since Master had raised the subject, Sky dared a question. "Where was that, Master?"

"Omaha," Master answered absently. "About as far away as you can get from the ocean." Then he shook himself and turned to grin at Sky. "Ready to run back?"

When they returned to the loft, Master told Sky to wash his clothes and then take a shower. The hot water was wonderful on Sky's overworked muscles; he might have stayed in the shower all day if he'd had a choice. But of course he *didn't* have a choice; so, clad in his underwear, he followed the smell of bacon down the stairs and into the kitchen.

Master waved from the kitchen island. "Hurry up and eat. You have an appointment." He didn't say for what. Sky obeyed, smiling to himself at the novelty of a master who prepared breakfast for his slave.

Master lent Sky a pair of sweatpants and a tee. A driver waited for them outside the building and then took them to a neighborhood of grand old Victorian houses, most with shops on the first floor. He let them off at a corner near their destination, Bay City Spa.

The small lobby was done up in a warm reddish wood and smelled of herbs. A pretty black woman with shiny slave bracelets bobbed her head at Master when they entered. "How can I help you, sir?"

"I'm Morgan Wallace. I have an appointment for Sky." He settled one of his big hands on Sky's shoulder.

Morgan. It was the first time Sky had heard his owner's given name.

"Of course. This way, please." She led them to a room in the back that, to Sky's considerable relief, did not remotely resemble a torture chamber. "Undress and lie on the table, please," she said to him.

Master watched as Sky complied. The air was pleasantly warm against his bare skin, and smooth jazz played quietly. "Your technician will be with you in a moment," the woman said to Master. "Can I get you something to drink?"

"No. Thanks."

Seconds after she left, another slave came in, this one much older and rather stout, her steel-gray hair shorn almost to her scalp. Master nodded at her. "I have some errands to do. You'll take good care of him, right?"

"Of course, sir." She had a deep, rich voice. Sky wondered if she ever sang.

Master gave Sky's leg a quick pat. "I'll be back in a little while. Survive this and I'll take you to lunch, okay?"

Sky gave a small smile. "Yes, Master."

Having all his body hair removed was not the most painful experience Sky had ever faced, but it wasn't exactly fun. The technician seemed quite competent, however, working quickly and without fuss. She handled Sky's most sensitive bits carefully but dispassionately, like a fruit seller arranging delicate produce. And when Sky was as sleek as could be, she told him to lie facedown on the table and administered a massage that quickly turned him into a moaning puddle of goo. "Your muscles are tight," she said as she worked his shoulders.

Not very surprising when he considered the stresses of the past several days.

Master returned, heavily laden with shopping bags, just as she was finishing. He set his purchases down, gestured for Sky to stand, and then walked around him, giving a close visual inspection. "Looks good," he said. He brushed his fingertips across Sky's pecs, and when he spoke again, his voice was slightly hoarse. "Very good."

The technician nodded. "Thank you, sir. He should exfoliate regularly. Those are some products he can use." She pointed at a plastic bag emblazoned with the spa logo, then left the room.

Master seemed almost in a trance as his fingers, with exquisite slowness, trailed across Sky's chest and down his belly. Between the waxing and the massage, Sky's skin was acutely sensitive, and the light touch hovered in a giddy space between discomfort and pleasure. By the time Master moved his fingers to the smooth area where Sky's pubic hair had been, Sky's cock was half-hard. Sky blushed when his master looked down at Sky's dick and then up at his face.

"You like being touched?" Master asked in a husky voice.

"I . . ." Sky swallowed. "Yes."

Master ran a fingertip from the base of Sky's cock to the tip, making Sky hiss and throw back his head. Sky nearly whimpered when Master took his hand away. "Not the time or place," Master said—it was unclear whether to himself or Sky. Then he rooted around in a couple of the bags before tossing Sky some clothing. "These ought to fit better than my stuff."

Sky pulled on briefs, a pair of tight black jeans, an equally tight white T-shirt made of the silkiest cotton he'd ever felt, and a soft cardigan in dark gray. He had socks and short black boots as well.

Master gave him another visual inspection and seemed pleased with the results. "You were accurate about the sizes. That's good, because I got you several outfits like this, and some exercise wear too. You're still going to need clothes for when we're out at night, but we can get those tomorrow. I've had enough shopping for today."

"At night?" Sky asked.

Master frowned and pursed his lips. "Let's go."

Sky carried the bags to another waiting car, which took them home. They stayed only long enough to drop off their purchases, then walked a few blocks to a restaurant with a sign out front boasting about the cassoulet. "What do you think of French food?" Master asked.

"Um . . . I really don't have an opinion."

"Is there any food you love? Or can't stand?"

It wasn't as if slaves were given menus. At Club Paradiso, as at the other clubs, Sky and the band members ate whatever the kitchen had left over. "The food at the warehouse was . . . not very good."

Master sighed. "This isn't a date. I know that. You sure as hell know that. But I can't . . . Let's just eat."

The restaurant host spied Sky's bracelets immediately, and a frown flitted across his face. Master stepped forward with his chest thrown out. "I want one of those tables in the window, not something hidden near the bathroom. And I want a nice meal with an attentive waiter. If I get those things, I'll leave a nice tip. I'll probably even come back again and spend a lot of money, seeing as how I live nearby. If I don't get those things, I'm walking out, and the only way you'll hear from me again is via a nasty letter to your manager and a one-star review on Yelp."

The host opened his mouth, closed it, and attempted a smile. "Of course, sir. Right this way."

They were seated at one of the windows.

The waiter managed to hide any displeasure at serving a slave, although he never spoke or looked directly at Sky. Master did the ordering, both because Sky didn't know what most of the dishes were and because Master wanted to enforce Sky's new healthy diet. And, well, because he was the master and Sky was the slave. The food was delicious: butternut squash soup, salad with tuna and eggs, and a little bit of crusty bread. Master ate the same, although he drank whiskey while Sky had water with lemon. As they ate, Master talked about rugby, a subject Sky knew nothing about, but that was fine. It was really nice just to have someone talking to him as if he were a real person.

When the food was gone, Master ordered coffee. Together they watched people walking outside. Almost all the pedestrians were free people, most of them nicely dressed. A few slaves in bright-yellow coveralls went by, maintenance workers of some kind, Sky supposed. He wondered how hard they had to work and whether their handlers were cruel.

"Now what are you thinking?" Master asked quietly.

"I've been very lucky, Master."

"How so?"

"Singing—it's an easy job for a slave."

"Yeah, I guess so. I saw a thing on the internet about slaves in mines somewhere. They live under brutal conditions. A lot of them only see the sky a few hours a week. And most of them don't last more than a few years before they get hurt or are exposed to toxic chemicals, and then they die." He shook his head. "That's not right."

Sky had heard stories about places like that—sometimes as threats made by handlers and owners, or as horrible tales slaves whispered to each other at night. But he'd never seen such things himself, and he was surprised that Master had searched out information like that. Even more surprised that Master had told him those conditions were wrong.

"Do you like singing, Sky?"

"I used to, very much." Sky gambled on the truth once more. "Not as much lately."

"Why?"

Sky searched for words to explain something even he didn't fully understand. "Nobody . . . nobody wanted to listen anymore. I mean, not really. They'd come to the club, but I was just . . . Whatever I sang, whether I was having a good day or was off my game, it didn't matter. They hardly heard me."

Master's gaze was sharp. "You want people to appreciate you."

"It's not my place—"

"I'm not asking what you're supposed to do. I'm asking how you *feel*."

Sky took a deep breath and met his master's eyes. "Yes. I want people to appreciate me."

"Sure. It's human, right? We need to feel like we matter to someone. We all do." Master looked out the window. "I used to love my job too. I don't think I do anymore."

Sky was shaken by Master's admission that Sky, too, was human, that he couldn't think how to respond. He tried to change the subject instead, to ask what Master's job was. But just then, the waiter came by with the bill, and by the time he left, the mood was broken.

After the restaurant, they went to a grocery store, where Master grumbled about having to do more shopping. Despite that, he seemed to be in a good mood, pausing often to ask Sky whether he liked a particular food. After the fifth or sixth time Sky said yes, Master shook his head. "Are you really this easy to please, or are you saying what you think I want to hear?"

"Master, I'll be thankful for whatever you give me to eat."

"Yeah, I'm sure that's true. But I'm trying to figure out what you want." He grimaced and rubbed his brow. "I guess I'm hoping it'll soothe my conscience a little if you're at least enjoying your meals."

Sky didn't like the implications of that, but he nodded. "I'll try to be more helpful, Master." And he did try; although, truth be told, he'd gone hungry enough times that there were few things he was unwilling to eat. He'd managed to swallow that horrible stuff in the warehouse, hadn't he? In any case, Master selected mostly fish, lean meats, whole grains, and fruits and vegetables, all of which looked delicious to Sky. The produce here was nicer than what Sky had been used to in New York, although he didn't know if that was due to the location or because the clubs that had owned him had skimped on the quality of their supplies. Maybe Club Paradiso wouldn't have needed to sell him if they'd served better food.

They ended up with so many groceries that they took a taxi, although the apartment wasn't far. Even getting everything up the one flight of stairs and down the hallway was a bit of a struggle. Master told Sky where he wanted things to go, and in the process, they danced around each other in the kitchen, both of them laughing a little as they maneuvered. When they were through, Sky folded the paper grocery sacks.

"Did you know the city makes stores charge ten cents per bag?" Master asked, tucking the folded sacks into a cupboard. "It's supposed to cut down on trash or something, but I think it's stupid."

Sky shrugged, wondering why a man who'd just paid several hundred thousand dollars for a slave would care about spending a few extra cents.

Master gave him another of his considering looks. "I don't suppose you know how to cook."

"I'm sorry, Master."

"No big deal. You can watch me and you'll pick it up. We don't need to do anything fancy." He glanced at his watch. "Damn. I'm still on East Coast time. Okay, I need to get some work done. What do you want to do while I'm busy?"

Nobody had ever asked Sky what he wanted to do; the question was so strange that he took several moments to process it. And then all he could do was look down at the floor and feel his heart race, because he had no idea what Master wanted him to say.

Master waited a few more seconds, then huffed a heavy sigh. "I think maybe this is a good opportunity for a couple of those rules we talked about last night."

Sky nodded eagerly. Rules were good. Rules were safe.

"Rule number one: tell me the truth. I've been fed so much bullshit in my life, it's a wonder I haven't burst. Don't say what you think I want to hear or what's easy. Give me honesty. Even if I can't return the favor. I'll never punish you for telling the truth. Can you do that?"

After thinking about it for a moment, Sky said, "I'll try very hard, Master."

"Good. And rule number two: if you don't understand what I want or what you're supposed to be doing, for God's sake, ask. I know you'll be paying attention—slaves have to—and I don't think you're stupid. So if you're not getting something, it's probably my fault for being unclear. Ask me to explain, and if I can, I will. Got it?"

"You won't get angry?" Sky asked.

Master snorted. "Well, I can't promise that because I'm an impatient bastard with a shitty temper. I might bluster. But I won't punish you for needing clarification, and when I calm down, I'll realize that it was my fault and I was being an asshole."

Even though Sky wasn't sure he believed any of this, he couldn't resist a small grin at the mental image Master had drawn. Master smiled back and thumped Sky's shoulder a couple of times. "Yeah, you've already got that part of me figured out, haven't you? My mom used to tell me she should've named me Calm Down, seeing as how she yelled it so often. So. Back to my original question. What do you want to do while I'm working?"

Sky gave the question serious consideration. He wasn't even sure what his options were. He wasn't sleepy, he didn't especially want to watch TV, and he hadn't seen anything in the loft to read. They'd already established that he couldn't cook. He looked around and spied the bags containing the clothing Master had bought him that morning; they lay in an untidy pile where Sky had left them before lunch. The breakfast dishes still sat in the sink, unwashed. "I could clean up a little," he offered.

"That's really what you want?"

"I'd like to keep busy, Master." That was true. Sitting around with nothing to do would just give him more chance to worry.

"Yeah, okay. I understand that. Do you know how to clean?"

"Yes, Master." Well, that was a small stretch. Sky had never cleaned a house before—he'd never lived in one. But he'd spent plenty of hours sweeping and mopping, wiping down tables, and generally getting a club ready for the next evening's customers. He figured the same principles would apply.

"Knock yourself out, then."

Master sat on the couch with his laptop perched on his thighs while Sky put away the clothing. Master had already told him to use one of the dresser drawers and as much closet space as he needed, and it gave Sky a weird feeling to see his own things hanging next to Master's as if they belonged there. He took the empty bags downstairs and stored them with the grocery sacks, then carefully washed and dried the breakfast dishes and put them away. Next he wiped down the stove and countertop and wiped fingerprints off the refrigerator. After that, he had to search for a few moments before he discovered a small closet stuffed with cleaning supplies. He extracted the broom and dustpan so he could sweep the kitchen. And when that was finished, he decided he might as well tackle the rest of the floor even though it wasn't very dirty.

"What's that song?"

Sky stopped chasing a dust bunny around the legs of the dining table. "Master?"

"You were humming."

"Oh." Sky swallowed. "I'm sorry I disturbed you. I won't—"

"I'm not complaining. I was just curious. I don't follow music much."

Since Sky hadn't even been aware he was humming, it took him a moment to dredge up the tune. "It's an old song. 'Midnight Special.'"

"I liked it." Master tilted his head. "You know, I haven't actually heard you sing yet."

"You want me to sing for you, Master?"

Master shook his head. "I'm not asking for an impromptu concert. Just . . . if you feel like singing while you work, go ahead. It won't bother me." He turned his attention back to his computer.

Sky returned to sweeping; he didn't sing, but he thought about it. Back at the club, he'd saved his vocal cords for practice and performances, but just now he'd been humming without even meaning to. Because he was . . . content, he realized. It was pleasant to have a full belly and nice clothes, to know he'd probably get to sleep in a warm comfortable bed, to have small domestic chores to keep him occupied. Maybe he could even pretend for a while that he had a home.

He padded over to the couch, where he stood awkwardly until Master looked up. "Can I get you something, Master? To drink, maybe?"

Surprise flitted across Master's face, followed by a slow smile. "I bet that beer's cold by now."

Sky hurried to the refrigerator and pulled out a bottle. After trying three drawers, he found and used the opener and then took the uncapped bottle and a glass to the couch. Master took the bottle, swigged from it, and grinned. "I'm a barbarian, so we can skip the glass. But what prompted this?"

"You were busy. I thought you might like—"

"That's right. I forgot you used to wait tables. Well, thanks for this. It hits the spot." He took another drink and made a small salute with the bottle.

Sky turned to resume his sweeping, but Master gently caught his arm. "Rule three: if you're hungry or thirsty, help yourself or let me know. When I get caught up in stuff, sometimes I forget to eat or drink. There's no way I'll always remember how long it's been since you had something."

"I can remind you when you need a meal or drink, Master. If you like."

Master gave Sky's arm a quick squeeze. "Someone to look out for me. That's a nice change. Don't know if you'll still be feeling it later, though."

"Master?"

He let go of Sky and nodded toward the laptop. "Back to the grindstone."

Night fell, and Master continued to squint at his computer screen. By then Sky had finished all the chores he could think of and stood at one of the big windows. There wasn't much to see since the view consisted mostly of a nearby brick building. But he could hear sounds—sirens, honking cars, braking trucks—and they created a discordant little city symphony. Like pattering rainfall or tumbling waves, the noises wrapped him in a soothing cocoon.

He caught Master's reflection in the window, gazing up at him instead of at the laptop. "Now what song?" Master asked.

Sky didn't turn around, and instead of answering, he began to sing the words about David and Samson. He let his voice soar on the chorus, and the *hallelujah*s echoed as beautifully in the loft as in any concert hall. His audience of one listened, transfixed, dark eyes wide and mouth slightly open.

Master waited for the last echoes to fade before reacting, and even then all he managed was a hoarse whisper. "Jesus Christ."

Sky turned back toward the room, his eyes prickling with unshed tears. He didn't know why. Maybe it was the hopeless beauty of the song—music sometimes did that to him.

After what felt like a very long time, Master cleared his throat and snapped the laptop shut. "How about some dinner?"

After Master cooked and they both ate, Sky washed up. They sat on the couch later with the television on. Master's attention was focused on two cell phones, though. He alternated between them, sending and receiving a barrage of texts. Sky wondered why anyone needed two of the gadgets, but of course it wasn't any of his business.

His yawns must have caught Master's attention. "Go on up to bed, Sky. I'm going to be a while."

"Can I get you anything?"

Master seemed distracted, but managed a small smile. "Nah. Get some sleep."

Sky moved slowly upstairs, where he undressed. He considered showering again, but Master hadn't told him to, so instead he wiped himself down with a washcloth and used some of the goos and creams he'd carried home from the spa. It had been a long time since he'd been waxed, and his hairless skin felt strange under his fingers, as if it weren't really his own. Which, in fact, it wasn't.

Clean and smooth and smelling faintly of citrus, he turned off the lamp and climbed into the big bed. A bit of light made its way from downstairs, and because sound carried well to the bedroom, he heard the TV and the click-clack of the laptop. But he still felt decadently alone under the skylight, wrapped in soft cotton sheets. He tried to pry apart his conflicting emotions, especially the ones about Master. Fear and confusion and a bit of anger, yes, but also gratitude and affection and the deep taste of desire. Far too complex for the likes of a simple slave, who was put on earth only to serve and obey. Those wretched creatures who were confined to the mines—Sky certainly didn't envy them, but at least their lives were simple. Even abject misery could be survived when that misery was predictable.

Nothing about Morgan Wallace was predictable.

When Master came upstairs, Sky pretended to be asleep, although he had to suppress a smile when he realized that Master was trying not to wake him. Master wasn't very good at being quiet. The floorboards creaked under his weight, and he banged hard into something and swore under his breath. He undressed and spent some time in the bathroom, then came tiptoeing back to the bed. The mattress dipped as he lay down.

Sky's back was to Master, but he could feel hot breath against his skin, paradoxically giving him gooseflesh. Master didn't touch him, though, and Sky felt the space between them as both a buffer and an absence. Those few inches of Egyptian cotton were like the iron bars of a zoo cage.

Tonight Sky couldn't resist. He had to pet the tiger.

He rolled onto his back and slid his hand across that empty expanse, tentatively reaching. When his fingers skimmed Master's hard belly, Master hissed and Sky froze. Three, four, five thudding heartbeats passed. Then Master gently pressed his own hand against Sky's, urging more pressure.

Sky had been fucked many times—by freemen who worked at the clubs, by men who paid his owners to use him for a night. On rare occasions, women had rented him instead. But male or female, the people who'd used him were in charge, and they'd strictly controlled the congress of bodies: who touched whom and with what. Sky had no choice in those matters. Yes, over the years he had occasionally been able to steal a few minutes with another slave, but even then, what they did with each other was determined by haste and expedience rather than preference.

Now, though, Master moved onto his back and allowed—almost encouraged—Sky to explore him at will. As Sky tentatively petted and stroked, Master guided him only with soft moans of approval, keeping his fingers threaded loosely in Sky's hair. Sky learned the smell of him—toothpaste, soap, and a faint hint of beer. He mapped the hair on Master's chest, traced the stiff peaks of his nipples, felt the smooth hills and narrow valleys of his abs. And when his hand reached lower, he found the hard column of Master's cock and the furry plumpness of his balls.

Master lifted his hips into Sky's caresses, but it was his breathy groan that prompted Sky to try more. Moving quickly, Sky burrowed under the blankets into a soft cave scented with the heady musk of lust. He curled himself against Master's long legs and pressed his lips against the tip of Master's glans.

"God, yes," Master said. "Please!"

When had anyone ever begged Sky? Just the sound of that one word went straight to his head—and to his groin—and Sky swallowed Master to the root. At the same time, he grabbed his own dick with his free hand and started tugging as he sucked. Master held Sky's hair with both hands now, a little more tightly but not enough to hurt, and uttered a guttural stream of the filthiest curses and blasphemies Sky had ever heard.

Sky's jaw hurt from being stretched over Master's considerable girth, his throat felt raw as Master's hot flesh rubbed against it, and his lungs and heart strained as hard as they had during his morning jog. But oh, sweet heavens, Master tasted good and *felt* good, both in him and beneath him. So much power, willingly tamed.

Sky was so caught up in the thrilling wonder of the experience that his orgasm caught him by surprise, rushing through his body like a winter gale. His hand, stomach, and groin were hot and sticky, his nerves almost too sensitive, and yet he stroked himself until Master uttered a choked howl and came in Sky's throat.

Slowly, as if in a dream, Sky disentangled himself from Master and pushed his overheated head and upper body out of the blankets. He expected Master to shove him away, or at least to simply roll over and fall asleep. Instead, Master pulled their bodies flush and skated his lips along Sky's neck and cheek.

"You wanted that," Master whispered into his ear. "As badly as I did."

"Yes."

"Even though I own you. Even though you've seen the playroom and . . . I've warned you."

Sky shuddered. "Yes."

"You are an interesting man." And then more quietly, perhaps to himself or as a sort of prayer: "God, please don't let me break him."

CHAPTER FIVE

Master was in a good mood when he woke. He laughed at the flaking mess of dried semen on their groins and bellies, but instead of showering, he tossed Sky a damp washcloth. "Lick and a promise now, proper bathing after our run."

They ran a little farther and a little faster this morning, the thick fog chilling them despite their vigorous movement and fleece clothing. They paused at the halfway mark again, this time several piers up from the Ferry Building, and Master did some stretches while Sky rasped for oxygen. Sky's legs were rubbery by the time they returned to the loft, and he was too used up to be hungry. But then Master joined him in the big shower and, with soapy hands, rubbed firmly at Sky's tender muscles until he nearly melted into a puddle of pain and bliss. Laughing, Master wielded a loofah over most of Sky's body. "You have to exfoliate, remember," he said with a grin. "They said so at the spa."

Sky returned the favor by massaging shampoo into Master's thick dark hair. Master moaned almost as much as he had over last night's blowjob, and by the time Sky was finished, Master was impressively erect. Yet he rinsed quickly, turned off the water, and hurried out of the enclosure. He tossed Sky a towel before taking one for himself. "We have things to do."

The first thing was breakfast. Sky watched carefully as Master stirred protein powder and mixed berries into oatmeal and then scrambled some eggs. Fortunately, by then Sky had found his appetite; he ate everything Master gave him.

"You can do the dishes later," Master said when Sky headed toward the sink. "We need to go."

Sky didn't know their destination, but jeans and light sweaters were apparently appropriate dress for them both. A hired car was again in front of the building, the driver a freeman who looked as if he'd be better suited to professional wrestling. Traffic moved in excruciating increments, their car stopping often to avoid delivery vehicles, road construction, and wayward pedestrians. Master kept his attention on one of his phones, leaving Sky to view the city spectacle.

As Sky watched people hurrying by, each of them wrapped up in everyday concerns, he wondered what it would be like to be free. So many choices and responsibilities. After all, a slave never had to worry about paying the bills, impressing his in-laws, or deciding whether it was time to buy a new car. When it came down to it, a slave had only one concern: pleasing his master. And if he was fortunate enough to be owned by someone who made the rules clear and the tasks manageable, pleasing his master was a simple task.

In theory.

Not long after 2Nyte was disbanded and Sky was sold to a Broadway production company, he'd been assigned to the chorus in a revival of *Oklahoma!* The theater was dark on Mondays, so most Sunday nights, the director took one of the chorus boys home with him; he seemed to favor Sky, choosing him almost once a month. On those Sunday nights, Sky slept in the director's slave quarters, which were nicer than the dorm at the theater and also offered fresh gossip. Sometime after lunch on Monday, the director would fuck him while his wife watched and occasionally called out instructions or encouragement. And Monday evening, the director and his wife would host a small dinner party, where Sky was expected to stand in the corner and look pretty during the meal, then serenade the guests afterward.

During one of these meals, the subject of slavery had come up, and a skinny woman with frizzy hair had argued that skilled slaves ought to be given part of their earnings so that eventually they could buy their own freedom. "It would give them an incentive to work harder and better," she said, "and that would benefit us all."

The director's wife had scoffed loudly. "That's nonsense! If they were freed, they'd end up a drain on society."

"Not if they were given some help adjusting—"

"We could give them all the help in the world and it wouldn't matter. They are psychologically and cognitively incapable of caring for themselves."

Another guest, a portly man who wore too-small shirts, nodded vigorously. "We're doing them a favor by guiding them, giving them shelter, food, health care, something to occupy themselves with. Without us, they'd spend their lives in violence and squalor. And most of them don't even have the acumen to appreciate all we do for them. Ungrateful, witless creatures."

"But I really think," the skinny lady began, only to be interrupted by the director calling loudly for another bottle of wine. The conversation shifted to grape varietals.

Nobody had so much as glanced at Sky during the discussion, not even the skinny woman, which didn't surprise him. He was used to being treated like furniture. But in the years since then, he'd given thought to what those people had said, and he considered the issue again now as he watched a young man in a suit ride an electric unicycle down the sidewalk.

Look at what he had now, with Mr. Wallace. A nicer place to live than most freemen, not to mention more expensive clothing and better food. At least so far, his workload had been extremely light. And what if someone waved a magic wand and freed him? The previous day he hadn't been capable of making even a simple decision as to what groceries to buy. He'd certainly be unable to provide for himself. And he even *liked* his master. Wanted to touch him. Wouldn't be repulsed if Master used him sexually. Shouldn't he be thankful?

But he wasn't.

Maybe that fat man at the dinner party was right, and Sky was just too stupid to understand.

After some time, the car left them on a street lined with cafés, bars, and shops. A few people—most of them women with baby strollers or with little dogs—sat at outdoor tables. The front door of a Pilates studio was propped open, and the voice of the instructor wended through, exhorting the students to put the small blue ball between their knees and drop their shoulders. Master took Sky through an archway into a courtyard and then to a building at the far end. Sky thought that a hundred years earlier, the building might have been a carriage house for the grander mansion in front. Now it was painted wine-red with a matte black door. The metal sign on the door said TRAPPINGS.

As soon as they entered, a slender young slave with bleached-white hair glided over. He wore nothing but iron bracelets, a matching collar, and a black leather loincloth. He dropped gracefully to his knees in front of Master. "How may I serve you, sir?" he asked softly.

Master told him to stand and then said some other things, but the meaning of the words was lost on Sky as the blood rushed through his skull. This shop sold clothing, but the items were very different from the things Master had bought him yesterday. Here were mesh shirts, leather collars and leashes, gladiator skirts, zippered thongs, cock cages, assless latex shorts, and hundreds of similar pieces intended to fetishize and display the men who wore them.

Master gave Sky's shoulder a hard shake. "Undress," he growled, his tone suggesting he was having to repeat himself. Trembling, Sky complied. Nobody seemed to be in the store except Sky, Mr. Wallace, and the slave who worked there, yet Sky felt exceedingly exposed.

He did his best impression of a mannequin while Master chose items and the slave dressed Sky. Just the touch of the fabrics—leather, plastic, nylon, metal—made Sky ill. He'd worn some of these kinds of things when he was onstage, but those had been costumes. He was fairly certain Master didn't intend any usual sort of performance.

Master selected quite a few items—Sky didn't pay attention to which ones—and finally the store's slave topped off the pile with a PVC thong with a fishnet front. The thong had itched—not that anyone had asked Sky's opinion. When the store slave realized how much Master intended to spend, his grin widened. "Just a moment, please, sir." He scurried to the back, and Master stood with a tight jaw and narrowed eyes.

When the slave emerged from the back room, a solidly built man with short, silver-gray hair accompanied him. He was wearing a well-tailored suit and shiny black shoes, and he gave Master a wide smile. "Welcome to Trappings," he boomed. "It looks as if you have quite a shopping list today. I'm Roger Fischer."

Master shook his hand. "Morgan Wallace. New acquisition," he said, inclining his head toward Sky.

"Ah. May I?"

With a nod, Master granted permission.

Mr. Fischer looked Sky carefully up and down. Then he prodded Sky's arms and measured Sky's waist with his hands.

"He's going to add a little more weight and muscle," Master said. "I want to make sure everything will continue to fit."

"Of course." Mr. Fischer examined the pile of items his slave had accumulated on Master's behalf, then turned to Master. "Can I suggest a few things?"

"Sure."

Mr. Fischer spoke quietly to his slave, who hurried to collect things. Meanwhile, Master and Mr. Fischer had a conversation in which Master said that he'd just moved to the city and didn't know the area well. "But you'd like to get to know it better?" Mr. Fischer asked with a friendly grin.

"Definitely."

"Let's get your gear all set, and then I can give you some ideas."

The slave returned, and Sky modeled more things, until finally Master gave an odd, tight smile. "I think that's enough to start me off."

"A very good start. My boy will ring everything up, but if you'll follow me, I can offer you those ideas I promised. And a drink."

"Sounds good." Master followed him toward the back of the store as the slave gathered up the substantial pile. Sky was sickly certain he was going to have to stand there, naked, but just before Master entered the back room, he turned around. "Get dressed, Sky. And have a seat somewhere."

"Thank you, Master." Sky was deeply relieved. He scrambled into his clothes and sat on a chair near the cash register. He watched as the other slave examined all the price tags, punched buttons on the register, and carefully placed the items in bags. "Master won't be happy about being charged extra for the bags," Sky said, mostly because he was too unsettled to remain quiet.

"We can throw them in for free."

"Your master won't mind?"

The kid shook his head. "With the amount of money your master's spending? No way." He bagged the last of the items and walked out from the counter to crouch in front of Sky. "Are you new to . . ." He waved his hand to indicate the store's contents.

"Yes."

"You're a little old for the first time."

Since the statement was true, Sky didn't take offense. "I used to sing."

"Well . . . I don't know exactly what your master has planned for you. He looks strong. And a little angry. But whatever he does to you, you can think of it as a performance, maybe. That might help you get through it."

"Is that what you do?"

The slave shrugged. "Sometimes." He gave the door to the back room a hasty look, rose gracefully, and returned to the counter.

Master had Sky store all the things from Trappings in the playroom wardrobe, and then acted as if they didn't exist. For the next few days, Master and Sky went running together, ate together, and watched TV together—even slept together—but didn't speak much. Master spent a lot of time on his laptop and phones. Sky tried to stay busy with cleaning, which didn't really take up much time, and cooking, which only occasionally resulted in something edible. Master didn't scold or punish him over the ruined food, not even when Sky burned chicken breasts and made the smoke detectors blare. Over all those days, they didn't touch each other.

Four days into this, when Sky was sweeping the perfectly clean floor for the third time that day, Master looked up from his computer screen. "You're bored silly, aren't you?"

"No, Master. I—"

"Rule one."

Right. The truth. "I don't have much work to do," Sky admitted.

"And you're miserable. No humming." He rubbed his cheek, where the stubble had almost grown into a beard. "I guess maybe I can do something about the boredom, anyway." He closed his computer, stood, and stretched. Then he crossed to the front door, where he slipped into shoes and a jacket. "Stay here. I'll be back in a while."

Sky paced the room after Master was gone. He'd rarely been left alone like this, but instead of freedom, he felt as if his chains were tighter than usual. It wasn't as if he could run away, since he'd be tracked down immediately if he tried. He would never be able to just walk out the door and take a nice stroll because he was restless or because the weather looked nice. He was no tiger, yet he'd spend his entire life caged.

The more he paced, the angrier he got. It would be so much easier if Master stopped pretending Sky was a real person and instead treated him the way his other owners had—as simple property. It would be so much easier if the playroom didn't lurk behind its walls in the corner, constantly reminding him of the unspecified fate lying in wait. He finally spoke into the empty room. "It would be easier if everything they said about slaves were true." If he didn't feel and hope and fear like a human being.

When the open space loomed too large, he decided to go upstairs. He knew that was allowed; Master had given him freedom to roam the apartment at will. He thought maybe he would take a bath or even a nap. But when he got there, he saw that the drawer to the nightstand on Master's side of the bed wasn't completely closed. Curiosity killed common sense, and Sky slid the drawer open.

It held a gun.

Sky had never seen a real handgun before, and might have wondered whether the dull black object was a toy, except the drawer also contained a cardboard box of cartridges. Why would Master keep a gun at his bedside?

Sky was nearly felled by his sheer lack of knowledge about the man who owned him, the man who slept with him. Master had shared so little about himself, and even those few scraps might be lies. Of course, while every day of a slave's history was available to his master, every crevice of his body open for inspection, a slave was entitled to nothing. A freeman's truths were irrelevant to the chattel he owned.

But oh, sweet heavens, those truths were the key to Sky's future.

Moving like a robot, he returned the drawer to its original position, carefully stopping it that slight bit before full closure.

He walked downstairs. And then he stood at the window, looking at nothing.

Sky startled violently when Master burst through the front door, carrying a large paper bag. His face was slightly flushed. "Take this."

When Sky rushed over, he discovered that the bag was heavy. Before he could ask what to do with it, Master kicked off his shoes, let his jacket fall to the floor, and pushed past him, striding toward his laptop. "You can have those later," Master said. He opened his laptop and punched some keys, but didn't look up at Sky. "I wasn't sure what you'd like, so I got a sort of random selection."

Bravely, Sky peeked inside. "Books, Master?"

"To entertain you. But not now. Go upstairs and clean yourself very thoroughly. Shave, too. And don't bother getting dressed before you come down."

The odd thing was that Master sounded almost as tight and apprehensive as Sky felt. But no use asking why, so Sky simply hurried to obey. He left the bag of books on a side table, experiencing a slight pang at not being able to inspect them now—and a funny little twist in his heart because Master had bought them for him. Then he ran upstairs.

He used all the special products in the shower, scrubbing his hair and cleansing every bit of his body. Even though it wasn't really *his* body, he reminded himself. As he lathered his skin, he felt an odd detachment, as if that surface was no more a part of him than the kitchen counter or the refrigerator door. When he was through in the shower, he dried off, shaved his face, and brushed his teeth. He eyed his hair thoughtfully in the mirror. Hair products lined the bathroom counter, but Master had never instructed him to use them. In the end, Sky simply towel-dried and combed his pale amber locks, which now fell nearly to his shoulders in soft waves. He preferred it short, but nobody cared what he preferred.

He took a few steadying breaths before walking downstairs.

Master looked up from his phones when Sky descended, and for a moment or two, Master froze. When he swallowed, the sound was loud. "Jesus, you're beautiful," he rasped.

Although Sky was accustomed to being stared at, he felt his cheeks flush, and he ducked his head.

"If I were *really* a free man," Master said, "I'd bend you over this couch, lick every inch of you, and make you come so hard you'd forget how to walk."

Sky snapped his head up, mortified to feel his cock harden. How could he not become aroused when Master looked at him like that, as if Sky were the most desirable man he'd ever seen, as if Master wanted nothing more than to make Sky's nerve endings sing with joy? But then Master blinked, tightened his shoulders, and gazed at Sky with something that looked more akin to regret.

"But I can't, Sky. I'm . . . Christ, I'm sorry. Come with me." He put down the phones and walked toward the playroom.

Sky followed, but slowly because his legs were disobedient. By the time he entered the enclosure, Master was waiting with a hard expression. Yet at the same time, he caressed one of the pieces of bondage furniture, stroking the padded bench slowly, as if doing so comforted him. He didn't say anything, and the uncertainty twisted Sky's stomach.

"D-do you want me to lean on that, Master?" If he pretended the straps weren't there, he could probably force himself down onto the bench.

But Master shook his head. "We're going out." He turned and marched to the wardrobe, then took what seemed like a long time making his selections. Finally he turned around with a pile of clothing, all black, and held it toward Sky.

Biting his lip, Sky took it and got dressed. The first item was a black leather kilt. While the pleated front and back hung almost to his knees, the sides were open except for two thick, buckled straps around his waist and hips. The shirt was sleeveless and made of sheer mesh with a studded leather strip down the center and a shorter strip on each shoulder. The short socks he covered with a pair of heavy ankle boots.

Stone-faced, Master looked him over. "Honestly, I prefer the unadorned version. Hell, I think you look great in jeans and a button-down." He sighed. "Dress code. Okay, my turn. Just . . . wait for me."

Sky hoped the rule about asking for clarification still held. "Here, Master?"

It must have, because Master didn't seem angry. "No. I'll be a little while. Go eat something light."

Sky's leather clothes squeaked as he walked, and the eyelets on his boots jangled. Master had turned him into a musical instrument of sorts. At least the outfit was fairly comfortable, although he'd be cold outside.

Eat something light. After some consideration, Sky decided that whole-grain toast and a salad would work. He could prepare that without burning down the building. Master hadn't said anything about whether he would eat too, so Sky compromised by toasting two pieces of bread for himself but making a salad big enough for them both. If Master didn't want it now, one of them could eat the rest later.

He heard the shower running upstairs, followed by the thumps of Master walking around. Sky thought about the gun.

Just as he was finishing his meal, Master came downstairs. He had followed Sky's color scheme, dressing himself in black trousers and a black silk shirt. Everything was tightly fitted, showing off the trimness of his waist and the imposing muscles of his chest, arms, and thighs. He'd shaved too—although Sky suspected dark stubble would sprout within hours—and he'd gelled his dark hair. "Well?" he asked, spreading his arms.

"Perfection," Sky whispered.

Master walked closer—very close—and gently tugged Sky off the counter stool. With their chests nearly touching, Master lifted Sky's chin with his finger. "You're a very good actor."

"Master?"

"You almost make me think you really want me."

Sky's throat felt like it had been scoured with sandpaper. "Rule one, Master."

One corner of Master's mouth quirked. "But truth is a slippery substance, isn't it? Believe me, I know." His expression turned sober, and he let Sky go. "Doesn't matter. You won't want me after tonight anyway."

With that grim prediction, he fetched his coat.

They hurried to the waiting car—this time a sleek limo—but Sky was shivering by the time they dove into the back. As the driver pulled away from the curb, Master gathered Sky to his side and wrapped an arm around his shoulders, lending him heat. Master's scent of spicy aftershave and wool overpowered Sky's own citrus and leather, as if Master were intent on claiming all aspects of Sky's body. Sky couldn't help but wonder what Master's cock would feel like inside his ass, solid and hot; and for no discernable reason, that thought soothed the edges of Sky's fear.

The limo came to a halt at the top of a steep hill, in front of a large house. Warm light spilled from the house's rounded front windows, and strings of lights lined the layers of ornate balconies. A uniformed slave with very dark skin opened Master's car door and waited for him to get out. Master gestured impatiently at Sky to follow.

"Your name, sir?" the slave asked quietly.

"Morgan Wallace."

The slave referred to an iPad, nodded, and gave Master a bow. "Welcome, sir. Please step this way." He waved an arm toward the sweeping front stairs.

Like a strange, small parade, the three of them ascended. Another liveried slave opened the door as they arrived; he looked so much like the first man that they might be twins. "Welcome, sir. May I take your coat?"

Master shrugged out of his jacket and handed it to the slave. It was warm inside the house, much to Sky's relief, and thudding music played somewhere, muted except for the beat. A third male slave appeared, this one with pale brown skin, wearing nothing but a tiny pair of tight white shorts and brushed-steel bracelets. "This way, please, sir."

The foyer was an intimate space with warm, gleaming woods that Sky suspected were original to the house. The foyer led to a room that was bare except for a few marble statues of men in chains and a broad staircase with carved wooden railings. At the top of the stairs, they crossed a carpeted hallway to a pair of intricately painted doors. When the slave opened them, Master strode confidently in, Sky at his heels.

Someone must have alerted the host that Master had arrived, because a tall man came at once to greet him. He and Master exchanged pleasantries and lapsed into small talk as they wound their way through the crowd. Sky didn't catch anything they said; he was too busy trying to process the situation without collapsing. Everyone in the room was male. There were perhaps fifty freemen, all of them dressed like Master, most of them with drinks in their hands. And kneeling beside most of them were slaves. *They* were dressed more or less like Sky, if they wore anything at all. But it wasn't the kneeling or nudity that scared Sky—he feared neither of those things—but rather the bruises, welts, and burns visible on the slaves' skin and the dull despair in their eyes.

When Master and the host stopped to talk to a group of men, Sky was almost thankful that Master pushed him to his knees. At least that way, there was less danger of Sky's legs giving out. And he couldn't as easily see the chains and bondage devices lining the walls of the large room—or the slaves who hung on those walls, bleeding.

A haze enveloped Sky. He dimly felt the ache in his knees—alleviated only occasionally and briefly when Master tapped him to rise before moving to a different part of the room and then pushed him back to kneeling. He barely registered the touch of men's fingers on his hair, on his shoulders and neck and back; the scents of food and alcohol; the sounds of music and talk and screams.

Then Master tapped him again, but this time, instead of leading Sky through the crowd, he stood there as three men watched. One of them seemed familiar, and then Sky remembered—Mr. Fischer from Trappings. He was grinning widely. "It's a good look on him," Mr. Fischer said.

Master nodded. He stood impassively while one of his other companions lifted the back of Sky's kilt and smoothed a palm over his ass. "Nice," said the man. "Could use some color, though."

"Yeah. But look, he's brand-new to this. I don't want to break him."

The man laughed and pinched Sky's ass hard enough to make him yelp. "But breaking them is the fun part."

"Aw, you know that's not true, Vince," chimed in the other man. He lifted the front of the kilt and gave Sky's balls a hard squeeze. "It's the folding, spindling, and mutilating that are the good parts."

All of them laughed that time, even Master, and Sky was trapped between the fingers delving into his ass crack and the palm enclosing his balls. He tried to keep his face neutral and his thoughts far away, but just breathing seemed to take all his strength.

Vince's blunt finger poked at Sky's sphincter, not quite inside. "He's pretty old for a newbie, Morgan. Why him?"

"I don't have much taste for delicate. Besides, this one has other talents."

"Such as?"

"Voice like an angel. He used to be in one of those boy bands."

To Sky's considerable relief, both men let go of him, allowing the flaps of his kilt to fall back down. Then Mr. Fischer trotted off, returning a moment later with the host, who smiled at Master. "Roger tells me your slave can sing."

"He can."

"How about an impromptu concert?"

"It would be a pleasure."

They led Sky to the rear of the room and stood him before a bank of curtained windows. He tried not to see the slave a few yards to his right, a naked young man with almost translucently pale skin marred with vivid red lash marks; he was faceup chained to a wooden cross, his cheeks streaked with drying tears.

The house music stopped abruptly. The host clapped his hands, and all the freemen turned to look, anticipation clear on every face. "We have a little treat for you," the host boomed. "Courtesy of our new friend, Morgan Wallace."

Master gave the crowd a small wave. Then he turned to Sky. "Sing." There was an odd message in his eyes, one Sky couldn't decipher.

"Yes, Master. What song would you like?"

Master shrugged. "Something to please this crowd."

And it was strange, but his response was like a tacit vote of confidence, an acknowledgment that Sky was an expert at this. Sky's uneasy stomach settled. He looked out at the freemen, then at the miserable slaves, and decided nothing bouncy would do. After a few deep breaths to stretch his lungs, he launched into "The House of the Rising Sun."

It was a good performance. His vocal cords were well rested, and the song was an excellent showcase for his deepish tenor and wide vocal range. He hadn't been allowed to sing it often at the Paradiso, but tonight the result was an enthusiastic round of applause.

"One more?" the host asked Master.

"Sure. Do you have a favorite?"

The host considered for a moment, stroking his narrow chin. Then a slow smile spread across his face. "'Beast of Burden.' Can you do that one, slave?" His gaze held nothing but contempt—and perhaps a hint of challenge.

Sky stole a quick glance at his master, who nodded. "Yes, sir," Sky said meekly to the host.

He didn't mind this song, but he understood that the host intended it as a cruel joke at Sky's expense: a slave claiming he'd never shoulder another's burden, a slave begging a woman to make love to him. All the freemen were in on the joke too, grinning as Sky sang—even Master. There was something menacing in Master's smile, although Sky didn't understand why.

This time the audience hooted and called when Sky was done. Then the host made a signal with his hand, and the house music came back on. He turned to Master. "You're right—you've found yourself a treat. Shall we see how well he sings under the lash?"

"Yeah," said Master.

Sky followed them numbly to the side of the room. At Master's command, he stripped off his shirt and unbuckled his kilt, letting them both fall to the floor. Master grasped the back of Sky's neck and forced him to bend forward over wooden stocks until his neck nestled into the notch. Master placed Sky's wrists into the two smaller notches, one on either side of his head, and brought down the corresponding piece that locked Sky in place. Somebody kicked Sky's legs apart and secured his ankles with straps. A padded bar under his belly held much of his weight. Sky was dimly grateful for the bondage, because he couldn't have forced himself to hold still for what he knew was coming.

At first, there was no pain. Just hands roaming over his back and ass, inside his thighs, over his hanging cock and balls. That was bad enough, really—a parody of tenderness that made him want to cry.

But then Master began to paddle him. Softly at first, then harder, every loud smack of wood against flesh drawing an appreciative noise from the crowd. Master was a powerful man, and soon the blows came so fast and heavy that they blurred into a single hammering agony. All of Sky's muscles shook, he tasted blood, and despite his efforts to remain silent, harsh cries tore from his throat.

At some point, the paddling stopped. But people smoothed their palms over the hot bruises, and even those gentle touches hurt. They were talking about him. He recognized Master's deep voice but not the meaning of any of his words.

And then, without warning, a crack sounded and a whip bit into his back.

This time, Sky screamed. He might have begged as well—he had no idea—but it didn't matter. The lash worked over his back, leaving strands of fire that consumed him.

By the time the torture stopped, there was nothing left of him. He barely noticed when someone rammed a slick cock into his ass and began to fuck him.

CHAPTER SIX

He got to the car, but he didn't remember how. He seemed to have lost some time. But as the limo rolled through the streets, Sky found himself sprawled on his side on the backseat, his head pillowed in Master's lap and his face buried in Master's silk-covered belly. Master was silently running his fingers through Sky's hair.

When the limo stopped again, Master took one of Sky's arms over his shoulders and the driver took the other and together they dragged Sky up to the loft. Even with his mouth clamped shut, Sky groaned and whimpered the entire way. And then there was another flight of stairs, and he was settled stomach-down atop Master's expensive sheets on his soft bed.

Time slipped away from him again, like clouds dissolving in a summer sky. He grunted when Master repositioned him and removed his boots and socks, hissed when Master applied some kind of cream to his back and ass. But the cream numbed the pain a little, which was good, and soon afterward Master gave him some pills and a cup with a straw so Sky could swallow them. The liquid felt wonderful slipping down his throat.

"Are you warm enough?" asked Master.

Sky tried to nod, but it hurt too much. "Yes," he whispered.

"Do you need to pee?"

"No." Actually, Sky thought he might have pissed himself during the beating, although he wasn't sure. Urine didn't feel much different from blood and sweat when it ran down his legs.

"Rest, then. I'll be back in a little bit with more water. Maybe some crackers or a smoothie if you think you can handle it. You need potassium."

Sky had no answer for that. He just closed his eyes and enjoyed the crisp feel of the pillowcase against his cheek. He flinched when Master touched him, but all Master did was pet his nape using tiny, soft circles that made Sky's eyes fill with tears. "Rest," Master said again. The mattress shifted as he stood.

Perhaps Sky dozed a bit; he wasn't sure. At some point, however, he became aware of Master's voice rising to the bedroom, tight with what sounded like anger.

"—do this, Trish. It's not fucking . . . Yeah, I know. God *damn* it, I know! . . . That was different. I had choices. I *wanted* it. And it wasn't . . ." A long pause, and then Master sounded resigned and tired instead of furious. "Yeah, I am. I'm making progress. Just tell me it's worth it, okay? . . . Thanks. You too."

A few minutes after that, a blender whirled and water ran. Master came up the stairs, set something on the nightstand with a clatter, and sat on the mattress. He tucked a strand of hair behind Sky's ear. "Think you can manage something in your stomach? It'll help."

Sky made a noncommittal hum. The pills Master had given him hadn't exactly stopped the hurting, but they'd separated Sky from it, as if the pain were a mildly interesting television show. He was floating somewhere a few inches outside his head.

Master grunted, lifted Sky's pillow a little, and stuck a straw in Sky's mouth. Sucking took supreme effort, but he was rewarded with the sweet taste of bananas and strawberries and the wonderfully cold creaminess of milk. He managed several slurps. Then Master took the straw away and replaced it with a bit of saltine. "Crumbs in your bed," Sky mumbled after swallowing.

With a soft chuckle, Master stroked Sky's hair. "I'll survive." He gave Sky some more sips of the smoothie.

They continued like that for some time, Master alternating the smoothie with crackers and water and Sky placidly swallowing whatever was in his mouth. But Master seemed to sense when it was almost too much. Then he simply sat there, his fingers gentle in Sky's hair. Sky's eyelids were too heavy to open, but that was okay.

Master left for a few minutes and returned smelling of alcohol. He resumed touching Sky, sometimes pausing for a bit—to refill his glass, judging by the sounds of gurgling liquid and then glass against wood.

Sky heard soft singing, and at first he thought he was doing it, but after a moment he realized his throat was still and his mouth closed. Besides, this singing was off-key enough to have earned Sky a beating back at Club Paradiso, and he'd already been beaten beyond endurance today. The lyrics were mangled too. But he recognized the song—Steve Miller's "Winter Time"—and then the singer.

"Master?" Sky whispered.

Master stopped singing. "Do you need something?"

"Singing."

"Oh. Sorry. It's probably painful for you to listen to me. I know I suck."

Sky pressed his head more firmly against Master's hand. "'S nice."

"You're only saying that because you're on good drugs. Back in fifth grade, my music teacher took me aside and begged me to just mouth the words when the class sang. I haven't improved since."

"Don't care." Nobody had ever sung to him before, not even badly.

"God, Sky, when you sang tonight? It was amazing."

A bolt of anger cut through the drug haze and pain, and Sky was medicated enough not to care about the consequences. He shifted to more easily look into Master's eyes. "Doesn't matter how well I sang. It could have been the best performance ever. But all you wanted from me was suffering."

Master jerked his head back. He pressed his lips together, and if Sky had possessed the capability, he would have braced himself for more punishment. But all Master did was reach for the whiskey bottle and refill his glass, his hand shaking. He drained the glass at once. "Suffering can be a gift. It can even be beautiful when it's willingly taken, willingly given. But when it's stolen, that's an abomination." His tongue stumbled a little over the final word, slurring it.

Sky was too far gone to understand what he was talking about.

After another refill—this one sipped rather than guzzled—Master shook his head. "*I* wanted your songs. Still do. 'S why we're both fucked."

He said nothing more. Sky allowed his eyes to remain closed, and Master resumed playing with his hair. Sky's anger dissolved like sugar on the tongue, and he allowed the haze to swallow him.

The bedside clock read 12:18 p.m. when Sky stirred, but the San Francisco fog kept the sun from streaming through the skylight. His body was one big bruise, and he had no desire to move, but his bladder felt otherwise. He was just wondering if he could manage a timely crawl to the bathroom when a hand settled on his arm. "Awake?" Master asked.

"Yes, Master. I . . . Please . . ."

Luckily, Master understood Sky's incoherent plea. He stood, groaned, and fell back onto the mattress. "Shit. My head feels like your ass looks. Hang on." He regained his feet and shuffled to Sky's side of the bed. He'd taken off his shoes, socks, and trousers, but nothing else, and his nice silk shirt was now a wrinkled mess. His hair stood up in wild spikes and his eyes were red, but he was gentle as he helped Sky stand. "Let me take your weight," Master ordered, wrapping Sky's arm around his waist.

The walk to the bathroom was long and painful, and Master had to prop Sky while he peed. "No blood," Master commented when he saw the urine. "Good. At least that fucker didn't get your kidneys." Which implied, Sky supposed, that Master hadn't been the one who'd lashed him. Had it been someone else who'd fucked him too?

Sky felt a little better when he was done peeing. Master, on the other hand, stared into the flushing toilet as if he might be considering puking into it.

"Does it give you any satisfaction to know I feel like death?" Master asked.

"No."

"Rule one?"

Sky met his gaze. "I don't want you to hurt, Master."

Master made a *hmm* noise, then a noisy sigh. "I smell like death, too, and my breath could kill a rabid hippo at fifty yards. How about if I get you back to the bed so I can . . . decontaminate myself. Then I'll figure out something for you to eat. I've got some ointment for your back, too."

"Thank you, Master."

"Don't. Just . . . don't thank me, okay? I feel shitty enough already." With Sky attached to him, he took two steps toward the door, then stopped. "Do you want more of those pills I gave you last night? Or will ibuprofen be enough?"

The pills had insulated him from the pain, but Sky didn't like the fuzzy feeling. He was afraid of what else his drugged tongue might say. "Ibuprofen."

"Okay, good." Master steered them to the sink, and Sky leaned with his belly against it. Master dug around in the medicine cabinet, found a plastic bottle, and dumped out a couple of caplets. Grateful for any pain relief, Sky was ready to dry-swallow them, but then Master filled a plastic cup from the tap and gave him that too.

Collapsing face-first onto the mattress was a huge relief. As Sky listened to the shower, it occurred to him that he must reek too—he felt filthy—but Master hadn't mentioned it. Not that Sky would be able to withstand a shower. Even the thought of water hitting his skin made him shudder.

After Master finished in the bathroom, he pulled on sweatpants and a T-shirt, then gathered assorted glasses, cups, and bottles from the bedside. "Back in a few." He disappeared down the stairs, and soon the sounds of clattering pans and dishes wended their way up, along with the faint smell of melting butter. Sky realized he was hungry.

It wasn't long before Master returned with a tray. "Can you roll onto your side?" he asked as he approached the bed. Sky could, and although his skin pulled and his muscles complained, the pain was a dull ache instead of a sharp one.

Master sat next to him. "Open up," he said, smiling down at Sky.

"I can—"

"Let me. The less you move around, the better."

So Sky opened his mouth like a baby bird, and Master slowly fed him spoonfuls of a delicious, creamy egg-and-cheese concoction, along with sips of orange juice through a straw. "None for you?" Sky asked when the plate was empty.

"I can't even think about eating right now. I deserve a medal for cooking and feeding you without barfing up my guts." But he smiled as he said it. Then he set the tray aside and tapped Sky's shoulder. "Onto your stomach—it's time for that ointment."

Despite dreading the touch on his back, Sky obeyed. At first Master's fingers on his skin made him flinch, but Master kept the pressure gentle, and the cool gel soothed Sky immediately. Still, he tensed when Master finished his back and reached his ass. "Just the ointment," Master assured him, and for some reason Sky believed him.

Eventually Master finished ministering to Sky, but still he remained on the bed, his brow furrowed. "What a fucking mess," he mumbled.

"I'm sorry."

"Jesus, Sky! Not you. And if you never say *I'm sorry* to me again, I'll be perfectly happy. You're . . ." He started to rub his face, but stopped and grimaced when he realized his fingers were still greasy from the ointment. "I used to think the answers were all so simple, you know? But now it seems like I can't even figure out the right questions."

"I don't know either the questions or the answers," Sky said.

"I doubt that." Master scrunched up his face. "I have to work. You'll be all right for a couple of hours?"

"I think I'll sleep," said Sky, even though he'd already slept for hours.

"Good. Use your energy for healing. I might be capable of eating by dinnertime. Any requests?"

Sky shook his head. "Everything you make tastes good."

The grin on Master's face made him look years younger. "I've never had anyone around to appreciate my food before. It's nice. Makes cooking more fun."

"Why do you— Shouldn't you have servants cooking for you? Slaves?"

"I like doing it. It's like magic, almost. Anyway, most of my life I had to do it if I didn't want to go hungry." When Sky blinked at him, Master shook his head. "Yeah, I know what you see when you look at me. Fancy apartment, hired cars, enough ready cash to buy an expensive slave. But it's not . . . I was poor as a kid. Single mom, right? She worked two, three jobs just to pay the rent on our shitty rat-hole apartments. Even when she was home at dinnertime, she was too wiped to cook. And believe me, we didn't own anyone to do it for us. So I taught myself how."

Sky wasn't as surprised at this revelation as he might have been. He'd seen his master's rough edges and heard them in his voice. "What happened to your father?" he asked hesitantly.

Master didn't seem to take offense at the question. "He was a two-bit drug dealer who got himself shot before my second birthday. I don't remember him. You know, every time I saw roaches in the kitchen or got laughed at in school because my clothes were old and my shoes had holes, I'd make this promise to myself. *Someday I'm gonna be better than this.* And here I fucking am." He shook his head as if his obvious success didn't meet his standards.

Shifting in the sheets, Sky tried to relieve some of the soreness in his back. Master helped by pulling a blanket out of the way and repositioning a pillow. "How about you?" he asked.

"I'm a slave. I always have been." It was possible for a freeman to be sentenced to slavery for committing certain crimes, or to be driven into slavery by debt, but those people would generally end up in the mines or somewhere else where they were watched carefully and didn't cost their owners too much if they were worked to death. They didn't adjust well—that was the official explanation. But Sky wondered if the truth was that no freeman wanted to see them around and be reminded of the capricious line between freedom and slavery. Besides, all their claims about the slave gene were harder to argue when the slave in question had once been as free as them. Better to hide the wretched souls away and forget about them.

"But you had parents," Master insisted. "Slaves don't grow on trees."

The hurt was so ancient Sky barely felt it. "My mother was owned by a bordello in Los Angeles. The bordello's owner sold me when I was eight."

Master *visibly* flinched, and a sound somewhere between a gasp and a groan escaped him. "Eight. Jesus. Do you remember much about her?"

"She was pretty. Obviously, considering how she served. She was quiet. But she liked to sing, and she was good at it. There was a bar in the bordello, and sometimes the management had her sing to customers there." Such little scraps of nothing, but that was all Sky had.

Master nodded. "Your father?"

"I don't know." But he remembered rule one, and besides, a strange feeling of intimacy had settled in the room. "My mother told me he was a famous rock star."

"Was he?" Master didn't appear appalled at the idea that Sky's father was a freeman. Not that it mattered—the child of a slave was also a slave, no matter who'd fathered him. But it wasn't a topic freemen liked to discuss.

"I have no idea. She said her owner was hoping to produce a slave who'd fetch a high price—attractive and talented."

"Shit. Like breeding show dogs. I guess people do that, though, don't they?" He scrutinized Sky, open-faced and raw, as if he expected Sky to somehow comfort him.

"They do," Sky confirmed. "And usually the bordello was really careful about not letting the slaves get pregnant. Less income that way. But my mother did, and nobody ended the pregnancy. Famous musicians and movie stars visited the bordello all the time, so it's plausible that he did."

"Who's *he*?"

Sky hesitated only a moment before answering, because what difference did it make? "Jonny Walsh."

Master stared at him for a moment, then whipped out a phone from his back pocket. He pressed at the keys, and whatever he saw made his eyes widen. "Holy fuck. You look like him. Same chin, same nose. And those amazing eyes."

Sky knew this already because he'd seen photos of Jonny Walsh. His irises were clear cerulean with a navy band at the edge—the same color eyes that had inspired Sky's name.

"Does Walsh know about you?" Master asked.

"Why would he want to?"

"Because—"

"Because what?" Another stab of that stupid, dangerous anger, and again Sky couldn't hold his tongue. "Would *you* want to know that a slave was carrying your DNA around? Would you want to know that you'd spawned *this*?" He waved a hand to indicate his battered backside.

Master studied him for a long moment before bending close and cupping his hand over Sky's nape. "Anyone with half a brain should be proud to be related to someone like you." Then he stood very quickly. "I have work."

Sky ate his dinner in bed, and afterward he made it to the bathroom by himself, with Master watching him closely. When Sky emerged, Master gave him a sad smile. "I bet you're feeling well enough to be bored. Would you rather stay up here and watch TV or come downstairs? I can help."

Choices. Master gave him these small ones. Did he think that helped make up for never having control over anything important?

"Downstairs, please."

Master helped him into a pair of fleece pants—silly and unnecessary, yet for some reason the clothing made Sky feel slightly better. Even the softest shirt would only hurt Sky's back, so Master turned up the heat to warm the loft. With Master steadying him, Sky made his way down the stairs.

Perhaps Master had planned ahead for this. When they reached the main floor, he took Sky over to the couch, where a familiar bag waited. "I don't know how comfortable it'd be, but you could try putting a book on the floor and reading like that," he suggested. He looked uncharacteristically insecure. "Or at least, you can see what I brought you. If you want."

In truth, Sky was curious to see the titles. He lay belly-down on the couch, his head and shoulders hanging over the edge. He'd previously disliked the modern design of the furniture, wishing there were padded armrests, but now he was thankful for their absence.

Master had bought him ten paperbacks. Some were nonfiction—one about the Titanic, one a history of tea, and the other a tourist's guide to San Francisco. The remaining books spanned a range of fiction genres, from young adult, romance, and fantasy to prize-winning literature. "I didn't know what you liked," said Master, hovering nearby.

Sky didn't know what he liked either. He'd rarely had access to books, and the few he did get were fairly random. When he was with 2Nyte, the manager would sometimes toss a few volumes into the back of the truck, mainly to keep the band members from getting too irritable with one another. At Club Paradiso, Bill occasionally brought him something he'd read or a book he'd discovered abandoned on the subway. Sky had devoured whatever came his way, sometimes rereading the same book so many times that he could recite whole passages. What Master had given him was a feast. And a puzzle, because the "Approved for Slaves" seal was conspicuously absent from most of the covers. He didn't know whether Master had deliberately chosen books meant only for freemen or whether it had been an oversight. Either way, Sky decided, it was best not to question the decision.

After considerable indecision about what to start with, Sky settled on the shortest book, reasoning that he had the greatest chance of finishing that one before . . . whatever happened next. It was a mystery about murders on an isolated island. Master sat at the free end of the couch and opened his laptop, and Sky was soon so engrossed in the story that his aches and discomforts receded.

Eventually his shoulders protested the awkward position, and Sky regretfully closed the book. With a few pained grunts and a little help from Master, Sky repositioned himself on the couch so he lay on his side, facing out.

Master stuck a couple of throw pillows under Sky's head. "How about some TV?" he suggested. At Sky's nod, Master clicked on the TV and began to scroll through the channels. He stopped when he got to a movie. "*Big*. I can live with this one. Okay with you?"

Sky smiled. He hadn't seen it in years. "I like *Big*."

So that was what they watched, both of them chuckling over the funny parts. When that movie ended, *You've Got Mail* began. Apparently the channel was doing some kind of Tom Hanks retrospective. Sky and Master watched that one too. By the end, Sky couldn't hide his yawns. Master stroked Sky's fleece-covered calf. "If I gave you something soft to sit on, do you think you'd like a bath?"

Sky sniffed. "I stink."

"You're not exactly fresh as a daisy, no. But I can put up with it if a bath's too much."

Good heavens, it would be nice to be clean. In addition to the ointment, his skin was covered in dried sweat and a little dried blood. Dried come itched between his legs. "I'd like a bath, please."

"Good." Master closed his laptop. "Wait here."

To Sky's considerable surprise, Master put on shoes and jacket. He paused at the front door. "I'll be back in fifteen minutes, okay?"

"Yes, Master."

As soon as Master was gone, Sky slowly sat up. If he'd been able, he'd have put on his own shoes and hoodie and left the apartment, disappearing into the city. Master would have found him soon enough—his phone undoubtedly had an app to track Sky's chip—but Sky would have enjoyed probably an hour or so of freedom. Yes, the price would be dear, but maybe it would have been worth it.

But the temptation didn't matter because Sky could barely make it across the room to the bathroom. He had to hold the wall for support while he used the toilet, and shuffling back to the couch was painful enough to make his eyes water. He was relieved to lie down again.

His thoughts, inevitably, turned to Master. Not to what had happened the previous night or was likely to happen again in the future—those things were too distressing to contemplate. Instead he lingered over the puzzle of Morgan Wallace. Over the past days, the solution to that puzzle hadn't become any clearer; if anything, Sky had discovered more stray pieces that didn't fit anywhere.

Was Master a drug dealer? It would explain a lot, like having money even though he didn't seem to go to work, the two phones he used constantly, and the gun. He'd already told Sky that his father had sold drugs. The idea was disquieting not because Sky cared about the morality of it, but because it meant Master was vulnerable. And if that was the case, Sky was in even deeper trouble than he thought.

Before he'd belonged to Club Paradiso, Sky had sung at a different place called the Fireside Lounge. It was kitschy, decorated like an enormous midcentury living room, but it was popular with tourists.

Sky and the other singers had worn suits and crooned tunes by Dean Martin and Frank Sinatra, and Sky had been relatively happy. But one afternoon as the club was getting ready to open, police had stormed in and seized paperwork and computers from the manager's office—along with all the slaves. For several weeks, Sky, the other singers, and the kitchen and cleaning staff had languished in a warehouse not much better than the one where Sky had ended up after Club Paradiso. They'd heard the guards at the warehouse talking about how the owners of the Lounge had been indicted for tax evasion and money laundering. And then all the slaves except the singers had been sold at auction, ending up who knew where. Sky had considered himself very lucky to be bought by the owners of Club Paradiso.

If Master were arrested and Sky sold again, who would buy him and for what purpose? He was no longer so young, and nobody remembered or cared that he had been almost famous. His lack of prospects made him shiver.

And then his thoughts turned toward the even more immediate aspects of the puzzle. What did Master truly want from him? Why was he so kind so much of the time, offering Sky liberties few slaves were given? Treating him . . . almost like a person. Expressing regret when Sky was beaten senseless, even as Master administered part of that beating himself and kept a room full of devices intended to inflict pain and suffering.

Sky had no answers to any of this. Even worse, he realized that he was a significant part of the puzzle himself. Despite all his fears, despite the bruises and welts that made simple movements agony, he was drawn to Master. He wanted . . . well, he wasn't sure what he wanted, but he knew that he enjoyed watching TV, exercising, and learning to cook with Master. He knew that his own breaths drew in and out in rhythm with Master's when they lay in bed. Sweet heavens. Maybe it was just because Sky had never belonged to a single owner, had never been the focus of anyone's attention in this way. Master made him feel valued.

Oh, Sky was truly a stupid slave.

Master returned home after exactly fifteen minutes, laden with plastic bags. "It's a good thing there are a zillion CVSs and Walgreens in this city," he said, grinning, as he kicked off his shoes. "But man, I keep forgetting to bring my own bags."

Sky wasn't sure whether he should help with the purchases, but when he started to stand, Master shook his head. "You wait there. I'll get everything set up for you and then come help you up the stairs."

Soon Sky heard water running in the upstairs bathroom. He wondered what Master meant by "everything." It looked as if he'd bought a lot of things.

The upstairs tub was enormous and took a long time to fill. Sky had nearly dozed off by the time Master returned to the couch.

"Ready to tackle the steps?"

"I think so."

They walked slowly across the room, and then the stairs loomed like Mount Everest. Sky wrapped his arm around Master's strong torso and struggled up the first step.

"When I was a kid, Mom and I moved around a lot," Master said, slightly breathless, as he nearly carried Sky. "We spent a few months in a sixth-floor walk-up. Wasn't so bad for me, but Mom was on her feet all day at work and— Hang on." They stopped midway to catch their breath. Then Master inhaled deeply and they began again. "And it sucked for her to face that climb at the end of the day."

"Does it make you hate me?" Sky asked when they finally reached the second floor. He disentangled himself from Master.

Master looked puzzled. "Why would it make me hate you? You didn't put us on the sixth floor without an elevator. Hell, you were probably a baby. I was still pretty little."

"Because I'm a slave, yet I've lived an easier life than she did. She worked so hard. I just sing."

"No." Master brushed a fingertip against one of the marks on Sky's back, but not hard enough to hurt. "I don't think you've had an easy life."

Master had to help Sky take off his sweatpants because bending hurt. Then he led Sky into the bathroom, which was warm and steamy and smelled slightly medicinal. "I put some oil in the water," Master explained. "It's supposed to be soothing."

He also had an inflatable donut-shaped pillow, affixed to the bottom of the tub so it wouldn't float. He helped Sky get in. "Is the water too hot? I can add some cold."

Sky smiled at Master's concern. "It's fine." In truth, the water stung a bit when he sat, but the cushion provided some comfort for his bruised ass. Besides, it felt wonderful having another rare opportunity to take a bath. "It's really nice," he said.

That made Master beam. "Good. It'll help with any soreness in your muscles. A beating like that doesn't just leave marks. Which you know." He sat on the edge of the tub and reached into one of the plastic bags. "This will help too," he said, holding up a bottle of Kahlúa. The liqueur surprised Sky, who thought that whiskey and beer were more to Master's taste.

But what happened next deeply shocked him: Master unscrewed the cap and handed Sky the bottle. "There you go. Not very civilized, but we've already established that I'm a barbarian."

In all the years Sky had worked in clubs, all the times he had served drinks to others, he'd never had one himself. "B-but . . . I'm not supposed to—"

"Sky, it's just you and me here. If you don't tell anyone I gave you booze, I sure as hell won't."

Sky looked dubiously at the alcohol. He even took a sniff—coffee—but didn't drink.

Master sighed. "Look. It'll kill the pain better than ibuprofen. I could give you more of the heavyweight pills instead, but I don't think you liked the effects very much."

"But slaves aren't—"

"I know. Screw it. I'm getting really fucking tired of *supposed to*s. Drink up. Um, slowly though." He grinned. "I chose Kahlúa because I thought it might go down a little easier for you, but it's still pretty strong."

Feeling daring, Sky took a sip—and promptly choked as the sweet, thick liquid burned its way down his throat. But Master just looked on encouragingly, so Sky braved another taste. And another.

Master gently pried the bottle from Sky's hand right about the time that Sky's residual discomforts floated away like water vapor. His head was full of clouds, though, which made him laugh.

"What's so funny?" asked Master, smiling at him.

"Sky is full of clouds." Saying it out loud was even funnier. Sky giggled like a child.

Master laughed with him. "It's great how a little booze can make all your problems shrink, isn't it? Until you sober up and the problems are twice as big as before."

Sky shrugged and traced a finger along the surface of the water, creating patterns in the sheen from the medicated oil. Then he looked up at his master, who stared at him intently. Heat and moisture had tightened Master's dark hair into curls and brought a subtle flush to his cheeks.

"You broke your nose," Sky announced.

"More than once," Master said with a chuckle. "You shoulda seen the other guys."

"It's good."

"Yeah? You picturing how satisfying it would be to plant your fist in my face?"

Sky shook his head. Slaves who struck freemen were punished horribly. "Makes your face more interesting. You'd be too beautiful with a straight nose."

"You're drunk," replied Master, who seemed amused.

"Still true. Rule one."

Master nodded, but his expression turned sad. His gaze traced the marks on Sky's back. "Have you been beaten this badly before?"

"Yes."

"And I bet nobody gave you painkillers or anything afterward."

That was true. After those beatings, the only mercy Sky had received was a day or two's reprieve from his duties. He'd spent those days lying stiffly on his cot, trying not to move. "But last night was worse," he said, looking directly into Master's eyes.

"Because that sick bastard raped you?"

So it hadn't been Master who'd fucked him. Interesting. "Slaves can't be raped."

"Call it whatever you want, it's the same thing."

Sky shook his head, which made him dizzy. "Lots of men have fucked me. Some of them were rougher than that. I didn't choose any of it." Those statements alone would make most masters strike him, but he didn't think this master would. Not today, anyway.

Sure enough, Master's voice was soft when he responded, and he showed no anger. "Then why was last night worse?"

"Because the other times, those were punishments." Sky tried to find the right words inside his sodden brain. "I . . . I did things to earn those beatings. Not last night. Whatever I did last night didn't matter."

Master frowned at him for a long time—not angry, but thinking. Then his eyes widened and he nodded. "Control," he said.

"What?"

"Jesus. That's it, isn't it?" Master got off the edge of the tub, only to kneel at its side, and then he leaned in close to Sky. "If you're being punished for screwing up, you're still sort of in control, right? Because you're the one who screwed up. And it means you're still a person who makes choices, even if they're bad ones. But last night . . . If someone beats you just for the hell of it, you have no control at all, and you're not even really a person anymore. Just a . . . a thing that stuff happens to."

Sky had to sort those words in his head. When he finally understood, he whispered, "Yes, Master."

The earth didn't open and swallow him; God didn't rain down fire. Master didn't even raise his voice. "I get it, Sky. Christ, I really do." And then he didn't say anything more. But after a short while, when the water cooled, he pulled the plug, helped Sky out of the tub, and wrapped him in an oversized towel. He even remembered not to rub the towel against Sky's backside.

Sky swayed on his feet, exhausted and sore and more than a little sloshed. "Hair," he said to Master, because he hadn't washed it in the bath, and it was a tangled mess.

"In the morning. Come on."

Master took the towel and tossed it onto the floor, then grasped Sky's hand and towed him to the bed. He must have changed the bedding while the bath was running, because the sheets were clean and smelled of fabric softener. The cool cotton felt wonderful against the warm skin of Sky's chest and belly. He would have fallen asleep immediately, but Master held a cup with a straw and ordered him to drink some water.

"Not thirsty," Sky mumbled. Even through exhaustion and the alcohol, he was surprised by his own defiance. Surprised and a little thrilled. Maybe that was why slaves weren't supposed to get drunk—it made them careless.

Master didn't seem offended by the refusal, only insistent. "You'll thank me in the morning."

So Sky drank. And *then* he fell asleep.

CHAPTER SEVEN

Sky spent the next few days living like a pampered prince. Master encouraged him to sleep in and wouldn't let him do even the simplest chores. In fact, Master insisted on waiting on him hand and foot. Sky suspected that guilt was a major part of Master's motivation, although he didn't understand why. Sky was a slave, and he had been used like a slave; what did Master have to feel guilty about?

Every night before bed and every morning after Sky's shower, Master applied soothing ointment onto Sky's back, yet his touch remained clinical and chaste. Sky found himself longing for something a bit more intimate, but didn't say anything.

Despite some lingering discomfort from the beating, these days were a treasured luxury. It was lovely to stretch out in a warm room on comfortable furniture in soft clothing, a pile of books within reach, and a handsome man fetching food and drink. That memory could be a comfort later, when things inevitably grew bad.

Four days after the party, as Sky sat on a stool in the kitchen, Master gave his shoulder a quick squeeze. "Do you feel up for a run today? We can take it slow and easy."

Master had lately gone for daily runs by himself, leaving Sky alone for a little while. Aside from a quick grocery trip, those were the only times Master had left the apartment.

"I think so," Sky said. "I'd like to spend some time outside."

"Good. Let's get geared up."

Sky found himself smiling as he laced up the running shoes Master had bought him, and then grinning full force when they stepped outside.

"You look happy," Master said as they did a few stretches to warm up.

"It's nice to be outdoors." And it was, with the air smelling of wet pavement and the sea, and passersby going about their business with no clue that the blond man was wearing slave bracelets under his hoodie. As Sky and Master began a slow jog, Sky grinned at a group of brightly dressed children with name tags around their necks, all of them being herded by some frazzled adults. He blushed a little at a lingering look from two businessmen in suits, sniffed eagerly at the scent of roasted chicken wafting from a food cart, and chuckled at a clot of tourists who goggled at everything.

His back and butt hurt a little, but Master kept their pace slow and steered them toward flat terrain. If Master was frustrated over such an unchallenging run, he didn't show it. But he checked with Sky often, looking him over and asking whether he was all right.

They ended up at the Ferry Building, maybe because Master realized it was one of Sky's favorite places. Sky liked to lean against the railing and observe the boats, but it was just as entertaining to face the other way and watch the gulls try to steal food from people. Today a young couple in slightly ragged clothing was occupying one of the benches. The boy strummed a guitar while the girl munched on noodles from a cardboard container. The backpacks and sleeping bags piled beside them suggested the couple was homeless, but they looked content.

"You're humming," Master said quietly to Sky.

Sky blinked up at him. "Sorry."

"Don't be. I like it. It's a mood barometer—whenever I hear you hum, I know that you're happy."

"And you care whether I'm happy?" A brash question, but Master had not punished his impertinence so far.

"I actually do. I know that's hard to believe, but it's true. Rule one."

"You're my master. You don't have to worry about rules."

Master shook his head. "You have no idea how wrong you are about that. My rules are different from yours, but just as oppressive." He turned to face the bay. "Anyway, when it comes to interacting with other people, I like rules. You want them so you know how to act without getting in trouble. I want them because . . . because they mean someone else is making the decisions for a change."

Sky tried to wrap his head around that. "You want somebody else to make decisions?"

"Sometimes. It's that control thing. You know what it's like not to have any, and I'm sure that sucks. But can you imagine what it's like to be . . . to carry the burden all the fucking time? And sometimes you make mistakes, and when you do, people suffer." He turned his head to look at Sky. "*You* suffer."

Master's gaze was so intense, so *heavy*, that Sky shivered—although not from fear. Master gave him a wobbly smile. "You're getting chilled. C'mon. Let's see if you can manage another mile."

They jogged up Market Street, where the streetcars rattled past and towering buildings cast perpetual shadows even on the sunniest days. An old black man sat at a shoeshine stand, calling out to passersby. Sky had heard freemen talking about how elderly slaves ought to be grateful their owners found a use for them, but Sky thought that this frail old man must spend many of his days cold and miserable, wishing for a comfortable spot in a warm home.

Sky and Master were waiting for a crossing signal, jogging in place, when someone called out, "Wallace! Hey, Morgan Wallace!" On the other side of the street, a man was waving in their direction. He was in his late thirties, pale and handsome, dressed in a conservatively cut suit.

"Shit," Master muttered, but he pasted on a smile and waved back. That was when Sky recognized the man as one of the people from the party—the one who'd squeezed his balls and joked about mutilation. Master shot Sky a brief, unreadable look, and when the light changed, they waited for the man to cross.

"Hey, Scott, how's it going?" Master shook the other man's hand.

Scott narrowed his eyes at Sky, who stood beside and slightly behind Master. "Isn't that your *slave*?" Scott asked with undisguised contempt. He said it loud enough that several passersby gave Sky hard stares.

"Yeah," Master said easily. "I'm getting him in better condition."

"I just chain mine to the treadmill."

"I don't have a treadmill."

Scott nodded. "That's right. You're still settling in to our fair city. Do you live near here?"

"I'm renting a loft south of Mission. I'll look into buying once I have a better feel for the city."

"Which is crazier—real estate here or in New York?"

Master's laugh sounded slightly forced. "I think it's a draw. There's fewer options here, I guess, since it's a much smaller city."

"True, true. Well, when you're ready to enter the market, let me know. My sister's a real estate broker. I do some investing myself, actually."

"Great. Thanks."

Scott turned his attention back to Sky. "Mind if I take a quick look, Morgan?"

"Go ahead."

Sky stood absolutely still as Scott lifted Sky's hoodie and T-shirt and scratched his fingernails over the healing welts. When Sky hissed in pain, Scott chuckled and dug his nails in a little deeper. Then he let the hoodie go, but tugged at the waist of Sky's sweatpants and briefs to peek down at his ass. Sky kept his jaw locked and face blank.

"The bruises are faded already," Scott said, letting the clothes snap back into place and then smoothing his palm over the curve of Sky's ass. Still stroking, he smirked at Master. "Tell you what. I have a little get-together planned for tomorrow night. Will you join us? And bring this?" He gave Sky a stinging slap.

"Hey, that sounds great. Thanks. I'm trying to make more local connections, you know?" Master put a little extra emphasis on the last part.

Scott swatted Sky again before digging in his pocket for his wallet. "Here's my card," he said, handing it to Master. "Text me tonight and I'll send you the details." Then he and Master shook hands again, and Scott continued down the sidewalk.

As Scott walked away, Master scowled furiously. Yet he set a gentle hand on Sky's shoulder. "Let's go home, okay?"

Master spent the rest of the afternoon and early evening texting. For dinner he ordered a pizza—usually disallowed on Sky's diet. Afterward Sky read a book and watched old reruns on TV. As the closing credits for *Friends* began to roll, Master turned to Sky. "Tomorrow . . . I doubt it'll be any better than last time."

Not knowing what response Master wanted, Sky stared at his own lap. "Yes, Master."

"This isn't my choice, Sky."

"It isn't mine either. Master."

"Most masters would beat you for that," Master warned.

Sky steeled himself and matched Master's glare. "Then beat me. Fuck me. Make me bleed."

After a long pause, Master's eyes widened. "Shit. You're trying to get me to punish you. Do you think if I use you hard enough tonight, you won't have to go to Scott's thing tomorrow? Rule one, Sky."

"I think that if I'm going to hurt, I might as well deserve it."

Master startled Sky by dropping his phone on the couch and moving closer. But Sky held his spot, and all Master did was cup Sky's face in his palms. "You don't. Deserve. *Any* of this," Master ground out. "You need to believe that."

Sky's sanity must have slipped—it was the only explanation for what he did next: he pulled Master close and kissed him.

Sky had been kissed only a few times in his life, and he'd never initiated. He was shocked when Master gave into him almost at once, opening his mouth for Sky's tongue and moaning as Sky tasted him. And sweet heavens, he tasted good, like the elaborate ice cream treats Sky had seen freemen eat but had never been allowed to try. The rasp of Master's stubble contrasted deliciously with the softness of his lips, and the heat of his body traveled into Sky, pooling low in his belly.

It was Sky who pulled away first, but only a few inches. Panting, they stared at each other.

"Wh-what was that for?" Master asked, the uncertainty in his voice making Sky's cock twitch.

"I don't know. I wanted to."

"Even though tomorrow I'm going to be responsible for . . . whatever happens to you at Scott's."

"Even though," Sky said, letting out a heavy breath.

A strange gleam appeared in Master's eyes. He licked his lips. Moving slowly, he reached over and set his hand on Sky's crotch. He didn't squeeze or stroke but simply let the weight of his touch settle there. Sky had been half-hard already; now he grew fully erect and allowed his eyes to fall closed. That pressure—*yes*—right there.

"Will you come upstairs with me?" Master asked in a whisper. Like it was a real question, one that Sky could refuse.

Sky did not refuse. As a matter of fact, it was Sky who took Master's hand and led him across the floor, up the stairs, and to the bed they shared.

"Get undressed," Sky ordered as he released their hands. It was as if he'd been possessed by some outside force that— No. No outside force. This was *Sky* doing exactly what he wanted, although where he'd found the courage he'd never know.

A slow smile spread across Master's face, and he began to unbutton his shirt.

Sky remained fully clothed, but soon his master was naked. And hard. His thick cock stuck up at a jaunty angle, and it remained that way as Sky stood and admired him. It occurred to Sky that although he was Mr. Wallace's slave, Mr. Wallace was *his master*—and for the moment at least, it meant the ownership went both ways. Or at least Sky could pretend that was the case, and Master seemed willing to go along with it.

"Has anyone truly made love to you, Sky? I'd like to do that."

Nobody had, but Sky shook his head. "That's not what I want. Lie down on the bed."

"On my back or stomach?"

Oh, sweet heavens. That question led to such impossible possibilities that Sky felt momentarily dizzy. Would Master really allow— But no. Sky didn't want to push this game too far. "Your back."

Master scrambled to obey as quickly as any slave, spreading himself out atop the duvet. He kept his body still, but his breathing increased and a flush spread from his face to his upper chest. He looked beautiful and delicious and vulnerable.

Sky prowled closer, still wearing his T-shirt, sweats, and socks. He grasped Master's ankles and moved his legs farther apart, then knelt on the mattress between them. When he slowly rubbed Master's thickly muscled thighs, Master threw his head back and made a throaty purr. Sky moved his palms along the V of Master's hips and traced the line of hair on his lower belly, not quite touching Master's twitching cock.

Master lifted his hand once, only to groan and let it drop.

Sky smiled. He let his hands roam over the rippled abs and the thick slabs of Master's pecs, along the curves of the shoulders and upper arms, even across the width of the strong neck. When he daringly pinched the hard nipples between finger and thumb, giving them a bit of a twist, Master cried out and arched his hips off the bed. A bead of clear moisture appeared at the tip of his cock and dripped slowly onto his stomach.

"Holy shit," he rasped. "That's—"

Whatever he was about to say ended with a choked growl when Sky swooped down and swallowed him whole.

Sky had expected Master to grab his hair or at least to thrust upward. But Master's hands remained at his sides, and although Sky could feel the tension in Master's hips, he stayed still.

As Sky bobbed his head, his own dick throbbed urgently. Of course, he could have shoved a hand down his pants and jerked himself off. But somehow he felt more excited, more *powerful*, as he ignored his body's demands and instead exulted in the jumbled stream of profanities spilling from Master's lips. Sky was doing that to him. Was making him tremble and swear and mewl with need. Morgan Wallace was a strong and powerful man, a free man, yet Sky didn't even need ropes to keep him in place; the force of Sky's will was enough.

And knowing that a gun was almost within Master's reach? That only made the experience more exhilarating.

"Sky . . . Sky, *please*," Master whimpered. "Please."

Sweet heavens. Master was *begging*.

With an evil smile, Sky slid off Master's cock with a loud *pop*, then rose up on his knees. Master's hair, usually carefully styled, was a wild mess, his pupils were enormous, and his fists were clutching the duvet in a death grip. The head of his cock was nearly purple. "Please," he repeated.

Sky smoothed his palms over thick chest hair before giving Master's nipples another twist, this one harder than the first. The noise Master made went straight to Sky's balls, and Master's cock pulsed hard, emitting a thick stream of clear fluid.

Sky took pity on him. He bent, took Master all the way to the back of his throat, and hummed.

Master roared when he came—without moving from the position in which Sky had placed him.

And then, while Master stared up at him with dazed eyes, Sky shoved his own pants down, grabbed his cock, and gave a few firm strokes. He spurted onto Master's chest and face, and when a glistening droplet landed on his mouth, Master stuck out his tongue and licked it away, making them both groan.

Sky pulled his sweats back up and collapsed alongside Master, who still hadn't moved.

"Jesus Christ," Master said after a very long time.

Sky only smiled.

CHAPTER EIGHT

They went for another run in the morning. Master had given Sky the option of refusing, since a long night loomed ahead of him, but Sky laced on his running shoes. "It's better if I'm already tired, I think." Besides, working off some of the tension was better than nervously pacing the loft.

Master cooked them a hearty lunch, and afterward they headed upstairs to the bathroom. Sky sat on the closed toilet and watched Master shower, smiling when his gaze made Master hard. Then, still naked, Master helped Sky bathe. He was careful to scrub even the most private parts of Sky's body, but his touch remained gentle. Sky was too tense to react to the almost-caresses, although he did appreciate them.

Master spent the afternoon on his phones and laptop while Sky tried to read. He didn't know whether Master's quick glances and general skittishness were due to what they'd done the night before, or to what they would be doing in a few hours. He also wasn't sure of his own feelings about the previous night. He was astounded by his daring; and he was equally astonished that Master had not only allowed it but enjoyed it.

Although Sky might not understand the tangle of emotions in his own head, he knew he was scared of what might happen tonight.

He wasn't hungry at all come dinnertime, but Master made him eat some soup and crackers. Sky noticed that Master didn't eat much either.

They went upstairs, and Sky watched Master dress in expensive trousers that showed off his powerful ass, a closely tailored shirt in forest green, and a black leather motorcycle jacket. He looked tough and dangerous and very handsome. He spent a long time on his hair, arranging it just so and applying a lot of product.

Then he turned to Sky and ran his fingers through Sky's locks. "I think you look perfect just like this." He sighed. "But you need a costume."

They headed to the playroom, which they'd both avoided all week. Master must have been planning this, because he didn't hesitate before assembling Sky's outfit: a pair of tight-fitting cobalt pleather briefs with open lacing on the sides, a white pullover fishnet shirt with long sleeves, and a padlocked steel chain for around his neck.

Sky held up the chain. "The bracelets already mark me as a slave. Isn't this redundant?"

"Probably. But like I said, it's a costume. You're fueling fantasies."

"Yours?"

The corner of Master's mouth quirked. "No. At least, not exactly. But tonight's not for my benefit."

"Then whose? What's the point?" Sky was almost growling with frustration. "If you don't want this, why do it? Rule two!" Sky wasn't even surprised anymore to be shouting.

Master answered him softly. "I can't tell you. It's for your safety and mine. But . . . it's worth it. At least, I thought it was when I started this. Now I'm not so sure."

It was stupid that Sky felt the impulse to comfort him. Master wasn't the one who'd end the night in agony.

Frowning, Master handed Sky plain black flip-flops. No jacket, so Sky was grateful when Master ran with him through the cold to the waiting limo. The driver must have known where to go, because without a word other than "Good evening, sir," he pulled away from the curb.

Scott lived in a wood-shingled three-story house that probably had a lovely ocean view on clear days. Tonight, though, there was nothing to see but fog. No liveried slaves met the limo, and the entrance wasn't grand—just a plain wooden door after a short flight of stairs. Scott himself answered the door, wearing jeans and a sweater and holding a glass of white wine. "Morgan!" he said, as if Master's appearance were a pleasant surprise. "I'm so glad you could make it. Please come in."

The foyer was drab. Off-white walls, an abstract painting, and a long table holding a glass bowl and a pair of carved wooden bird statues. There was no pounding music. But after Scott led them down a hall and into a rectangular room, all the breath left Sky's lungs.

The room itself, although large, wasn't nearly as big as the one at the previous party. Bright overhead lights glared off of white walls, white area rugs, white furniture. Even the fireplace was surrounded by white tile. The space was almost entirely free of ornaments—except for one wall, which was decorated with two slaves hanging side by side. One was white and the other black, but they were roughly the same height and had the same slender build. Their heads were shorn bald. They were naked, and their penises had been doubled over and fastened in place somehow, fully exposing their scrotums; their nipples were pierced with heavy silver rings. Thick black thread crisscrossed their lips, sewing their mouths shut. Their shackled arms held the weight of their bodies, and their legs were spread and fastened to the wall with iron clamps. They writhed, moaning through their sealed mouths, sweat glistening on their skin.

And the worst of it was that nobody in the room was paying the least attention to their suffering. Fewer than two dozen freemen milled around, with roughly as many slaves kneeling or crawling beside them. The freemen were drinking wine, eating bacon-wrapped bites from white china plates, chatting and laughing with one another. The slaves suffering on the wall received no more notice than the empty fireplace or the bland light fixtures.

Sky wanted to sob with anger and grief.

But he didn't. He followed respectfully behind Master, falling to his knees as soon as Master stopped to talk to other men, keeping his face carefully blank. He tried to concentrate on the soft music—Mozart, he thought—but all he could hear were the freemen's light conversation and the slaves' muffled whines.

After an hour or so, Sky noticed that Master seemed to be strategically placing himself in conversations so that Sky could kneel on a rug instead of the hardwood floor. And whenever another guest seemed to take an interest in Sky, Master steered the talk elsewhere.

That changed, however, when Scott walked over and handed Master a fresh drink. "It's a good group tonight, isn't it?" Scott asked, looking around the room with a proprietary air.

"It is. I appreciate the invitation."

"I always enjoy the opportunity to get like-minded people together."

"Well, as the new kid in town, it's nice to make some connections."

Scott smiled. "For business or pleasure?"

"I always thought it was more efficient to combine the two."

Master and Scott laughed. Sky had the feeling there was a subtext to their discussion, but as a slave, it didn't matter whether he understood.

He startled when Scott rested a hand on his head. "He's pretty enough, but I'm wondering why you didn't buy one trained as a companion. A younger one." He tugged hard at Sky's hair, then settled his palm on Sky's scalp again.

"My tastes run differently," Master said.

"Oh? How so?"

"Well, for one thing, I like them a little older. The young ones are too . . . delicate."

Scott chuckled darkly. "True enough. But you could have found an older companion. It would have been a bargain. I know plenty of men who like to trade in their used models for fresh ones, and those old ones have depreciated."

"Sure, but cost isn't an issue. I'm perfectly willing to shell out big bucks if it means getting what I want."

"Which is?"

Master didn't answer at once, and although Sky kept his head bowed, he rolled his eyes to sneak a look upward. Master had a crooked smile—a cruel one, Sky thought—as he inched closer to Scott, and when he spoke, his voice was quiet. "I don't like my slaves to be too easy. I prefer . . . a bit of a struggle."

Scott nodded. "And this one gives you that?"

"A little bit. Honestly, I had to settle with him. It's hard to find what I like. Attractive, not too young, but not yet broken."

"Hmm." Scott's fingers were still entwined in Sky's hair. "And have you found that combination in the past?"

"A couple of times. Criminals condemned to slavery."

"Ah."

Master had told Sky he'd never owned anyone before. Was that a lie? Or was he lying now to Scott—and if so, why? Besides, unless they had specialized skills, condemned criminals were supposed to belong to the state. They ended up leased for farm work or the mines.

Scott dropped his voice too and echoed Sky's thoughts. "Individual owners aren't supposed to have access to criminals."

"I had a . . . connection."

"Had?"

"It was in New York. And unfortunately the gentleman in question caught the wrong kind of attention and had to flee the country. I've heard he's in Turkey now, which doesn't do me much good."

After a lengthy pause, Scott said, "You know Sebastian Dash?"

"Knew. We weren't besties or anything. Let's say we engaged in the mutually satisfactory exchange of goods."

"Interesting," Scott said.

Master shrugged and drained his wineglass. "I suppose. Doesn't much matter now, anyway. In fact, Dash's issues have caused me a host of problems."

"How so?"

A slave came by to offer a tray of shrimp hors d'oeuvres. He was naked and thin to the point of near starvation, his pale skin tight against his ribs and his gray eyes deeply shadowed. Master grabbed a few pieces of shrimp by their decorative toothpicks and set them on his plate while Scott popped one straight into his mouth. When the slave turned away, Sky saw that his back and ass were terribly scarred with lash marks and small circular burns.

"Your Dash-caused problems?" Scott prompted, tugging again at Sky's scalp.

"Right. Two-fold, really. I was, uh, a little concerned the official attention might turn from him to some of his business associates. Things got just a little too hot in New York for my taste."

"So you relocated to our nice chilly little city."

Master grinned. "Exactly. Although I think San Francisco has its charms. And in the event that I end up heading back to the East Coast, it'll be nice if my partners and I have expanded business out this way."

Behind Sky, someone let out a garbled screech. With Scott gripping his hair, Sky couldn't turn to look, but he suspected the sound had come from one of the slaves hanging on the wall. His stomach churned. Neither Scott nor Master paid any attention to the noise.

"So moving out here maybe wasn't so much a problem as an opportunity," Scott said.

"Maybe."

"What was the other issue?"

Master gestured carelessly at Sky. "What we've already covered. My last freeborn slave . . . well, he's out of commission. Permanently. And this is the best replacement I could get my hands on. And don't get me wrong—he's not bad. But when I'm done with him . . ."

Sky felt the blood drain from his face, and he struggled not to vomit on Scott's expensive shoes. He didn't know whether to trust this version of Mr. Wallace or the one who treated him kindly and let Sky order him around. Either way, his master was a liar.

Scott finally removed his hand from Sky's hair. "I can understand your problem," he said.

Master gave a wry chuckle. "Yeah. Well, if you hear of a solution, let me know. Like I said, money's not an issue if I get what I want." He looked around. "Excuse me, will you? That wine is fantastic. I'm going to hunt down another glass."

"I'll get you one myself," Scott said.

After Scott walked away, Master gently smoothed a few strands of Sky's hair back into place without looking at him.

Master drank more wine after that, and Sky shuffled along and knelt silently beside him, trying not to wince once his knees began to ache. The slaves on the wall grew silent, and when Sky glanced at them, they appeared to be unconscious. Sweet heavens, he hoped so. But as the party guests grew more intoxicated, they turned their attention to the other slaves in the room. Nothing as . . . showy as when Sky had been beaten. No paddles or whips were in evidence. Instead, tonight's entertainment involved the thorough use of fingers and hands on sensitive body parts, as well as liberal attempts to humiliate. A freeman sat on a white couch, spanking the slave draped over his lap. Near a corner, one slave was being fucked while he rimmed another slave in a cock cage.

It was inevitable, perhaps, that Sky would be used as well. Master was first, sticking his cock down Sky's throat. And yes, it was the same dick that had been in Sky's mouth the previous night, but this act was nothing like the other had been. Sky wasn't aroused at all—in fact, he had to be careful not to choke and spit. By the time Master was through with him, several other men had lined up for their turns.

It was very late when Master grabbed Sky's arm and dragged him outside to the waiting limo. Master weaved slightly as he walked and his eyes were unfocused. Collapsing onto the plush seat and closing his eyes, he filled the car with the scent of alcohol. He said nothing to Sky, who sat beside him.

But when the car stopped at a light several blocks away, Master opened his eyes and regarded Sky. "Are you all right?"

Sky didn't know how to answer that. He wasn't bruised and beaten like last time; he was even still wearing the clothing Master had given him. But his throat hurt, his jaw ached, his hair was filthy with dried come, and his knees were protesting the night's treatment. He was scared and confused and more than a little lost. "No," he whispered.

Master squeezed his eyes closed as if he were in pain. Then he turned his head away and remained silent for the rest of the ride.

Inside the loft, Master took off his jacket and shoes while Sky just stood with hands at his sides. "Shower and go to bed," Master said. "I have to . . . Shit. Have to work." He ran his hands through his hair, making it stand up wildly.

When Sky got upstairs to the bathroom, he didn't know what to do with his clothing, which reeked and was filthy. Mixing it with the other laundry didn't seem right, and it would be ruined in the washing machine. He left it in a little heap on the bathroom floor. Let Master punish him for that, if it pleased him to do so.

The shower felt like heaven. He stayed under the hot water for a long time, scrubbing until his skin was nearly raw and his scalp was sore. He drank a cup of water from the tap and then climbed into bed, which smelled of him and Master and sex.

But he couldn't sleep because Master was shouting into his phone.

". . . goddamn drunk, Trish! Am I supposed to stay sober at the goddamn party? . . . Doing my job just fine, thanks very much. Why, you think Delancey can do it better? Then tell him to get his ass out here . . ." Master was quiet for so long that Sky thought the call was over, but then Master spoke again, this time without yelling.

"I'm working my way in . . . Don't know yet. I think it's Scott Simpson, but I'm not sure . . . Not even close, not yet . . . I don't know . . . Okay, fine. But when I'm done here, I want a vacation . . . Denmark. I want to go to fucking Denmark. Can you make that happen, Trish?" His voice broke, almost as if he were holding back tears. After another long silence, he said, "Okay. Christ, it's almost morning for you. Get some sleep . . . Yeah, you too."

Sky fell asleep before Master came to bed, and when he woke up late the next morning, Master's side of the bed was empty. Sky used the bathroom and got dressed—sweatpants and a T-shirt—before padding downstairs. He found Master seated at the breakfast bar, laptop in front of him and coffee mug at hand.

"I can make you some breakfast," Master said quietly.

"I'll do it myself."

"Sky . . ." Master stopped himself, then looked away.

After waiting a moment, Sky entered the kitchen. He really wasn't very hungry, but he'd eaten little the night before and knew he should have something. He put toast and a small cluster of grapes onto his plate and, after some indecision, sat on the stool next to Master. He wondered whether Master was feeling hungover—and then wondered why he cared.

He chewed his toast and washed it down with some orange juice, while Master stared blankly at his screen.

"Let's take the day off from running," Master finally said, rubbing his forehead. "Go ahead and use the weights and stuff if you get bored." He waved vaguely in the direction of the exercise equipment.

Sky didn't answer.

After a while, Master sighed. "A senate committee introduced a new bill the other day. It would prohibit nongovernmental entities from importing slaves from overseas."

"It's already illegal except for a few big agencies, isn't it?" Sky said.

"Yeah, but it happens anyway. Too many loopholes, you know? And crooks who don't give a shit about licensing."

Sky nodded. He'd heard stories of free blacks kidnapped in Africa and brought to the United States, where no blacks were free. He'd even heard freemen justify the practice, arguing that blacks were better off in slavery, where their owners could see to their needs, rather than living as savages in the wild. He didn't know whether to believe that, but nobody asked him what he thought.

"The bill would close the loopholes, increase penalties, and nationalize the existing licensed agencies," Master said. He shot Sky a quick look. "It would also allow for manumission. Slaves could buy their freedom, or owners could simply choose to free them."

Sky snorted. "That bill will never pass."

"Yeah, it died in committee last time. The president's already said she'll veto it if it gets to her. But it's progress. Just a few years ago, no senator would have dared to support a bill like this. Now several of them have. The idea's gaining momentum. And kids . . . I've seen polls that say a growing number of college students want to end slavery completely. The trade unions are in favor too."

"But that doesn't really matter as long as the wealthy and powerful want to keep their slaves," Sky said.

"Sky, I . . . Fuck. There's nothing about this situation that I want."

Sky firmed his jaw. "Your cock was hard enough last night, Master."

Master flinched. He looked down at his lap for a moment, then back at Sky. "Viagra. I took a goddamn Viagra so I could be part of the show too. And I thought . . . Look, I know what happened to you last night was . . . But it could have been worse. Nobody fucked you. And they didn't whip you."

If Master expected Sky to thank him, to tell him it was all right, he'd certainly be disappointed. Sky simply gazed at him until Master looked away.

Sky stood, gathered his dishes, and took them to the sink, where he washed and dried them before putting them away. "I'd like to read," he said quietly.

"Yeah, that's fine. I have work."

For a couple of hours they remained like that: Sky on the couch with his books, Master at the breakfast bar with his laptop and phones.

But then Sky heard dishes clattering in the kitchen, and a short while later Master came over to the couch with two plates. "Lunch," he said.

Sky put down his book and took the offered dish. "Thank you." It was his favorite omelet, made with spinach, cheese, and mushrooms, set off with sliced fruit along the side. Everything was arranged carefully, as if it were a meal in a fancy restaurant.

Master sat beside him and handed him a fork. "It's that cheese you really like. The kind I buy at the Ferry Building? I added some herbs too."

Dutifully, Sky took a bite. "It's delicious," he admitted. Suddenly ravenous, he gobbled the rest. When he was through, he set the plate onto the coffee table and stared at Master, who was picking at his food. "I wish you'd tell me the truth," Sky said.

"I wish I could. The situation is fucked." Either he was genuinely distressed, or an excellent actor.

"I'm frightened," Sky said. He didn't know why he admitted it. And honestly, he couldn't explain why he was so scared. He'd been in more perilous positions. Recently, even. Sitting in the cage in that miserable warehouse, he could have been sold to anyone, for any purpose; and he'd known he was past his prime. His emotions then had centered around dread and despair, whereas now he was terrified. Not just about his future—he'd never imagined a happy ending for himself—but about whatever was going on in his head. He didn't just distrust Master; now he distrusted himself.

"You want to know the truth?" Master asked. "Me too. I usually have a strong grip on what I'm doing, but with you, not so much. I'm losing it."

"Then stop. Stop . . . whatever's happening."

"Can't. Too much at stake. Not just me and you either, but bigger things. Important things. Shit. Not that you're not important too."

It was an impasse. Master wouldn't or couldn't come clean with him, and Sky couldn't detach himself emotionally. Sooner or later, something was going to give. But for now Sky sighed, nodded, and picked up his book.

"What are you reading?" Master asked, tilting his head to see the title.

"About the tea."

Master chuckled. "That one was kind of a random choice. I don't know anything about tea—don't usually even drink the stuff. But I liked the picture on the cover." It was a beautiful photo of an emerald-green tea plantation, the plants in rows over rolling hills, almost like an abstract sculpture.

"The book says tea originally came from China. That's far away, isn't it?"

"It's . . ." Master gave him a funny look. "I forget sometimes. You never went to school. Nobody ever taught you even the most basic things about the world."

"They taught me what I needed to know in order to do my work."

"Right." After a moment of thought, Master got up and hurried over to the kitchen. He returned with his laptop and sat so close to Sky that their thighs touched. He clicked a few keys. "Look," he said, angling the screen slightly toward Sky. "This is the world."

Sky peered at the image. He knew it was a map—he'd glimpsed maps before—but he had no idea what the different shapes represented until Master began to point. "This whole blob here is the United States. We're right here, up against the Pacific Ocean, and New York City is way over here on the other side. And this is China. Far away."

It didn't look so distant on the little computer screen. "Where's Los Angeles?" Sky asked.

After a brief hesitation, Master showed him. It was very close to San Francisco—or at least it seemed to be.

"Let me show you something else," Master said. He clicked a bit more, bringing up a new map. This one showed the same shapes, but now they were covered in broad swaths of color.

"Everything in green, that's a place where slavery is legal. All the Americas, almost all of Europe, Africa, the Middle East, these big blobs in Asia."

"It's a lot of green," Sky said.

"Yeah. These yellow places in Asia and Africa are under tribal control, mostly. At least in theory. It's probably a few multinational corporations calling the shots in those places. The media claims there's a lot of chaos and bloodshed in those countries, and of course everyone places the blame on the people who live there, call them savages, but I don't know if any of that is true. Christ, we probably caused the mess ourselves. We fucked them over when we stole their people after the Red Death, and we continued to fuck them over with colonialism."

Sky paused in his questioning, astonished to hear a freeman admit that his people had caused other people's problems. But since he didn't really understand what Master was talking about, Sky decided to save that issue for a later conversation and concentrate now on the map. "And these small red spots?" he asked, pointing.

Master leaned back. "Scandinavia."

"No slavery."

"We have treaties with them. If someone brings a slave to Norway, Denmark, or Sweden, that slave's not freed. He remains the property of his owner, and if he runs, all these countries promise to help catch him and give him back. But they pretty much discourage foreigners from bringing in slaves in the first place, and even if they do bring them in, they can only stay thirty days max, unless they get special permission."

Sky remembered what Master had said on the phone last night about vacationing in Denmark. "Why are you showing me this?"

"I don't know." Master rubbed the back of his neck. "I guess so you can see that there are pockets of hope. Little pockets, but they exist."

"I see," Sky said, which was a lie and a violation of rule one. He didn't understand at all.

But Master was chewing his lip thoughtfully. "I have a bunch of . . . meetings I need to go to over the next few days. Not parties, Sky. You won't be going with me."

Sky let out a small sigh of relief and cocked his head at Master. He didn't understand where this was going.

Master smiled at him. "Would you like it if I gave you access to my laptop while I'm not here?"

"You would do that?"

"Sure. I'll give you your own log-in and password and stuff. Um, you know how to surf the web, right?"

"Yes," Sky said. "Ms. Avery had me learn new songs on the internet." His use of the computer then had been carefully monitored, and he'd been allowed to visit only a few specific sites.

"Good. I figure this way, if you have more questions like *Where's China?* and I'm not here, you can find the answers. Or you can just play. Watch movies. I'll give you my Netflix account info. You can even order some more books from Amazon, if you want. You're almost done with the ones I bought you."

If this was some weird trap, Sky didn't get it. "I can . . . do these things?"

"Yeah. Shit—I should have thought of it before." Master typed for a few moments before grinning. "Here we go. Your log-in is Sky, and your password is Blue, with a capital B. Which is a lame password, but I'm not too worried about someone hacking into your laptop account. Hang on a sec and I'll get you set up on Amazon and Netflix."

When he was through, Master smiled at Sky. "Consider this an extension of rule three—you can use the laptop anytime you want, as long as I'm not needing it. And don't go completely nuts ordering stuff, but when you're ready for a few new books, go ahead and buy them."

He handed the computer to Sky, who let it sit in his lap untouched. He knew he should hold his tongue, but he was afraid that if he kept his thoughts bottled up, they'd come out even more explosively later. "Is this supposed to make up for what happens to me when we're with your friends?" he asked.

Master's face went blank, and he blinked a few times. "No," he rasped. "Time on YouTube and a small shopping spree don't exactly make up for repeated rape and abuse, do they?"

"They don't."

"And here I am acting like it's a big deal that you get to do something that all freemen take for granted. Something that won't cost me more than a few bucks, which I can well afford."

Sky looked at him—really *looked* at him—and saw that Master did understand, and that his eyes and downturned mouth reflected either true sadness or a damned good imitation of it. "I don't understand why you bother to do nice things for me," Sky said.

"Because I want to. Because . . . God, when you hum to yourself or smile, it's like a heavy burden lifted off my heart. Because you're stronger than me and braver than me, and I'm fairly certain you're smarter than me too. And because I want . . . . I want to do what I can within the cage I've built us both."

Although Sky's eyes burned, he kept his chin firm. "I wish I could believe that."

Instead of getting angry, Master exhaled loudly. "But you can't trust me, and I can't afford to trust you either. Not fully." He ran his fingers through his hair and rubbed his scalp. "But I hope that'll change soon."

Sky hoped so too, but he wasn't holding his breath. He'd never been in a position to trust anyone. If you were a slave, trust only set you up for a fall.

CHAPTER NINE

The next morning a hired car drove them across the city. Sky was nervous as they passed through the neighborhood where the last party had been, but then he realized they were heading to Lands End park for a jog. The terrain proved to be hillier and more difficult than the mostly flat areas south of Mission and along the Embarcadero, but the eucalyptus-scented path gave them stunning vistas of the open ocean and the Golden Gate. Master patiently allowed Sky to pause often and gape at the views.

"Beautiful," Sky said as they watched a huge cargo ship maneuver under the bridge and out to sea. "I've never seen anything like this in real life."

"It's a lot better than on TV, huh?"

Sky nodded and waved toward the western horizon. "It's so big. So much world." And no safe place for him within it. "Where do you suppose that ship is going?"

"China, I'd guess. It probably arrived here a few days ago with a cargo of cheap electronic gadgets or shoes or something."

"Made by slaves in factories there," said Sky, who'd spent a good part of the previous afternoon and evening on the internet learning about slavery.

"Probably." Master turned to him. "Have you ever wondered what ships like that take back to China?"

Frowning, Sky shook his head. "Not really."

"Machines, vehicles, pharmaceuticals, chemicals, foodstuffs. If the cargo's legal. If not, drugs. Counterfeit goods. Slaves."

Sky's throat tightened. "Master?" he whispered.

"Not you," Master said quickly, grasping Sky's arm. "Jesus, not you. God, I didn't mean to sound threatening. I was just thinking out loud. I'm sorry—I'm incredibly stupid sometimes."

"I know it's illegal to import slaves, but I thought it was okay to export them."

Master looked grim. "It depends on how you obtained those slaves."

Before Sky could respond—and he wasn't sure what to say anyway—Master's phone buzzed. He pulled it from his hoodie pocket and looked at the screen. "Shit," he said, typing something with his thumbs. "We have to go back. Sorry. I wanted to spend more time out here. We'll come back soon, okay?"

He must have contacted the driver, because the car pulled up to the curb shortly after Sky and Master reached the street. "How'd you like to walk across the bridge sometime?" Master asked when they were settled in the backseat. "We could have dinner in Sausalito, maybe somewhere on the water. Take a car home."

"Sounds nice," Sky answered.

Master nodded, looked out the window, jiggled his leg, and then turned to face Sky. "Someone's coming over to our place. He's a . . . business associate. He won't touch you, I promise."

Our place. Sky was so caught up in that phrase that he barely noticed the rest. Yes, the sense of implied joint ownership was entirely false, yet Master had said it so easily, as if he hadn't given the idea a second thought. Sky's heart suddenly ached for one of the many things he would never have—a home.

"Are you all right?" Master asked, leaning toward Sky and gently touching his shoulder. "Really, this guy's not—"

"It's not that."

Master frowned but didn't ask more.

Traffic was heavy, so even though San Francisco was a fairly compact city, their progress was slow. Sky looked out his window at the shops, bicyclists, and pedestrians, at the buildings crowded close to each other and the occasional splashes of green. He wondered what kind of food the restaurants served and who lived behind the curtained upstairs windows. He smiled a little at a man holding hands with a small child.

Inside the loft, Master gave Sky's back a quick pat. "I'm going to change."

"What do you want me to wear?"

"Whatever you want. This isn't a show, Sky, and I repeat—he's not going to touch you. That's not why he's coming over."

Sky elected to remain in his running clothes, even though he was a little sweaty. They were warm and cozy, and although Master's business associate undoubtedly would know Sky was a slave, it felt good to have the hoodie hide his bracelets. He put the kettle on because his recent reading had put him in the mood for tea, and he munched on an apple as he waited for the water to boil. When Master came down to the kitchen in jeans and a plain black T-shirt, Sky held out a mug. "Want some?"

Master looked delighted. "Yeah, thanks. That was nice of you to think about me."

Who else was Sky going to think about? And wasn't it a slave's duty to think about his master?

They didn't say anything after that, but there was something oddly relaxing about standing side by side in the kitchen, leaning against the counter and sipping their drinks. The tense lines around Master's eyes and mouth smoothed slightly.

"Why are you looking at me like that?" Master asked.

"I'm not sure." Sky tilted his head. "How'd you break your nose?"

"The first time? Got in a fistfight with another kid. I was twelve, thirteen. Tough neighborhood. We didn't have any insurance, so Mom couldn't afford to have it set properly."

"You could afford it now."

"I suppose. But I'm used to it. Plus, I've busted it a couple times since and probably will again, so there's really not much point in making it pretty. Anyway, I thought you said you liked it crooked." He grinned.

When Sky reached up and traced the bridge of Master's nose with his fingertip, Master drew in a noisy breath but didn't move away. Sky ran his thumb along Master's lips, back and forth, and stroked the bristles on his chin, enjoying the rasp against his palm. "I shouldn't want you," Sky said quietly.

Master answered in a hoarse whisper. "Jesus."

But then the buzzer announced his guest's arrival. Despite seeming reluctant to draw away, Master went to let the man into the building. Sky remained standing stiffly in the kitchen, his empty mug in hand, not precisely sure why his heart was beating so fast.

When Master opened the door to the loft, a large man nearly rocketed inside. He was as tall as Master but heavier—more with fat than muscle—and his short brown hair was going gray. He wore a dark suit and carried a briefcase. He pushed right past Master and started walking around. "Slick setup, Webster," he boomed, peering through a window.

"Wallace," Master said, closing the door and locking it.

"Right, right. Wallace. Morgan Wallace. You've got fancy digs. I'm stuck in a split-level with a huge mortgage out in Hayward."

"You know that wouldn't work for me, Teague. And this is temporary."

"Yeah, yeah. Guess it makes up for that shit-hole you were in last year in Jersey City." Still carrying his briefcase, Teague inspected the exercise equipment and the big-screen TV. He stomped over to the stairway and looked up but didn't ascend. Then he entered the kitchen, poking at the coffeemaker and running his hand along the cast-concrete countertop. He came to a stop in front of Sky. "Interesting choice," he said, looking Sky up and down.

Master rushed over and inserted himself between them. "Leave him alone."

"Touchy. I'm just looking. He ain't my type. I prefer . . ." He used his free hand to mime a set of protruding breasts on his chest.

"That's great," Master said. "Go find a girl with big tits."

But Teague didn't move away. He leaned slightly to see Sky around Master. "You know, I get that you like dick. But why this one?"

"He's what I needed." It sounded as if Master was fighting to control his temper. "Teague—"

"C'mon, lemme take a look. He looks familiar. Have we used him before?"

"No."

Teague reached toward Sky, who was trying to keep his expression neutral, but Master batted his hand away. "I told you to leave him alone." That came out as a growl.

"I swear I've seen him before."

"He used to perform in a club in New York."

"Perform?" Teague repeated, bushy eyebrows raised.

"He's a singer."

Teague snapped his fingers. "That's it! He was in one of those boy bands. I dated a girl who was into that crap. She made me take her to a concert once. My ears fucking bled."

"He's a good singer," Master said.

Teague snorted, but after another long look at Sky, he nodded and walked away. Master shot Sky an enigmatic glance before following Teague out of the kitchen. Sky's stomach clenched when they headed toward the playroom. He couldn't see them once they entered, but thanks to the partial walls and the loft's good acoustics, he heard them.

"Wow, impressive!" Teague said.

"I didn't equip it."

"I thought you were into this stuff."

"Not like this."

Something thudded—a paddle against a leather bench, maybe—and Sky flinched when a cane cracked against a hard surface. It hit three more times, and each blow made him jump. Then the hitting stopped, only to be replaced a moment later with a loud buzzing.

"Teague, you're not here for playtime," Master said.

"True. But I gotta check things out—the boss says."

"Fine. You've checked everything out, and—"

"This ain't gonna work. Not like this."

After a brief pause, Master said, "What do you mean?"

"All this shit is here to make a statement in case you have guests over, right? To prove you're one of them."

"So?"

"Everything in here's brand-new. I mean, I'm no expert, but even I can tell you haven't used any of it. What kind of impression will that make, Wallace?" He put a heavy emphasis on the name.

"Fuck. Look, Teague—"

"You don't want to fuck this up, my friend. Not when we're this far into it. You know what's at stake."

If Master answered, Sky didn't hear him. Soon afterward, Teague and Master exited the playroom and walked to the couch.

Teague set his briefcase on the coffee table, fiddled a bit with the lock, then popped it open. Both men gazed at whatever was inside; Sky couldn't see anything but the raised lid.

"We really came through for you this time, buddy," said Teague.

"Yeah? That's not enough."

Teague shrugged. "We're working on it. This'll get you off to a nice start, though, don't you think? Wet their whistles?"

"I guess so."

Seemingly satisfied, Teague nodded. "In case you're tempted to sample—"

"I don't do that."

Teague held up his hands and grinned. "Yeah, yeah. But we both know that sometimes circumstances call for desperate measures. All I'm saying is if you *do* sample, be careful. This shit is about as pure as it gets. It's gonna make your new friends very happy."

Master nodded stiffly and closed the briefcase.

Teague paused at the door, cast Sky a long look, then turned back to Master. "You sure you're cool? We can bring in Delancey in a pinch."

"Delancey doesn't know his ass from third base. He'd fuck it up for sure."

"Maybe. He did okay on that thing in Sacramento."

"Only because he had a lot of help. Besides, this job requires . . . delicacy. Delancey doesn't do delicate."

Teague laughed. "You're right about that. Okay. I'll give the boss a good report. Just remember what I said about your toys." He gestured toward the playroom. "Break 'em in a little. We'll talk soon." He shook Master's hand and left, leaving the briefcase behind.

Master closed the door and leaned his forehead against the wood, as if he were too exhausted to move. Finally he sighed, turned around, and gave Sky a weak smile. "Well, *that's* over."

Sky put down his mug and strode out of the kitchen, stopping very near Master. "You didn't let him touch me."

"I promised."

After a brief pause, Sky nodded. He was so relieved and grateful for Master's honored pledge that he could ignore Teague's warning about the playroom needing to be broken in. Ignore it for now, anyway. Instead he laced his hands behind Master's neck and tugged him down for a kiss. It began as an almost chaste brushing of lips, but Master moaned so loudly at that bit of contact that Sky became ravenous. He deepened the kiss, pillaging Master's mouth with his tongue, tasting the faint floral essence of jasmine tea. Master settled his hands on Sky's shoulders almost hesitantly, without any pressure at all, and pushed his lower body forward until their groins rubbed together.

Master was hard—Sky felt him through jeans and fleece—but then so was Sky, the blood rushing south so quickly that he felt light-headed. Sky broke the kiss, but only so he could lick the tender spot under Master's ear and then mouth at his neck. Sky didn't know where he found the courage to do these things. Didn't even know where the impulses to do them came from. But he knew that his actions made his master groan and thrust against him.

"Oh fuck," Master said, his voice an octave deeper than usual. He threw his head back to give Sky better access to his neck, and when Sky bit him lightly, Master jerked and made a sound low in his throat.

"Sky," Master whispered. And then he dropped to his knees.

As Sky peered down in astonishment, Master clutched Sky's legs and pressed his cheek into the cradle of Sky's hip, carefully avoiding the very evident erection. He stared up at Sky, eyes smoldering. "Can I? Please?"

"Yes," Sky said without knowing exactly what he was agreeing to.

Moving slowly and carefully, Master tugged at Sky's waistband, pulling his sweats and boxer briefs down. Master made a small hiss when Sky's aching cock bounced free, but he continued to painstakingly draw the clothing down Sky's thighs and past his knees.

Ordinarily Sky might have felt hobbled with his pants around his ankles. But when Master kneaded Sky's ass with his big palms and rubbed his nose along the crease of leg and torso, Sky forgot about the sweats.

"M-Master?"

"You can put your hands in my hair. You can pull, even. I don't mind." Master grinned up at him. "Actually, I kind of dig it."

Sweet *heavens*.

Sky did as suggested, enjoying the feel of messing up Master's carefully styled hair. He tugged experimentally—not too hard—and Master groaned and rewarded him by licking the length of his shaft.

There was nothing forbidden about freemen sucking slaves' cocks; after all, the slaves belonged to them and they could do whatever they wanted with their property. But in Sky's fairly considerable experience, the men who used him wanted to stick their dicks into his body, not vice versa. None of them had ever given him a blowjob. Sky *had* been sucked off by other slaves, but the last time had been rather long ago. The situations happened very rarely and also very quickly due to fear of discovery.

As Master took Sky's length into his mouth while stroking the base in his fist, Sky knew he wasn't going to last long. He pulled harder at Master's hair, which caused Master to move more quickly, humming over the flesh in his mouth and jerking his own hips in abortive little thrusts, even though he was still dressed and his cock remained untouched.

"Oh God," Sky moaned.

Still sucking, Master met his eyes, his expression an odd mixture of lust and humor. He pushed at Sky's ass, urging him in deeper, and when Sky gave a few experimental thrusts, Master swallowed him so far that Master's nose was buried against Sky's hairless groin.

Sky plunged his hips forward and yanked Master's head tightly toward him, and just as he had predicted, within moments he felt his orgasm building. "I'm g-going to come . . ." he rasped, loosening his grip so Master could pull free. But Master didn't. He just squeezed Sky's ass a little more until Sky renewed his tight hold on Master's hair, and when Sky cried out, Master took Sky's spend down his throat.

When Sky's thrusts stopped and his skin became too sensitive, Master patted his flanks, let him go with a slurp, and sat back on his heels. He licked his swollen lips and then grinned, his eyes sparkling.

Sky tried to find his voice. "D-do you want me to . . ." He waved his hand vaguely.

Master chuckled. "No need." He pointed at the large wet spot spreading across the crotch of his jeans.

That was when Sky's knees gave out completely. Luckily, Master caught him and lowered him to the floor until Sky knelt facing him. "Wow," Sky finally said.

"*That* didn't take Viagra. That was just you."

"You like—"

"I like you." Master laced his hands behind Sky's head, drew him closer, and gave him a kiss. Now Master tasted like Sky, which was almost enough to make Sky hard again. Master broke the kiss and leaned their foreheads together. "Jesus *Christ*. I'm so fucked."

Sky was inclined to agree.

CHAPTER TEN

Surfing the internet was a lot like wandering into the jungle. Sky would set out with a destination in mind—finding out the origin of the Titanic's name, perhaps. But then he'd get distracted by Greek mythology, veer off into the history of Greek wars, delve into Alexander the Great's biography, learn about typhoid fever, then antibiotic resistance . . . and become aware of himself hours later, lost deep in the wilderness.

Master didn't seem to mind Sky's internet explorations. In fact, he often looked up from his phones or returned from one of his meetings and asked Sky what he was reading. Master would listen with what seemed to be genuine interest as Sky lectured him about lions or professional boxing or the history of electric guitars or whatever had most recently caught Sky's interest. Master would ask him questions or eagerly look up details up on his phone, and they'd end up having some lovely conversations about things Sky had never before considered. It was wonderful. It made Sky feel so fully human that, for a few minutes anyway, he'd almost forget he was a slave.

During their long discussions, Sky learned that Master had passions for cooking and fitness—which didn't surprise Sky—and for rugby. One evening Master found a game on TV, ordered pizza, and sat with Sky on the couch, eating and watching the match. Sky didn't really understand the attraction of the sport, but it was fun to see Master cheer and yell at the players. Master also invited Sky to drink beer with him that night; Sky got a little tipsy, which he also enjoyed.

About a week after Teague's visit, Master came home from one of his meetings well after midnight, looking haggard and smelling strongly of booze. Sky was still awake, and Master collapsed next to him on the couch with a noisy sigh. "Did you have some dinner?" Master asked.

"Leftover chicken and salad. There's some left—do you want me to bring it to you?"

Master rolled his head sideways to smile at Sky. "No thanks. I've lost my appetite."

"Water then?"

"You don't have to wait on me."

"You're my owner. I'm supposed to wait on you."

Master flapped a hand dismissively. "Fuck *supposed to*. God, I hate this."

That was when Sky noticed the impressive erection straining at Master's fly. Master saw him notice. "Viagra again. Should wear off soon."

"Your meeting tonight . . .?" Sky prompted, already certain what the response would be.

"It was at Roger Fischer's house. The asshole who owns Trappings? It was . . . well, you've seen what goes on at those things. Picture more of the same, only this time with fifty percent more recreational pharmaceuticals." He leaned his head back on the couch cushion and closed his eyes.

"Why didn't you take me?" Sky asked.

Master answered without opening his eyes. "I told them you were— Fuck. I told them I beat you so badly yesterday that you couldn't walk."

Sky had no name for the emotion making his stomach flutter. "Why would you do that?"

"Because I was pretty sure I could get away with it, this once." He opened his eyes, sat up straight, and pinned Sky with his gaze. "Because I don't want them to hurt you."

Although Sky still had many more questions than answers about this man, he believed what Master had just said. "Thank you."

"You shouldn't have to thank me for not handing you over to get tortured and raped, Sky. Nobody should." Then he shook his head. "I can't think about this right now. What are you researching?" He pointed at the laptop.

Sky paused a moment before answering. "Manumission of slaves."

Master's answering laugh held no humor. "Or lack thereof."

"Slaves could be freed in ancient Greece and Rome. They could even become citizens."

"Yeah. It was allowed in the early years of the United States, too."

This was news to Sky, who hadn't read that far. "What changed?"

"Couple of things. In some places, people got worried that freed blacks would gain political power, and none of the whites wanted that. But the main thing was that a few folks started saying that it was morally wrong for one human being to enslave another. It was the Enlightenment, you know? People were saying stuff like that."

Sky had no idea what the Enlightenment was; he made a mental note to look it up later. "So what happened?"

"So they had to find a justification for slavery. The Greeks, the Romans, the Ottomans, they pretty much enslaved people that they conquered, or maybe even just people they managed to snatch away from their homes." He scowled deeply. "It was about power. But they didn't particularly need to rationalize why it was okay. They just didn't think that way. During the Enlightenment, though, they needed an excuse. They claimed that free people were inherently superior to slaves. That we have souls and they don't. We were doing them a favor, even. And if your whole justification is that this group is fundamentally inferior, it makes sense to pass laws saying they're never allowed to be free."

Because Sky had heard similar arguments, he nodded. "But I don't look different than free people," he pointed out. Then he gathered his courage and added, "Some of my ancestors might have been free. My father was."

"Yeah. But some ancestor on your mom's side was a criminal or a debtor. The excuse for enslaving them—for enslaving people like you—was they were hereditarily incompetent. Some eighteenth-century scientists even suggested that they were a different species—or at least a different race—simply mimicking real humans. They used to do experiments, cutting slaves up to find the bits that would prove they weren't really like free people."

Sky shuddered and his stomach lurched. "And now people say there's a slave gene," he said.

"Just a modern twist on the same old lies."

Sky was so shocked by Master's statement that he couldn't find the words to respond. He had his own doubts about the slave gene—and he *knew* he felt emotions deeply, despite what everyone claimed. But to hear a freeman say these things was nearly unthinkable. Perhaps Master's difficult life experiences had made him more cynical than most people and less likely to accept what he'd been told.

One of Master's phones buzzed, but he ignored it. He leaned back again, but this time he kept his eyes open, focused on Sky. "So many fucking lies," he said.

Sky watched his own finger tracing invisible patterns on the seat of the couch. "I wonder which crimes my ancestors committed." He'd never thought about it before.

"*Visiting the iniquity of the fathers on the children and the children's children, to the third and the fourth generation,*" Master said, and when Sky looked at him quizzically, he sighed. "That's from the Old Testament. Exodus. But we hold slaves well past the fourth generation, don't we? Besides, Ezekiel says, *The son shall not suffer for the iniquity of the father, nor the father suffer for the iniquity of the son.* And anyway, in your case, nobody accused your father of iniquity. He's in the Rock and Roll Hall of Fame."

"What's iniquity?"

"Wickedness. And let me tell you, Sky, the freemen I know—myself included—are far more iniquitous than any slave has ever had occasion to be."

"Master—"

"I need to go to bed. Feel free to stay up if you want to."

After a moment's consideration, Sky shook his head and shut down the laptop. "I'm tired too."

Judging by Master's expression, he was pleased to have Sky join him.

They got ready side by side in the bathroom, Sky passing the toothpaste to Master after he finished with it. Then Master undid the top two buttons of his collared shirt and pulled it over his head. He gave it a sniff. "I smell like . . . what I've been doing. I'm going to shower."

Sky put his hand on Master's shoulder. "It doesn't matter. Come to bed before you drop."

Master gave him a slow, tired smile.

In the end, Master swiped a damp washcloth over his bare body. By then the Viagra must have worn off, because his erection was gone. Still, when Sky stripped too, Master managed a wolfish grin. "So beautiful," he said.

Sky was thinking the same thing about him.

They lay under the duvet, their only illumination a bit of foggy moonlight sneaking through the skylight. They didn't touch, but Sky was very aware of Master's presence, the heat and bulk of him so very close. After a time, Master's breathing evened and slowed, and he began to snore. Sky was tired, but he couldn't fall asleep. Master had lied to other freemen in order to protect him, or so he had said. Not only did Sky believe that claim, but he believed that Master had kept him home not out of possessiveness—not because he couldn't stand the thought of others touching his property—but because he cared about Sky. Cared *for* Sky.

Where did that leave them? Especially when Master had apparently moved into a corner of Sky's heart as well.

An hour or so later, Sky was still wide-awake, but Master began to thrash and moan. At first his words were unintelligible, but then Sky was able to discern a few: "No! No! Please stop! Don't hurt her! No!" His movements became more frantic, and his voice became a scream. It wasn't the first nightmare he'd had since buying Sky, but it was the most violent.

"Master!" Sky grasped his shoulders and shook him. Master swung at him blindly, hitting Sky's face hard enough to jar his teeth and make him see stars, but Sky didn't let go. "Master! Wake up!"

Master cried out and his eyes sprang open. His chest heaving, he stared at Sky. "I . . . Oh fuck." He swallowed noisily. "Sorry. Dream."

"Can I get you some water?"

"No. I . . . I'm sorry."

Master sounded young and lost, and Sky acted instinctively. He draped himself halfway over Master's body and wrapped an arm around his waist, holding him close. Master moved a bit, but only to reposition one of his arms and embrace Sky with the other. He snuffled at Sky's hair. "God, you feel good."

"I don't want to have sex tonight," Sky said, confident that Master would respect that wish.

"Good, because I couldn't if I tried. This is nice, though. Don't . . . don't let go for a while, okay? Please?"

"I won't." The lullaby of Master's heartbeat soothed Sky to sleep.

In the morning, Master gave Sky a secretive little smile. "Run first, then a surprise," he announced. That sounded like a fine plan.

Although Sky was still nowhere near as fit as Master, his prowess had definitely improved. He now ran at a pace that pleased Master, and his endurance was good even if they took a hilly route.

"Do you hate this?" Master asked when Sky started to huff and puff. Master was jogging backward to look at him, not the slightest bit out of breath.

"No," Sky admitted between wheezes. "Feels good . . . Nice scenery . . ." He didn't add that running gave him a small sense of freedom. Judging by Master's knowing look, he was already aware of that.

Back at the loft, they took turns in the shower. Sky looked to Master for guidance on how to dress, then followed his lead by putting on jeans, a T-shirt, and a green sweater that covered his bracelets. They got in the waiting car, which took them into Golden Gate Park and stopped in front of a large low-slung building with an oddly twisted tower.

"De Young?" Sky said, reading the sign.

"Museum. I thought we were both due for some culture."

Inside, Master paid for both of them, grabbed a brochure with a map, and led the way. "I've never been much of a museum guy," he admitted as they entered the first gallery.

"Then why come here?"

"I thought you'd like it."

As it turned out, Master was right. Sky wandered in open-mouthed wonder, captivated by rooms full of colorful tapestries, moody photographs, beautiful sculptures and household goods, and stunning paintings. Master grinned the entire way, even as he waited patiently for Sky to read all the placards. Sometimes a particular item caught Sky's special attention; in those cases, Master made a note on his phone of the artist and the piece so that Sky could look them up later. By the time they'd toured the entire museum, Sky's brain felt as wonderfully full as his stomach after a big feast.

Before leaving, they browsed the gift shop. Master bought him a thick museum catalog and a soft blue-and-gray scarf that Master wrapped around Sky's neck, a tender act that made the pretty salesclerk smile. Although her smile would have faded fast if she knew Sky was wearing slave bracelets.

They took a quiet stroll around the park. Sky liked that there was so much green in the middle of a city. Of course, New York had Central Park, but in all the years he'd lived there, Sky had never been allowed to ramble and admire the scenery. Now, he wondered what the names of the trees and plants were. When he asked Master about one of them, Master shrugged. "No clue, sorry. City boy."

Maybe next time they came here, Sky would bring a book on local greenery. *Next time.* Sweet heavens—he was planning for the future. Planning for a future here, with Mr. Wallace, where Sky was given leeway to buy books and wander around parks. Stupid, stupid slave.

"Are you okay?" Master asked, looking concerned.

"Yes. I was just . . . I'm a little hungry." Not quite a lie, so not a violation of rule one. More a misdirection.

"Me too. What are you in the mood for?"

Sky had no idea, so he waited while Master tapped at his phone for a minute or two, and then directed them out of the park and up a few blocks. "Do you like Korean food?" Master asked.

"I've never had it."

"Time to try something new then."

It turned out that Sky loved Korean food. He ate something called bibimbap—rice mixed with vegetables, beef, egg, and a spicy sauce. Master made a magnificent mess with barbecued ribs, and when he licked his fingers clean, Sky felt warm from more than just the spices. But there were also lots of little dishes to sample, small bowls of vegetables, fish, eggs, and potato salad.

Sky ate a lot, but in between bites of food, he enthused about the museum exhibits.

"Your mind is so quick," Master said admiringly.

"Maybe because it's empty. There's lots of room for new things."

"Nothing empty about your mind."

When the meal was over, Master seemed reluctant for their outing to end. So they walked some more, this time along city streets, enjoying the temperate weather and varied sights. Eventually they found an outdoor table at a coffee house. Master went inside for a few minutes, and while Sky waited, a pair of policemen exited the shop, each carrying a coffee cup. Even though they barely glanced at him, Sky shifted uneasily. Few slaves felt comfortable around police, who tended to beat unaccompanied slaves first and ask questions later—not particularly caring that the slaves might be on legitimate errands for their masters and carrying passes that verified this.

Master returned with two large cardboard cups: coffee for himself and tea for Sky. He scooted his chair next to Sky, so they were both looking out onto the sidewalk. Sky smiled at all the dogs that walked by, and one of them—an enormous black beast—pulled its owner over and nearly plopped its head in Sky's lap.

"Sorry!" said the owner, a young woman with braided red hair.

Sky scratched the dog's soft ears. "It's okay. I don't mind."

After the dog and the girl had gone, Sky turned to Master. "Who was she? The one you dream about."

Master's expression turned so thunderous that Sky cowered a bit, knowing he'd finally crossed a line. But Master didn't strike him. Didn't even yell, actually. He just breathed hard for a few moments and then rubbed his face. "Lindsey," he said very quietly. "My sister."

Sky didn't want to push since it was obviously a very painful subject, so he said nothing. After a few seconds, Master sighed. "She was a year younger than me, so I was . . . I was supposed to protect her. But we lived in these god-awful neighborhoods. This man broke into our apartment one afternoon when Mom was at work, and he started stealing stuff. We didn't really have much worth stealing, you know, but he was probably too high to realize that. He screamed at me, asking where we kept our cash, and Lindsey made a run for the door. He caught her and . . . and he just picked her up and started bashing her against the walls, the floor."

Sky put his hand over Master's, who turned his own hand over and squeezed Sky's. "I tried to stop him, but he was stronger than me. I was ten. He just kept pushing and kicking me away, and I couldn't— A neighbor must have heard the screaming, because she started pounding on the door. The burglar took off running. Knocked the neighbor over as he left the apartment. I was just banged up a little, but Linds . . . There was so much blood." His voice cracked, and he rubbed his face with his free hand before taking a gulp from his cooled coffee.

"I'm sorry." Sky didn't know what else to say.

Master shook his head ruefully. "I've seen a lot of fucking awful things since then, but when I have nightmares, every victim has my sister's face." He huffed. "I'm sorry. I shouldn't be complaining to you. Not after what you've been through yourself."

"Do you think one person's pain makes another person's suffering less important?"

"No, I guess not."

They were quiet for a while after that, Master's fingers entwined with Sky's. The smell of fried food wafted through the air from the restaurant next door. More dogs walked by with their people, a guy in a suit and tie rattled past on a skateboard, and a police car raced down the street, siren blaring and lights flashing. Sky couldn't tell if it carried the same officers he'd seen before.

"Do you have other family?" Sky finally asked.

Master squeezed Sky's hand. "No. Mom died my senior year of high school. Cancer. We were never in touch with anyone else—no grandparents or aunts and uncles or anything. So then it was just me."

"What about a lover? A spouse? Kids?"

"None of that. I've never had anyone stick. My lifestyle's not real conducive to long-term relationships."

Sadness washed over Sky. It had never occurred to him that a freeman might be as lonely as a slave. He wanted Master to be loved. *Stupid.* "If you could wave a magic wand and have any kind of life at all . . .?"

Master gave him a long look. "I used to think I was doing exactly what I wanted. Lately, not so much. So, magic wand? I'd have a comfortable little house—maybe one with a small garden so I could grow a few things for my kitchen. And I'd spend my days cooking and exercising and . . . and being with someone special." He hung his head for a moment. "Dumb, huh?"

"Not at all." It was a pretty little dream, if it was true.

"How about you, Sky?"

Sky shook his head. "Slaves don't get magic wands."

CHAPTER ELEVEN

O ver the next few days, Master had more meetings. That was what he called them, anyway. Most were during the day, but one was at night. He didn't bring Sky along, and Sky knew that the story about him being too battered wasn't going to hold up much longer. Every time Master returned from one of the meetings, he looked more exhausted, more defeated.

Sky would have predicted that when Master wasn't at his meetings, exercising, or on his phones, he'd prefer to collapse comfortably by himself, maybe with Sky waiting on him. But instead, what Master most seemed to want was to putter around in the kitchen with Sky perched on a stool, prattling on about whatever had most recently caught his attention in books or on the internet.

What really made Master smile was when Sky hummed. So when Master had another screaming, kicking nightmare, this one even worse than the last, Sky ducked the flailing arms, pulled Master close, and crooned Beatles songs. Master quieted and his eyes fluttered open. "'Hey Jude'?" he rasped.

"I don't know any real lullabies." Nobody wanted lullabies in the middle of a show.

"'S nice." Master rolled to face Sky and then embraced him. He snuffled Sky's hair before placing a kiss atop his head. "Nice." And he promptly fell back into a sound, dreamless sleep.

They didn't run the next morning, although Master spent some time with the weights and treadmill. When he was done, he showered and came downstairs in what Sky had come to think of as his meeting clothes: expensive trousers, equally expensive silk shirt, and a gray sports coat that looked custom tailored. He rustled around in the closet where he'd stowed Teague's briefcase and emerged with a gray suede messenger bag. He slid the strap over one shoulder. "This'll take a few hours, so eat lunch without me. We can go out for dinner, if you like. Seafood with a view?"

"That sounds good."

"Do you have enough to keep you busy until then?"

Sky smiled. Nobody had ever worried whether he might get bored. "I got those new books yesterday, remember?" He'd ordered quite a few from Amazon, and instead of getting angry over the expense, Master had seemed delighted.

"Oh yeah, right." Master's usually confident stride was oddly hesitant as he made his way to the door. "Okay, see you in a few hours." The latch clicked as he left.

After considerable indecision, Sky settled down with a book about an Englishman who'd explored Africa in the nineteenth century. It was a fascinating read, but it assumed a much greater knowledge of history and geography than Sky possessed. He kept having to pause and google things. Photographs of the Zambezi River captured his attention during one of these research diversions. And as often happened, he ended up sidetracked, first reading about the agricultural benefits of deltas, then about plantations in the American South. By the time he came up for air, he was hungry. He ate a quick sandwich along with some carrots and an apple.

When he returned to the couch, he intended to pick up the book again, but the open computer distracted him. He set it on his lap, and when the search-engine web page stared him in the face, Sky found himself typing "Morgan Wallace." He found an actor he'd never heard of who'd died over sixty years earlier, a company that manufactured motor oil, and a store in Australia that specialized in clothing for big and tall men. He also found lots of men—and some women—with that name, but none looked or sounded remotely like Master. In all, Sky spent almost an hour creeping around the internet, but he couldn't find any mention of *his* Morgan Wallace. Hah. As if Master belonged to him.

Finally he gave up the search. He wasn't surprised to have found nothing. But instead of returning to his book, Sky keyed in a different name that brought up thousands of hits.

Jonny Walsh had grown up middle class in Massachusetts and, after dropping out of high school in the late 1960s, made his way to California. His versatile voice and his good looks—honey-colored hair and sky-blue eyes—caught a producer's attention, and before too long, Walsh was playing to sold-out concert halls. He'd taken an ill-advised detour into electronica and new wave in the eighties, which had dimmed his star considerably, but he experienced a resurgence in popularity around the turn of the millennium after a few of his songs were used in advertisements. Now he coasted along, singing the same playlist and padding his bank accounts with merchandising deals. He'd been married and divorced three times, and his only child, a daughter, died in a car accident in 2003.

His only child.

Sky didn't know for certain that Jonny Walsh was his father. But those eyes certainly looked familiar, as did the square chin and peaked cupid's bow of his upper lip.

"It doesn't matter," he said aloud. It didn't. The law was crystal clear: Sky could have been sired by God Himself, but because his mother was a slave, so was he. And so would he always be, until he one day died from untreated disease or injuries and his body was ransacked for viable organs and then burned along with the rest of the trash. Other than a few 2Nyte albums, some antique fan photos, and perhaps a few old sales receipts, there would be no sign that he'd ever existed.

Sky allowed himself the rare luxury of the what-if game. What if his mother had been one of Walsh's wives or girlfriends instead of a bordello slave? Growing up, Sky would have had a home, an education. Family. He would have had the opportunity to choose a career. Maybe he'd have been a musician, but maybe not. He might have opted to be a teacher, a scientist, a lawyer. Would he have owned slaves, and if so, would he have treated them kindly?

He might very well have fallen in love with someone and been loved in return.

Or maybe he would have died young in a car wreck or from an overdose. Maybe he would have been reckless and cruel, pandering for media attention and squandering his father's money on useless baubles.

He would have had choices. He would have had *control*. And he wouldn't now be sitting alone, waiting helplessly for the next time he was brutalized—and the next time he was sold.

Sky closed the browser window and carefully set the laptop on the coffee table. He walked to the entryway, where he put on his running shoes and hoodie. He opened the door, stepped into the hallway, and quietly closed the door. And then with his mind an eerie, almost perfect blank, he headed for the stairs.

Although he had no plan or destination, he wasn't surprised that he walked toward the Ferry Building. After all, he and Master ran there nearly every day; it was one of his favorite places. But today he didn't stop to watch the ferries or the seagulls, and he didn't browse among the shops that sold such tempting food. Instead he continued walking north along the Embarcadero, ignoring the tourists, stepping mechanically past the piers. When the sidewalk curved toward Fisherman's Wharf, he followed it. The scents of ice cream and hot dogs hit him as he passed Pier 39, and he heard sea lions barking and the slight tinkle of carousel music. He passed restaurants, the stands that sold crab, shops full of cheap trinkets for people to take back to Wisconsin or Delaware. He saw the old ships moored at Hyde Street Pier and wondered if, once upon a time, any of them had brought slaves from overseas. Maybe even his ancestors.

And then he came to Aquatic Park, where waves lapped endlessly against a little crescent of sand. He found a bench. He sat. And then he did nothing at all.

He didn't notice when the sun set, and he'd probably been shivering for some time before he realized it. But he just hunched his shoulders, crossed his arms, and lowered his head.

"Sir? You can't sleep here, sir."

Sky squinted up at two police officers. It was too dark for him to discern their features, but he knew they were inspecting him closely. Not looking for bracelets, because extremely few slaves were foolish enough to try to run away, but probably assessing whether he was high or mentally unstable. They certainly didn't appear to be searching for him specifically.

"I'm sorry," said Sky, managing not to *sir* the officers back. He stood uncertainly.

"Do you have someplace to go?"

Of course not. But he nodded. "Sorry. I was just here thinking."

"I understand, sir. Do you need assistance of some kind?"

Sky almost laughed. It would likely have come out high-pitched and hysterical. "No thank you. I'm just . . . trying to work things out."

The cops looked at him, exchanged a quick glance with each other, and nodded in unison. "All right, sir," one of them said. "You have a good evening."

With a tiny nod, Sky turned away from them and headed toward the sidewalk.

After that, he just walked. He didn't pay attention to where he was going, but it seemed as if all the streets were uphill. He kept expecting sirens, running feet, angry shouts, blows from big men who carried electric prods. But none of those things happened. He passed a few homeless people who had hunkered down in doorways for the night, a small group of drunken twentysomethings, a straight-backed old man walking his tiny dog.

Master could track him. The chip embedded in Sky's body meant Master could find him as easily and precisely as a misplaced or stolen phone. He wouldn't even need to get the police involved if he was avoiding them; he could simply hop in a taxi or hired car and follow the signal from the chip. Surely he'd returned to the empty loft hours ago.

But as the night dragged on, he didn't appear.

Sky became thoroughly lost, which didn't matter since he had no goal. His empty stomach complained, but although he passed a few markets and restaurants that stayed open all night, he had no money. When he found himself miraculously back within view of the Ferry Building clock tower, he very nearly climbed over the railing separating the sidewalk from the bay and jumped in. At that moment, he didn't care that didn't know how to swim.

At that moment, though, his life was his own to keep or end.

He chose to keep it.

He turned away from the water and trudged back to the apartment building. The outer door was locked, of course, and he couldn't bring himself to push the buzzer, so he sat huddled against the brick wall, waiting.

Minutes later, the main entrance burst open and a large figure hurtled through. "Sky!" Master yelled, catching sight of him at once. Sky tensed and readied himself for the blows.

But Master knelt in front of him, and his hands on Sky's shoulders were gentle. "Are you all right? Are you hurt?"

Sky blinked up at him, confused to hear worry instead of anger in Master's voice. "I'm fine," he whispered.

Master heaved a noisy sigh. "You're freezing. Let's get inside." He stood and held a hand to Sky, helping him up. Then he flung an arm around Sky's shoulders, drawing him close. After Master unlocked the door, they walked slowly up the stairs, down the hall, and into the loft. In the better light of the entryway, Master held Sky at arm's length, inspecting him. "Do you want a hot bath? Or tea? Fuck, I bet you didn't have any dinner. Soup?"

Unable to make sense of what was happening, Sky shook his head. The penalties for running away were severe—far worse than the beatings he'd endured so far. So why was Master offering him soup? "I . . . I ran away," Sky whispered.

Master nodded gravely. "It's really late. Let's go to bed, okay? We'll discuss it in the morning."

That didn't make sense either. But Sky docilely allowed himself to be led up the stairs and then stripped, obediently lifting his feet so Master could remove his shoes and socks and then his jeans and underwear. Master steered him to the bathroom to pee and to drink a cupful of water. They seemed to be skipping the rest of their usual nightly ablutions, because moments later, Master tucked Sky into bed.

Only when Master began to undress did Sky realize he was still wearing his meeting clothes, although the sport coat was gone and the shirt was badly rumpled. Master's hair was a mess too, standing on end as if he'd been raking his fingers through it.

After turning off the lights, Master climbed into bed and pulled up the covers. Sky waited for Master to hurt him, but all Master did was place a tentative hand on Sky's waist. "Can I?" he asked.

"Yes." Because Master had given him the option to refuse—and Sky trusted he'd respect that refusal—Sky consented, even though he wasn't sure what Master was asking for or why.

Master scooted close, pressed their bare bodies together, and exhaled loudly. "Thank you."

For what? Clearly, Sky's muddled brain wasn't going to provide him with any answers tonight. But the bed was warm and cozy, and Master felt good against him. It made Sky feel safe, as stupid as that was. So he decided to enjoy these comforts while he could, and fell asleep with Master's breaths puffing against his skin.

Sky awoke to the scents of jasmine tea and maple syrup. He pried his eyes open and discovered Master smiling down at him, a tray in his hands. "It's past noon, but I figured breakfast still works."

Glancing at the bedside clock—it was actually almost 1 p.m.—he tried to clear his head. "Breakfast?"

"Yep. A slightly decadent one, actually."

Although he was still deeply confused, Sky was also ravenous, and the food smelled amazing. Rubbing his face, he sat up and propped himself on pillows. He scooted his legs over a little so Master could perch next to him.

Master transferred the tray to Sky's lap. In addition to tea, there was a big bowl of oatmeal, glistening with butter and drizzled with syrup; a pile of small link sausages; four toast triangles with more butter; and a cup of sliced fruit. Sky looked down at the feast in astonishment. "But I ran away," he said.

"We'll get to that later. Food and a shower first. Unless you'd rather have a bath?"

"A shower is fine."

"Okay." Master raised his eyebrows, clearly eager for him to eat.

Neither of them said anything while Sky devoured his meal. He wasn't sure he had ever tasted anything so delicious. Although he would have thought that fear would make everything taste like ashes, he was no longer afraid. He felt an odd separation from himself, as if he were watching an actor in a movie. At least the actor was eating well.

After every last crumb had disappeared, Master set the tray on the bedside table. He gave Sky a hand up, as caring and solicitous as when

Sky had been beaten. He even turned on the shower, making sure to get the water temperature just right, and then politely backed out of the bathroom while Sky was under the water. Sky was tempted to take a very long shower, just to put off his punishment a little longer, but in the end he scrubbed, shampooed, and rinsed quickly.

Naked, he left the bathroom and focused on Master, who was pacing by the bed. Master stopped. "We're not going anywhere today," he said, "so feel free to wear whatever's comfy."

"But I ran—"

"Away. Yes. We've definitely established that." Master sighed. "Maybe it would be better to just get this over with, huh?"

Sky nodded. And when Master waited, foot tapping, Sky pulled on sweatpants and his softest T-shirt. Master, he noticed, was wearing jeans and a white oxford shirt with what appeared to be a few small spatters on the chest.

They went downstairs, and Sky wasn't at all surprised when Master guided him to the playroom. After they entered, Master turned to him, his eyes dark and serious. "I started tracking you as soon as I got home. At first I was afraid someone had kidnapped you."

"Stolen," Sky whispered.

Master ignored the correction. "But when I saw where you were, I figured you were on your own. And I watched you." He shook his head. "You walked for miles last night. Jesus Christ, I cannot tell you how relieved I was when you came back home."

"Why didn't you come after me? Or send someone?"

"I wanted to. Fuck, if someone else had found you . . . I *can't* let you go, Sky. But I really, really hoped you'd come back on your own. And you did."

Still not understanding, Sky shook his head.

Master looked around the playroom, no doubt taking in the various instruments of bondage and pain, then caught Sky's gaze. "We need to do this. Both of us. You've gotten so far under my skin that I'm messing up the job. My boss is pissed. I think this might help get me back on track."

It was a good solution to two problems, Sky thought. Master could punish him while at the same time breaking in the playroom equipment, just as Teague had advised him. Sky wouldn't struggle. He had chosen to run away—he had earned this.

And then Master began to unbutton his own shirt.

Sky gaped, dumbfounded, while Master let the shirt fall to the floor, followed by his jeans and briefs. Now completely nude, he scrutinized the room before walking to a multilayered bench padded in black leather. He climbed onto it belly-down. Cushioned boards supported his spread knees and upper shins, a wider part held his torso and head, and a pair of narrow planks bore his palms and forearms.

He had to twist his head a little to see Sky. "I'd rather you strap me in, but that's up to you."

"M-Master? I-I don't . . ." Sky choked over his own words. "Rule two." He really, really didn't understand.

"At least when we're in here, don't call me Master. Please. I'm Mor— Shit, no. I'm Mac. It's short for Mackenzie. Please call me Mac."

"Mackenzie Webster?" Sky asked, remembering the name Teague had used.

"Yeah. I should've said something sooner. A lot of people call me Web, but to my friends—not that I have many—I'm Mac. You can use it, but only when we're alone."

"Mac," Sky said carefully. "But why?"

"I like it. Hardly anyone uses my real name. And the rest . . ." He toyed with one of the leather straps that could hold his wrist in place. "I used to be into this. Not totally hard-core, but when I needed to relax, take the edge off. I talked to a shrink about it once. Christ, I didn't want to, but I had no choice. I thought for sure she was going to tell me I was perverted and crazy. Sick."

"Did she?" asked Sky, caught up in the story despite his bewilderment.

"No. She said as long as it was consensual and I was careful not to get injured, it was healthy. I've been responsible for myself since I was little. Sometimes it feels like I have the whole goddamn world on my shoulders and nobody to help take up the slack. She said this stuff"—he patted the bench—"is me giving up control for a short time. Like handing the burden to someone else for a little while. Letting someone else run the show."

Partial understanding dawned on Sky like a puzzle piece slipping into place. He and Mast— *Mac* had discussed this before, but in a different context. Sky had so little control that he almost didn't mind being punished for misbehavior—because he'd chosen to misbehave. And Mac had so much control that sometimes he needed to relinquish it. To put himself in a position where he *couldn't* decide everything.

"You like to get tied up," Sky said.

Master smiled. "Now and then. And while I'm bound, if my partner decides to hurt me a little, that's good too."

Sweet heavens. "You like pain?" Sky asked.

"Not exactly. Well, I like a little. When you pulled my hair, for instance. The shrink claimed that I'm punishing myself. I don't know if I believe that, though. I think if it's done right, your body can't even tell the difference between pleasure and pain, and that makes it all good. Like adding hot sauce to food."

Still not quite believing they were having this conversation, Sky moved closer to Mac. Close enough to touch him. And when Sky ran his fingers over Mac's spine and beautiful ass, Mac shivered and sighed.

"And you want *me* to do this to you?" Sky asked.

"I'm dying for it."

"But I'm a sl—"

"Don't. What you are, Sky, is the most remarkable man I have ever met. And here you are, tied up so tightly you ran away, even knowing you couldn't get anywhere. I can't imagine what it does to you to be so constrained. Controlled. I know it's a fiction, but just for now, let's drop all that. Right here, right now, you get to be in charge. I think it'll be good for you. I get to be *not* in charge, which I know will be good for me. Can we do this, Sky? Do you want to?" His questions sounded like pleas.

With his mouth dry as sand, Sky carefully buckled the straps around Mac's ankles and shins. As he did so, he saw Mac's cock—hanging so vulnerably between his legs—begin to harden. At least it was evidence that Mac was enjoying this. But to see the man who owned him naked, bound, and soon to be helpless made Sky's heart race so fast that he felt light-headed.

Sky reached for the straps near Mac's arm, but stopped. "How can you trust me?"

Mac didn't look alarmed or upset at the question. "You've never given me reason not to."

"I ran away!"

"You came back. Anyway, there's a world of difference between trying to escape a fucked-up situation and harming me."

"I could *kill* you." He thought of the gun upstairs. He didn't know how to use it, but he could figure it out. Or why bother—the kitchen was full of knives, and the playroom contained several devices that could be fatal, depending on how they were used.

"You could," Master said calmly. "But I don't think you'll choose to."

In fact, there were many practical reasons not to commit murder. It wouldn't help Sky escape, because eventually someone would figure out that Mac was dead and Sky missing, and then they'd track him down. And the penalties for slaves who killed freemen were unspeakable. Sky had heard of it happening only once before. He'd been with 2Nyte at the time, and the management had insisted that all the singers sit in a room and watch the televised torture of a woman who'd poisoned her master. The woman had begged for death until she had no voice to beg with, and most of the band members—Sky included—had vomited. Sometimes he still had nightmares about what he saw.

But it wasn't the practical reasons that made Sky shudder, but rather the thought of Mac dying. And not because Mac's death— even if not by Sky's hand—made Sky's future uncertain and ugly. He just . . . wanted Mac alive. Because he cared for him. Because he'd grown to crave Mac's laughter, his gentle touches, the soothing presence of his big body in bed. Because even if Mac was still a cipher, even if he had handed Sky over for brutal use and would do so again, Sky had become attuned to him, his own heart beating in harmony with Mac's. Because against all reason and common sense, Sky believed in him. Trusted him.

When Sky began to fasten the strap around Mac's right wrist, Mac groaned. "Thank you, Sky."

Sky worked quickly to buckle the rest of Mac's restraints, making each of them tight enough to severely restrict movement, yet taking care not to cut off blood circulation. When he was through,

Mac tugged at them with his powerful muscles—and wasn't that a lovely sight!—but he couldn't get loose. He grinned at Sky. "Perfect."

"What do you want me to do to you?"

"Anything you want."

It was a gift, Sky thought. Mac trussed up firmly, displayed for Sky's use and pleasure, a flush already coloring his cheeks. But deciding what to do next was like choosing one book out of Amazon's millions, one restaurant out of the thousands in San Francisco, one song out of the many Sky had learned. *Everything* tempted him. So he put off the decision by simply smoothing his palms across Mac's wide shoulders and tapered back, over the meaty globes of his ass, down the thick, furry width of his thighs. Mac responded to every bit of contact; he pressed against Sky's hands as fully as his bonds allowed, making throaty noises like a cat being stroked.

It felt as if Sky had grown extra nerve endings. Despite the lightness of his touch, he sensed every hair on Mac's body, every hill and valley of him, and he basked in the heat as it transferred to him. Then he surprised both of them by slapping one of Mac's butt cheeks—hard. The noise echoed. And then Mac laughed delightedly. "Good," he said.

Encouraged, Sky spanked him several more times. He put his strength into it, admiring the way pale flesh reddened and the way Mac began to gasp with each blow. When his hand began to sting, Sky stopped and trailed his fingers first across the pink skin, then—after a slight hesitation—down the crease between Mac's cheeks and onto Mac's tender, hanging balls.

Mac quivered.

Sky wanted more of that, and he looked around for an appropriate tool. His gaze settled on a black leather paddle with several large holes. He picked it up, swung it a few times, and struck it against his denim-clad thigh. He liked the feel of it in his hand, but what he liked even more was Mac's expression: wide-eyed and hungry.

Trying to hide a smile, Sky returned to Mac and stood behind him. He lifted the paddle and was about to bring it down when he remembered something he'd heard about. "Shouldn't you have a safeword?" he asked. Slaves, of course, didn't get safewords.

Mac chuckled. "It's fenugreek, but I won't use it."

"Fenugreek?"

"It's a plant. Its leaves and seeds are used in cooking. And it's not something I'd normally say during a scene."

Sky wondered what it tasted like. Perhaps he'd ask Mac—later.

Now, he raised his hand again and brought the paddle down on the roundest part of Mac's ass. The paddle was lightweight, the leather warm and sensual under his hand, and the *thud* it made was very satisfying. As was the hitch in Mac's breathing.

It wasn't exactly that Sky liked causing Mac pain. What he *did* like—what made his jeans feel far too tight—was watching Mac writhe and hearing him whine, seeing Mac's stiff cock jerk, feeling the heat in Mac's skin, and knowing that he was causing all that. He could do *anything* to this handsome man, and if he did it right, the man would beg for more.

Sky knew how uncomfortable an injured butt was, so he set the paddle aside after a while and, giving in to another impulse, trailed his tongue over the abused flesh. Mac tasted good. Salty.

"Oh God," Mac whimpered. His eyes were closed and he'd gone limp—well, *most* of him had; his dick was as hard as ever.

Sky tried out a variety of paddles and floggers and canes, inflicting only a few blows with each and always following up with soothing caresses or tender kisses. Mac seemed to have melted into a puddle of pliant goo, sometimes moaning or mumbling incoherent pleas.

At one point, Sky stopped what he was doing and moved around to crouch in front of Mac's face. He stroked a lock of hair off Mac's sweaty face. "Are you all right?" Sky asked.

Mac's eyelids fluttered but didn't open, and his mouth curled upward slightly. "Yeah," he slurred. "'S good." He looked more relaxed than Sky had ever seen him, even during sleep.

When Sky grew tired of swinging his arm, he looked around the playroom again. This time he found a small, spiked metal wheel with a metal handle. He gently rolled the wheel over the back of his forearm. Without pressure, it didn't pierce the skin and didn't hurt, but it made his nerves prickle. He imagined the feel of it on already sensitized skin and smiled.

Mac gasped loudly as Sky ran the wheel along the length of his spine, but when Sky guided the spikes softly along the curve of one ass cheek, Mac actually sobbed.

"You're mine," Sky said, tracing Mac's inner thigh. "Not legally. Not forever. But right this minute, you are truly mine."

Mac nodded.

There were a thousand more things Sky wanted to do to him, so many parts of his body yet to explore, so many sounds Sky could draw from him like a conductor of a symphony. But Mac's thick lashes were wet and his pulse fast, and Sky decided Mac had borne enough. He set the wheel aside and began to slowly unbuckle the straps.

Mac didn't move even when he was completely freed. "Can fuck me," he whispered.

Sky's balls ached. He'd never fucked anyone, and there was nothing he wanted more in the entire world right at that moment. But instead he bent and kissed Mac's cheek. "Let's just go lie down for a while."

Mac stumbled a bit when he got to his feet, and he was shivering, so Sky draped the white oxford shirt over Mac's shoulders and wrapped his arm around Mac's waist. They didn't so much walk as shamble, and Sky was so skeptical about their ability to get upstairs that he began to steer them toward the couch. But Mac dragged his feet, "Need room for you." He sounded like he was drunk.

They wouldn't both fit on the couch, at least not without discomfort and the risk of falling off, so Sky redirected them, and they managed to get upstairs with only moderate difficulty. Mac let the shirt slide off his back and collapsed onto the unmade bed, and Sky pulled the blankets over him. Then, remembering how Mac had cared for him after the first party, Sky fetched a cup of water and helped Mac drink. "Do you want something more substantial?" Sky asked. He could make a smoothie or soup or—

"You."

Sky felt good. His arousal had faded, but a feeling of peace remained. And power. He was strong. He'd given Mac what he craved and had cared for him exactly right, and now Mac needed him.

He skimmed off his clothes and slipped into bed, drawing Mac's pliant body into an embrace. Mac sighed loudly, and it was Sky's turn to kiss his hair.

"Fuck me later?" Mac muttered, then yawned loudly.

Sky hugged him more tightly. "Definitely."

CHAPTER TWELVE

After spending the better part of the day lolling in bed, Sky and Mac finally got up at dinnertime, threw on comfortable clothes, and ambled down to the kitchen. Stretching and yawning, Mac began to assemble a meal while Sky watched. Sky felt relaxed and decadent, and Mac was so calm that for a change he hummed—loudly and off-key. He kept pausing in his work to throw Sky lazy smiles, and sometimes he detoured to the breakfast bar so he could drop a kiss on Sky's cheek.

They ate steaks, steamed veggies, and baked potatoes, followed by enormous bowls of ice cream. And then they sat squashed together on the couch, watching the entire Lord of the Rings trilogy and munching on popcorn.

As the third movie was entering its zillionth farewell scene, Mac leaned his head on Sky's shoulder. "Before you, I never got to do this," he said. "With anyone."

"Me either," Sky said drily.

"Yeah. Shit. This is good though, isn't it?"

Sky stroked Mac's hand. "Yes. But it doesn't make up for—"

"For the shit I've put you through. I know. And there's probably going to be more of it soon."

"I know." Sky had made an uneasy sort of peace with that concept. Mac had said the parties were necessary, and although Sky didn't know *why*, he was inclined to believe him—despite the pain and the brutal sex. Mac trusted Sky; unexpectedly, Sky had discovered he could reciprocate.

"I am sorry. Christ, if I could trade places with you, I would. I realize that's an empty declaration, but I swear it's true."

Sky knew that. But he had to clarify a point. "What I did to you today is nothing like what they do to me. The equipment may be the same—"

"But the intent isn't. I get it. And I wanted what you did to me— hell, I loved it. Even if you'd beaten me more severely and left me marked, I would have enjoyed every second." He took a moment to pet Sky's hand. "I'm fully aware of how important consent is. What we did, that was bliss. For me anyway."

"Me too," Sky said softly.

"Good. But what they do to you is an abomination." He sat up and twisted to face Sky, his expression earnest and sad. "So will you believe me when I tell you some of them are doing something even worse?"

When Sky nodded, Mac looked relieved. But Sky had a question. "Why do you have to be the one to . . . do whatever you're doing?"

"With you chained to me and bearing the brunt of it. I just thought I was buying a slave, you know? A tool to help me do the job. I'm an idiot, and it never occurred to me I'd be dragging a *person* into this shitstorm. And it sure as hell never occurred to me I might end up falling for him."

Sky almost stopped breathing. "Falling?"

"Fell. Don't worry—it's my problem, not yours."

"I can't— I don't know . . ."

"Of course. Christ, you can't love someone if he has the kind of power over you that I do. I'm probably being selfish by even telling you how I feel. It's only that I've never been in love before."

After thinking about it for a moment, Sky gave him a small smile. "I'm glad you told me. It's nice to know. Nobody's ever loved me before."

Mac blinked a few times. "Your mother?"

Sky shrugged. "I didn't know her very well. She had other obligations. And she knew she wouldn't keep me long, so I suspect she avoided getting too attached." That was the reality for slaves, and it was important that Mac understood it.

"Fuck." Mac cradled Sky's face and leaned their foreheads together. "You're very lovable, actually."

"You too," Sky said with a small chuckle.

"Rule one?"

"Rule one."

"Thank you."

The credits were rolling, so when Mac let go, Sky stood and stretched. The past two days had churned with emotion, and he was exhausted. "Will you come to bed?" he asked.

Mac smiled. "Yeah." But when he stood, he caught Sky's arm to stop him from walking away. "That man who killed my sister? They never caught him."

Sky felt a bit whiplashed from the conversation's sudden veer. "I'm sorry."

"Here was a little girl battered to death by some junkie, and the cops didn't care because we were poor. They even threatened to arrest Mom because we were too young to be left alone. Child endangerment, they said. As if it was something she had a choice about."

Sky had just recently learned that even free people were sometimes in positions of little control. "That's terrible."

"Nobody cared that Lindsey died. And that's why I do what I do." He gave a half shrug. "I know that's sort of a weird explanation, but it's the truth. Even my shrink said so." He moved his hand to clasp Sky's, and together they walked upstairs.

Although they went to bed naked, they didn't have sex that night. Mac spooned back against Sky, his firm ass wonderful against Sky's groin. Mac gave every indication that he'd be willing, if Sky wanted to take him up on his previous offer. But Sky's emotional reserves were already depleted, and he didn't want the first—and possibly only—time he topped to be quick and clumsy. Instead he kissed Mac's nape and hummed them both to sleep.

They woke to Mac's phone buzzing on the nightstand. While Mac read the text, Sky checked the time. It was after nine. Another late morning for them. He shuffled to the bathroom to pee and brush his hair, and when he came out, Mac was sitting in bed looking profoundly unhappy.

"Are we going running?" Sky asked.

"We have a party tonight. Both of us."

Sky straightened his shoulders and nodded. "I think we should run now anyway." It was better than skulking nervously around the loft.

A light rain was falling, but the cool air felt good. Sky ran his fastest, and Mac—who might have been a bit sore from the day before—seemed pleased to finally be moving at close to his normal pace. He let Sky choose the route, and instead of their usual journey past the Ferry Building, Sky led them up through the Stockton tunnel and into North Beach, then over to Fort Mason and back down Van Ness. They were both winded by the time they reached the loft, and Sky's legs felt weak and rubbery. Good. The more he exhausted himself now, the better.

Mac was occupied with his phones for the rest of the day, so Sky did some housecleaning for the sake of keeping busy.

When it was time to get ready, Mac dressed simply in designer jeans and a pale green cashmere sweater that made Sky want to pet him. With his mouth tight, Mac led them into the playroom. "Fuck. I'm so tired of the goddamn costumes. Hang on." He dug out a relatively conservative outfit: snug-fitting leather pants that laced all the way up the sides, a black leather-and-fishnet tank top, and glittery red-and-black platform boots. Sky had performed onstage wearing considerably more risqué clothing than that.

Before Sky put on the pants, though, Mac held up a hand to stop him. "One more thing. I'm . . . Shit. This is probably a terrible idea, but I can't—" He reached into a drawer and pulled out a steel belt with a shield in the center.

Speechless, Sky simply stared.

"I know," Mac said, looking pained. "But if you wear this, they can't fuck you."

Sky believed that Mac was honestly trying to protect him. He didn't point out that none of Mac's acquaintances would be able to fuck him if he and Mac stayed home. He also didn't mention that the device wouldn't stop anyone from using his mouth or beating him bloody.

He took the belt, but putting it on was trickier than he expected, and Mac had to help. It fit snugly over Sky's hips, and the shield covered his cock and balls completely, pressing his dick down and slightly between his legs. The end of the shield attached to a thick metal tube that passed tightly between his butt cheeks. The tube flatted out to allow attachment to the back of the belt. The device wasn't exactly comfortable, but he'd be able to endure it for one night. And Mac was right—his most vulnerable bits were protected, and it would be impossible for anyone to stick anything in his ass.

Mac locked the belt and handed the key to Sky. "Keep this here. Put it wherever you want."

After spending a moment staring at the little metal key, Sky placed it on a shelf next to a scary-looking butt plug. Then he began to struggle into the leather pants. Even as tight as they were, the thin belt wasn't visible underneath them.

"God, Sky. I'm sorry. I'm hoping this will be the last time, okay?"

A weak promise at best, but it was all Sky had. "Sure." He pulled on the shirt.

Sky actually smiled after he put on the boots. "I'm taller than you now."

"Are you sure you can walk in those things without breaking your neck?"

"I could dance in them if I had to." He'd worn similar footwear in some of his stage shows.

Mac nodded but looked grim. "Let's get this over with."

The party was at a pretty Victorian in the Mission. Sky couldn't remember seeing the host before—a surprisingly young, tiny man with jet-black hair and porcelain skin. He reminded Sky of a doll, the evil kind that came to life in movies and murdered everyone in their beds. He frowned at Sky, perhaps peeved at the way Sky towered over him in his boots, but gave Mac a broad smile. "Glad you could make it, Morgan."

"Thanks for the invitation, Alan."

Alan took them to a living room done up with fussy antiques. No agonized slaves were chained to the wall. In fact, apart from two pretty young black men in frilly maids' uniforms who were serving canapés and drinks to the guests, there were only two other slaves in evidence. One of them was an older man playing a guitar, and the other, in his early twenties, was kneeling naked at his master's feet.

When several men came over to greet Mac, it was clear that they knew him well. They clapped his back and joked with him about the weather. They discussed the upcoming presidential primary, the expensive highway project CalTrans was working on in the East Bay, and football. Some of the men preferred the NFL, in which the players were free, but others liked the slave league better.

"My uncle is VP of media strategy for the slave league," said a skinny man with thinning hair. "He told me they're considering adding cheerleaders next year. Just like the NFL has, only these cheerleaders would be slaves."

"That might increase the fan base," Mac said.

A man Sky recognized joined the group: Scott Simpson, the man who'd examined him on Market Street and later hosted the party with the slaves bound to the walls. He gave Mac a huge smile and then a quick hug. "I was hoping to see you here tonight, Morgan. And I see your slave is no longer indisposed."

Mac didn't even glance at Sky, who stood behind him. "Yep, he's right as rain."

"Glad to hear it. But your interest in expanding your holdings still remains?"

Slaves were good at keeping their expressions blank, and for that Sky was grateful. Never mind that his insides felt like ice.

"Yeah," Mac said. "I mean, if the right opportunity comes along. I had to settle a little bit with this one. Don't want to do that again."

Simpson gave Mac a hearty clap on the back. "Don't blame you. We work hard, and we deserve to enjoy a few of the finer things in life. And who wants cubic zirconia when you can afford diamonds?"

All the men laughed at this, including Mac. Then someone mentioned a new restaurant that had opened in the Castro, and the conversation shifted.

For the next couple of hours, nobody paid Sky much attention, which was fine with him. He clumped around in the tall boots, trying not to wince at the way the belt dug into him and the leather pants chafed. He would very much have liked to put on a pair of sweats and cuddle up on the couch with one of his books and a cup of tea, some good music playing in the background. He would have liked to take a hot shower and then lie in bed with Mac's big warm body beside him and the fog-streaked moon overhead.

After a while, though, his dreams turned more prosaic—he needed to piss. He thought he'd be able to do so with the belt on, although he'd have to sit. But Mac didn't offer to let him use a bathroom and Sky couldn't ask. Sky tried not to watch while Mac drank what seemed like gallons of whiskey.

Mac was slurring his words and weaving slightly on his feet, talking loudly with several men about whether a '69 Mustang was better than a '69 Camaro, when Simpson rejoined the group. He was accompanied by a large, grim-faced man who looked as if he disapproved of everyone in the room in general and Sky in particular. For several minutes, the man stood silently nearby while Simpson joined the debate about cars. Then Simpson moved closer to Mac. "Got a few things to discuss with you, Morgan. Do you have a minute?"

"Sure thing," Mac said, grinning and nodding.

Simpson jerked his head toward a closed door and the big man and Morgan followed him. But when Sky tagged along in their wake, Simpson stopped and turned. "Leave him here," he said, gesturing at Sky. "He'll distract the guys so we can have a more private chat."

Mac shot Sky a quick look, fear and uncertainty flashing across his face. But then his expression hardened. "Stay here," he commanded, deep-voiced. He followed the other two men, and the big one closed the door behind them.

The remaining men pounced on Sky almost at once. One of them pushed him hard enough to make him fall, and then the others pulled off his boots and shirt, tossing them aside. They had more trouble with the pants because they were so tight, but they eventually peeled those off as well. The belt, however, stumped them.

"Why are you wearing that?" demanded the painfully skinny one, punctuating his question with a kick to Sky's thigh.

"Master told me to, sir," Sky answered quietly. And truthfully.

The man kicked him again anyway. "Take it off."

"It's locked, sir."

They grabbed his arm and hauled him to his feet, then tugged and pulled at the belt. The metal grated painfully against the skin on his hips, but the belt didn't give and wouldn't slide off.

The party host—Mac had called him Alan—grabbed a fistful of Sky's hair and yanked his head back. "Where's the key?"

"Master." That was a lie, but a reasonable one. After all, it was patently clear that Sky didn't have the key on him, and it made sense that his owner would keep it.

The party guests grumbled. It was obvious that they weren't willing to disturb Mac's private meeting, so they had to limit themselves to poking at Sky's exposed flesh. Alan even tried to squeeze a finger past the tube blocking Sky's ass, but all he managed was to scrape a sharp fingernail against tender skin.

"Stupid fuck," Alan spat, giving Sky's butt a hard slap. Sky assumed Alan was referring to him, but then Alan continued. "Who brings their slut to a party locked up like a bank vault?"

The skinny man scoffed. "He thinks the slave's got such a sweet mouth that his ass doesn't matter." When one of the other guests expressed puzzlement over the statement, the skinny man clarified. "The slave's a canary. Sings like an angel." He placed his palms together as in prayer and fluttered his pale lashes.

Alan gave Sky a smile consisting of very sharp teeth. "Sing for us, canary."

"What would you like me to sing, sir?" A respectful question asked in a respectful voice, even though Sky wanted to rage and scream.

This time, Alan slapped his face with a resounding crack. "Stop questioning me. I told you to sing."

Sky was fairly certain that no matter what song he chose, this audience wouldn't be pleased. But he had to do *something*, so he settled on "Total Eclipse of the Heart." It was an old song but a favorite of the audiences at the Paradiso. It showcased his wide vocal range.

He took a deep breath, steadied himself, and began the first line, belting it out as if he were on stage. The men took a few steps back, forming a ring around him, and for a few moments he thought it was going to be all right. Most of them smiling, they nodded to the beat. And he sounded good; the room had surprisingly fine acoustics and his vocal cords were well-rested.

But just as he reached a high note, his voice clear and steady and true, Alan pushed him hard from behind, sending Sky sprawling onto his knees. "You think you're better than us, don't you?" Alan growled at him.

Sky scrambled into a kneel. "No, sir, of course not, sir. I'm just a slave. I know I'm—" His babbling was cut off by a hard blow to his head.

They forgot about his singing after that. Instead, they shoved and battered him as if he were a ball in some vicious game, and they took turns making him suck their dicks until his throat hurt, bitter semen coated his tongue, and tears coursed down his cheeks. He'd hoped that would be enough for them, but it wasn't, because then they resumed the beating. More seriously this time, until he curled into a whimpering ball on the floor, his arms poor protection against fists and feet. They were drunk and angry, and like a pack of predators, half-mad with the taste for blood.

There was no pretense of showmanship, no toying with paddles or whips. This was nothing but pure brutality, the goal nothing but the infliction of pain. Sky tried to plead with them—or maybe remind them that Master could sue them for damaging his property—but one of them punched him hard in the face, filling his mouth with blood. He choked, rolled onto all fours, and spat frothy red liquid onto the carpet. That only incensed the men more. They kicked him onto his back. When one of them stomped on his chest with a heavy foot, something cracked. Sky screamed a burbling cry and finally voided his bladder, the hot urine puddling between his legs before soaking into the rug.

He couldn't see well anymore, and he didn't know whether it was due to swollen eyes or all the head blows. Everything wavered in the dimming light. But even as he lay on the floor too broken to react, the men continued to attack him, clearly undeterred by the potential legal penalties. He wished he understood why. He liked to sing and read and jog, and he was learning how to cook. He loved watching the steel-colored water of the bay slosh against the piers, listening to Mac breathe beside him, smelling coffee brewing. He liked silly comedies and sappy romances. He was obedient. And the only time he'd ever hurt anyone was when Mac had asked him to—*begged* him to—and even then the strikes had been as tender as they were firm.

Sweet heavens, why did they take such joy in ruining him?

Another stomp, another *snap*, and now every breath sparkled with agony, as glittery and sharp as broken glass.

"Stop it! Jesus Christ, you're killing him!"

Sky was dimly aware of the men drawing back and Mac kneeling over him. He couldn't make out Mac's expression.

"Sky? Are you with me?"

He couldn't answer, not even with a nod.

"What the fuck did you do to him?" Mac shouted.

Sky didn't recognize the voice that answered. "We were just playing. You had him all locked up, so you know . . ."

Mac snarled. Then he scooped Sky into his arms and stood. Sky was sorry to be getting blood and piss on Mac's nice sweater but didn't have enough control over his limbs to do anything about it. He felt the unsteady lurch of Mac's steps, the bite of cold air on his bare skin, the welcome warmth of a heated car. Then he felt nothing at all.

CHAPTER THIRTEEN

Strange, pain-sprinkled dreams danced through his mind. He dreamed of Bill, his handler at the Paradiso, standing beside Ms. Avery and yelling at him because the crowds were sparse. He dreamed of a bird singing in a cage. Of a woman with a messy ponytail, wearing a sweatshirt decorated with a sparkly American flag, carefully moving him around and poking him with needles. Of his bandmates in 2Nyte, whom he'd never seen again after they were sold. Of a faceless mother turning her back on him. Of Mac talking softly, making impossible promises. Of a ship sailing an endless placid sea.

When he slowly pried his eyes open, Mac was gazing down at him, brow creased with worry. "Are you back with me?" Mac asked.

Everything hurt, but in an oddly distant way, as if the discomfort belonged to someone else. He tried to answer, but managed only a hoarse croak.

"Hang on," Mac said. He reached away—Sky's vision was too wavery to track the motion—and when his hand came back into view, he was holding a glass of ice chips. He scooped one of the chips onto his fingers and placed it tenderly in Sky's mouth. Heaven.

After allowing a few more chips to melt on his tongue, Sky licked his cracked lips. "'S good."

Mac looked relieved. "Let's give the ice a few minutes to settle. If everything's okay, we can graduate to juice. Are you breathing okay?"

An odd question. But when Sky took a moment to consider, he realized that part of the pain was a jagged, tight band around his chest. "Sore," he concluded.

"I know. You have a couple cracked ribs. The doc said it's important for you to keep breathing deeply or else you might end up with pneumonia. Can you do that?"

Sky tried it. Air in, air out. More pain, but nothing about it felt urgent. "Yes."

Mac brushed a strand of hair from Sky's face. "You're on some meds at the moment. Let me know if things get to be too much as they wear off. I can give you more. Doc said icing your ribs might help too." He paused, looking uncharacteristically doubtful, his hand in midair. "Is there anything else I can do for you now?"

It took Sky a bit of time to understand the question—San Francisco's fog had obviously crept into his brain and settled. It took him a while longer to connect his mind to his body. "Pee?" he asked.

He fuzzed out almost completely as Mac moved him about, but Sky was dimly aware of pissing into a container and feeling better afterward, and then being allowed to sip a bit of sweet, sticky juice through a straw. He probably fell asleep after that, because when he became aware again, the room's light had shifted and his pain had become sharper and more real.

Mac was still sitting beside him, his face haggard. "Juice?" he asked immediately.

"Please."

Mac propped another pillow under Sky's head before maneuvering the straw between his sore lips. When Sky raised his head, it hurt and made him dizzy. His eyes felt puffy, and he blinked as he drank.

"The swelling's going down already," Mac said, sounding exhausted, "but you have a couple of really good shiners. The doc had to give you a couple of stitches inside your lip. Nothing's broken except those ribs, she says. Just a lot of bruising and a mild concussion. She was afraid your kidney got banged up, but there's no blood in your urine, so that's good news." He ran fingers through his messy hair and shook his head. "Do you want something for the pain?"

Sky thought about it. He was very uncomfortable, his body one throbbing ache. But he preferred pain to the muzzy-headed feeling from the drugs. "No."

"Okay." Mac took the glass away and fussed a bit with the pillows, then tucked in the blankets more tightly. "I'll make you something to eat. Oatmeal? Soup? Something easy on your mouth."

Sky wasn't hungry. He wondered how much time had passed since the party. He thought it was late the following afternoon, but he wasn't sure. Mac was wearing the same sweater, now crusted with dried blood and other body fluids. "You should sleep."

Mac buried his face in his hands. "Can't," he mumbled through his palms.

"Just lie down. I'm not going anywhere. I'll wake you if I need anything."

For a long time, Mac didn't respond. Then he sighed. "I'm not going to bother to apologize again. I *am* so fucking sorry, but that doesn't do you any good."

Tongue loosened by pain, medication, or exhaustion—Sky just didn't care anymore. At least his mouth was free. "You should have just let them fuck me. You shouldn't have left me alone with them."

"There's . . . this voice in my head that can justify almost anything and excuse the rest. That voice sounds so damn reasonable. All for the greater good. Sacrifices have to be made. You'd have ended up in some shit situation no matter what. And hey, I've given you books and decent food and blowjobs and that makes it all okay."

Sky wondered if all freemen had that voice. Was that what allowed them to sleep soundly after exploiting and brutalizing other human beings? When they sold a child away from its mother, when they dragged a man or woman into a mine to work until death, when they deprived an entire class of people of such basic things as love? If Sky had been born free, perhaps he would have heard that voice as well. The thought scared him.

Mac raised his head. "That voice tells a lot of pretty lies. But this is the truth: I'm done listening to what it tells me about you. I won't let any of those bastards near you, not ever again. I'll find a way to keep you safe forever. Don't care what it does to my mission."

"Mission?" Sky whispered, hoping to finally catch a glimpse of the real game. "Rule two."

Mac shook his head. "Can't. I want . . . I want to convince you that I'm a good guy, a white hat. But why the hell would you believe that after what I've done to you? I'm not even sure I believe it anymore."

If Mac wanted words of comfort or forgiveness, Sky couldn't give them. But his heart held neither hate nor anger, not right now. So he simply said, "Lie down for a while. Then you can make me some soup. Or eggs. I could probably eat scrambled eggs." Because Mac made them soft and velvety.

"All right." Mac stripped down to his boxer briefs and got into bed, taking great care to shake the mattress as little as possible. Even though the bed was big, he stayed near the edge, leaving a wide gulf between them. He didn't fall asleep right away—Sky could tell from his breathing—but he didn't shift around. Sky wondered what thoughts were going through Mac's head, and whether Mac wished they could have another session in the playroom right now, the thick straps holding him fast and a leather slapper leaving red marks on his back and ass.

"I think I'd fuck you this time," Sky said.

After remaining very still for a moment, Mac slowly rolled over to face him. "What?"

"If I had you tied down on that bench."

Mac's breath caught audibly. "For revenge?"

"No. I think it would feel good."

His eyes wide with wonder, Mac gave a small nod. "I think so too." Then his body shuddered with a heavy sigh and he closed his eyes.

The doctor returned the next day. Instead of a flag sweatshirt, she was wearing a pilled pink sweater with a tasseled hem. Her ponytail was neater, and her lipstick matched the sweater. She interacted with Sky much the way he imagined a pediatrician would with a toddler or a veterinarian with a dog: gently, but with all her comments and questions addressed to Mac. In the end, she even cooed at Sky for being a good boy and patted his head.

"He'll be fine," she said to Mac. "Three weeks of very light movement and lots of rest. Pain meds if he shows too much discomfort.

Continue to ice the chest after he's been up and around. Light duties for another four weeks after that."

"What about the stitches in his lip?"

"They'll dissolve."

"We like to—" Mac stopped himself. "I've been having him run with me. When can he do that again?"

"Not for at least six weeks, and even then, go easy. Watch his breathing, and stop immediately if he's laboring too badly or showing pain."

Sky scowled at her view of him. As if he were incapable of directly expressing how he felt.

The doctor gave Mac a few more instructions before he escorted her to the door and then hurried back to the bedroom. "That was awful," he said, sitting on the bed beside Sky.

"She tried not to hurt me."

"With her hands, sure. Jesus, that doctor acted like you're too stupid to understand a word, when you're actually one of the smartest people I know. Smarter than me, that's for sure."

Because nobody had considered Sky intelligent before, he'd never thought of himself that way. He'd have to chew on that one for a while. Right now he needed to make a point. "It's not just the doctor. It's every free man and woman, every day, treating every slave like an object. Maybe an expensive object, but still a thing. We feel, Mac. Just like you do. We want. Sometimes we even hope."

Mac nodded slowly. "I'm getting that. Bit by bit. I've spent my whole damn life allowing myself to be tricked by the illusion. It's not easy trying to unsee it, you know? But I'm trying, I really am. You've gotta give me a little time."

Sky smiled sadly. "I have no time to give you. I have nothing except what my master allows me to have, and even that can disappear at any moment."

"Would you believe me if I told you I wish I could give you everything—and for good?"

"When it comes to you, I don't know what to believe."

"Fair enough," Mac said. One corner of his mouth quirked. "I'll have to give you proof, then." He leaned down and kissed Sky's still-sore forehead, Mac's lips warm, soft, and soothing. Then he stood and walked away.

Mac's shouting startled Sky from sleep, but before Sky could scramble out of bed—no doubt hurting himself in the process—he realized that Mac was downstairs, probably yelling into his phone.

"...give a shit anymore, Trish. If you saw what they did...They almost killed him. And for no reason. And if they *had* killed him, what would have happened to them? A lawsuit? Trish, he's—" A very long pause ensued, although if Sky listened closely, he could hear Mac pacing the floor, his bare feet making little slapping noises on the wood.

"No, seriously. Delancey can go fuck himself. I'm gonna finish this thing without Sky and we're getting the hell out of here...I don't know. A week, I think. Can you get the shit to me by then?...Okay, good...Yeah, I've been thinking about that part a lot. Not here and not Simpson's place. I'm going to see if I can get him to take me to the holding facility...I don't know. He's been close-mouthed and I don't want to push too hard. I'm not sure how far he trusts me... He's dropped a few hints. I think maybe Oakland, which makes sense. That's where the big port is. But I'll let you know as soon as I know."

Another long pause on Mac's end of the conversation. He opened the fridge, uncapped a bottle with a noisy *pop*, and probably took a good swig during the lull before setting it on the counter with a little thud. That reminded Sky that he was thirsty too. He gave a small grin of triumph when he managed to take the bottle of water from his bedside, unscrew the cap, and swallow quite a bit of it—all by himself, without even a straw.

Then Mac was speaking again. His voice was quieter, more conversational, but the acoustics of the loft meant Sky had no trouble hearing every word. "What about that other thing," Mac asked. "Any headway on that?...Yeah, I know how impossible it is once they're sent overseas. But you're supposed to be able to do the impossible... Fuck." Mac sighed loudly. "Well, it would have been nice, you know?

But you're getting his paperwork in order?... You have to promise me that whatever goes down, you'll follow through with this. Promise me, Trish ... That's fine. Take every penny if you need to ... Yeah, well, I probably won't make it to retirement age anyway ... Thanks. Okay, I'll let you know ... Bye."

Sky wished eavesdropping didn't raise more questions than it answered.

Mac took the doctor's orders seriously. He hovered over Sky like a mother hen for the next several days, not allowing him to do anything for himself except use the bathroom and eat. Even bathing Sky became Mac's responsibility. He'd help Sky into the tub and gently soap and shampoo him, then rinse him clean with repeated cups of water. Sky could have managed a shower on his own, but he didn't protest. The pampering felt good.

In fact, by the time a week had passed, the pampering felt so good that when Mac lingered a bit over Sky's groin with a washcloth, Sky's cock hardened. Mac grinned wickedly, continuing his ministrations with additional enthusiasm until Sky climaxed with a gasp and a shudder.

"You're feeling better," Mac said smugly, sitting back on his heels beside the tub.

"I'm feeling really good right now."

Mac lifted an eyebrow. "I bet we can do better than good."

Sky wasn't sure what Mac meant but had no intention of complaining when Mac patted him dry, dressed him in soft clothes, and helped him down the stairs. He installed Sky on the couch with a new book and a big cup of fragrant tea, then hummed off-key while preparing dinner. They ate spicy-sweet noodles and crunchy vegetables, with homemade fruit sorbet for dessert. "I'm going to get fat," Sky said when they were done, rubbing his belly.

Mac shrugged. "If you want to."

"I wouldn't fit in any of those ... clothes." Sky gestured toward the playroom.

"You're never wearing any of that crap again—unless you feel like it. And if you *do* feel like it, we can always go shopping for the next size up."

As they sat on the couch, Mac kept a respectful distance between them. But Sky felt languid and comfortable, like a well-fed cat, and he scooted over to lean against him. They cuddled as Mac laughed at *Airplane!* and Sky dozed happily against him.

"Ready for bed?" Mac asked as the credits rolled.

"Yes."

Sky could have gone up the stairs on his own, but Mac's support was nice. Sky got himself ready for sleep while Mac fussed with fresh bedding. "I'm going to shower," Mac said as Sky climbed between the clean sheets.

"'Kay." Sky reached for the book at his bedside. It was a good one, a novel about imaginary kings and queens, and he was so engrossed that he didn't realize at first that Mac was taking an unusually long time in the bathroom.

He certainly noticed when Mac emerged though—naked, smiling, erect. He prowled to the bed. "You can say no," he said right away. "Say no and I won't touch you. But God, I've been thinking about this all week, and I hope you'll at least consider saying yes."

It was funny, but Sky wasn't afraid. He believed that Mac would honor his refusal. And Mac was gorgeous. So strong. The memory of controlling all that power—even if only for a short time and because Mac had allowed it—made Sky's blood heat. "I'll consider it."

Mac's grin widened.

Moving slowly, perhaps so as not to frighten, he pulled the covers off Sky, who was wearing nothing but his slave bracelets. "The bruises are mostly gone," Mac observed. That was true. Only a few yellow-blue reminders of the beating remained. "I won't hurt you, Sky. Never again."

"What will you do to me?"

"Tonight? I have a plan."

Apparently the plan began with Mac stretching out full-length against Sky, shower-warm and hair still damp, smelling of citrusy soap. He'd shaved his face, so when they kissed, Mac's cheeks felt smooth against Sky's bristly ones. Beneath the toothpaste mint of Mac's mouth, Sky caught a hint of spices from their dinner. Delicious. Mac threaded his fingers through Sky's hair while Sky devoured him, and when Sky daringly placed his hands on Mac's ass, Mac waggled approvingly.

"This is a good plan," Sky gasped when they broke the kiss.

"That's just step one. Ready for more?"

"Yeah."

Moving nimbly for such a large man, Mac scrambled to his knees, then turned head-to-foot to straddle Sky on all fours, his mouth over Sky's groin and Mac's ass—sweet heavens, his ass—right in Sky's line of view. As overcome as Sky was, he noticed that Mac was careful not to rest any of his weight on Sky's healing torso. He placed a soft kiss on Sky's right hip. "I'm already slicked up. All you have to do is stretch me out a little."

Oh God.

Sky tried to gather his scattered thoughts, but then Mac licked the length of Sky's shaft, and *poof!* Those thoughts were gone. Instead, all Sky could do was register how wonderful Mac's mouth felt on his cock, how delicious Mac's gasps and groans were as Sky pressed his fingers inside him, how *hot* Mac's tight channel was. Droplets of pre-come fell from Mac's cock and landed on Sky's chest.

Despite the orgasm only a few hours earlier, Sky was soon hanging not far from the precipice again. "M-Mac," he moaned in warning, pushing weakly at Mac's flank.

Mac immediately stopped sucking him and rolled to the side. "Okay. I'm stopping."

"No! Don't— I'm not saying no."

"What are you saying?" Mac asked, grinning widely.

"That if you have a step three in mind, you'd better move things along."

Mac laughed and stole a quick kiss. He tasted salty. With another graceful, careful move, he straddled Sky again. This time, though, Mac was on his knees facing Sky. "I haven't done this in a really long time," he said. With his tongue peeking out in concentration and his hand guiding Sky's cock into place, Mac slowly impaled himself.

"Oh fuck," Mac moaned when he'd fully engulfed Sky. "That's good."

Sky's garbled mix of vowels was intended as agreement. He'd never been inside a man before, and this most intimate of embraces felt so delightfully tight as the slick heat surrounded him. Welcomed him.

Mac looked down at Sky. "You okay? This doesn't hurt?"

"I am . . . not . . . in pain." Heck, Sky was fairly certain he'd have ignored imminent amputation of his limbs as long as Mac didn't move off him.

Mac rose on his powerful thighs, drawing himself up but not quite breaking their contact, then dropped down again in a slow glide that made both of them moan.

"This . . . will be fast," Mac gasped.

Sky nodded. He was already almost past the point of no return. When he gripped Mac's hips, Mac nodded back. "Good. Hang on tight."

Hanging on was all Sky could do. He was probably going to leave fingerprint-shaped bruises on Mac's skin. Good. And when Mac grabbed his own cock and began stroking as he rose and fell, Sky ignored his lingering soreness and arched his back, driving his cock even deeper into Mac.

"Sky," Mac rasped. He kept moving, and his gaze remained trained on Sky's eyes. His expression suggested that he wasn't fucking a slave—he was making love to a man, a specific man with a name and a history and a soul. "Sky. Sky. Sky . . ."

Mac's face and chest had gone red with effort and arousal, his dark nipples peaked amid the black hair, his plum-colored cockhead shiny-wet when it appeared through his fist. "Sky!" he cried once more, and Sky again pressed his hips upward, the crest of pleasure washing over and through him, making him jerk and roar.

He was still in the midst of his climax when Mac made a ragged sound and collapsed hard into the cradle of Sky's hips. Mac's seed shot onto Sky's chest, some of it even reaching his lips. He licked it away, which brought a desperate whimper from Mac.

Mac soon flopped near Sky's side, and it took several minutes for him to gather the strength to stand, pad to the bathroom, and return with damp cloths. He cleaned both of them, which was good because Sky felt as boneless as a jellyfish, his nerves too depleted to twitch.

"I didn't hurt you?" Mac asked, tenderly stroking Sky's stomach. Sky laughed. "No."

"That wasn't . . . I wasn't trying to make up for the bad shit I've done to you. I know things don't balance that way. I did that because I really, really wanted you inside me, and I hoped you wanted it too."

"Not an apology or excuse," Sky said, nodding his understanding.

Mac cupped Sky's cheek and brought his own face closer. "Nothing but desire," he whispered. "Rule one."

Sky believed him.

CHAPTER FOURTEEN

O ver the next several days, Mac spent a lot of time online and on his phones. He said he felt bad about hogging the laptop and disappeared one morning on a mysterious errand. He returned an hour later with a bag displaying the Apple logo. "For you," he said, handing the bag to Sky, who'd been content with a book.

Curious, Sky pulled out a box. "An iPad?"

"It's yours. If you want to use an external keyboard with it, let me know and I'll get one."

"You don't have to buy me things."

Rubbing the back of his neck, Mac sat next to him. "I know. I want to. Has anyone given you gifts before?"

Sky shrugged. Sometimes fans sent things to 2Nyte—or even threw items onstage during concerts. Sky and the other band members got to keep the flowers, but their handlers kept anything of value and tossed the fan letters and lacy underwear.

"Well," Mac said, "I've never had anyone to give to. The last gift was to my mom when I was in high school, for her birthday. She was already pretty sick. I was working a couple of part-time jobs to help cover the bills, but I saved up a little and got her some roses and a necklace. It was a cheap thing, silver-plated with rhinestones, but it looked nice on her. And she smiled all day."

Sky saw Mac's soft expression and realized that a present could be as beneficial to the donor as to the recipient. "Thank you for the iPad. Will you show me how to use it?"

Mac did so enthusiastically. Sky learned that the video quality was better than the laptop's and that he could download a reader for electronic books. Now if he ran out of things to read, he didn't even need to wait for next-day delivery. He could take photos with his new toy too. Mac patiently let Sky take some of him before grabbing the tablet and snapping a whole series of Sky. "Look at you," Mac said, holding up the tablet to display one of the pictures.

"I'm sitting on a couch."

"Yeah, and maybe tomorrow if you feel up to it, we can walk to the Ferry Building and take some there. I'd love to photograph you with the Bay Bridge behind you. But Sky, you'd break my heart wherever you were posed." Mac bit his lip and shook his head, then gave a sad smile. "You're the most amazing person I've ever met, and I'm in love with you. Rule one."

Thankful to be sitting, Sky took a shaky breath. "Mac, you— I can't—"

"I know. God, you should hate me."

"I don't hate you. Rule one."

"You're so much more than I deserve." Mac handed the tablet back to Sky and picked up one of his phones, which had begun to buzz.

After that, Sky spent a long time experimenting with the various apps. He liked the ones that allowed him to alter photos, but he also had fun with a couple of games Mac showed him. Maybe it was perverse of him, but Sky's favorite was one in which he played a gladiator leading a revolt against the Romans. It was fun to slaughter imaginary slave owners in the name of freedom.

Sky had just run his digital sword through a man in a toga when Mac shot to his feet. "Fuck!" Mac yelled. His face had drained of color.

"What is it?"

"Scott Simpson and his goons are on their way here right now."

Sky's stomach contracted into a hard ball. "Do you want me to—"

"Go upstairs. Get in the closet and don't come out until I tell you to."

"But—"

Mac crouched in front of him and laid his hands on Sky's shoulders. His eyes were wide with panic and his face had flushed. "I told them I got rid of you after Alan's party. I promised you—I won't let them touch you again. Go hide. Please. And don't make any noise."

Although Sky had serious misgivings, he nodded and stood. But before he walked away. Mac handed him the iPad, which Sky had left on the couch. "Take this with you. It'll give you something to do. Just keep the sound off, okay?"

"I wish you'd tell me the truth about who you are," Sky said.

"I will. Soon."

And just because he could, Sky paused long enough to give Mac a quick kiss on the lips. Then he climbed the stairs, trying not to grunt from the lingering ache in his chest.

The closet was at the far end of the upstairs area, separated from the rest of the bedroom by a partial wall like the ones for the playroom. Unlike the playroom, however, the closet had a door, a sliding panel of opaque glass. Taking his tablet, Sky went inside and closed the door. The space was big enough that he could have lain down and stretched out, but instead he grabbed an extra pillow from a shelf and sat on it. Otherwise, the wooden floor would have quickly become uncomfortable. He had plenty of light due to the skylight, and the closet smelled faintly of Mac's hair products and aftershave. It was a cozy hideout.

Only a few minutes passed before Sky heard a buzz. Shortly after that, Mac opened the front door. "It's good to see you, Scott," he said.

"Thanks for letting us drop by. Hope I'm not interrupting anything."

"Nothing too urgent. Come on in." Mac didn't greet anyone else, but the several sets of footsteps suggested Simpson hadn't come alone.

"It's an interesting loft," said Simpson.

"I got it on short notice. It'll do for now. If business goes well, though, I'll be looking to upgrade soon. Didn't you say your sister is a broker?"

"Yep. We can give her a ring when you're ready to start shopping. What kind of place do you have in mind? A house? No, you're a New Yorker. I bet you'd like an apartment in one of those new high-rises. The kind where the walls are mostly windows and you can see half of Northern California?" Simpson's voice had faded a bit as he walked away from the entryway—and the stairs. Then he whistled. "Quite a setup you've got here, Morgan."

"It's a start."

There was a muted thump, probably Simpson testing a paddle or flogger against the leather of the bench. "Good range of equipment. Too bad you've got nobody left to use it on."

Sky wasn't exactly surprised to learn that Mac really had told Simpson that Sky was gone—but the confirmation was nice. What Mac said next, though, made Sky's fists tighten.

"I was kind of hoping that's what you're here to talk about," Mac said. "Has that shipment arrived?"

"Soon. We had a few delays." A loud crack made Sky wince. Apparently, Simpson was trying out a whip. "You know how it goes. Some goods are harder to move than others."

"Sure. I guess I'm just . . . eager."

More footsteps, most likely as they moved out of the playroom. "I can see that. You seemed pretty attached to that blond slave."

"I don't like people damaging my property."

"But you said it yourself—you were settling when you bought him. The boy could sing, but he wasn't anything special."

Mac's response came out as a growl. "Like I said. I don't like damage to my property."

"Fair enough, fair enough. In any case, you're eager for a replacement."

"Yes."

Even upstairs in the closet, Sky could feel tension between them, although he didn't understand it. Simpson's tone had a light, teasing quality and Mac—who hadn't offered his guests a drink—was guarded and angry.

After a pause, Simpson spoke. "I've talked with my partners. Usually we operate on a cash-only basis, but they're intrigued by your offer. And by the prospect of future arrangements."

"I told you, that's part of what I was hoping for. I don't have the connections here that I did back east. I figure you and your pals could open a lot of doors for me."

"We could." Simpson continued to walk—pacing, Sky thought. He was trying to sound amused but he was nervous about something. Or keyed up. Then he stopped. "I need to see more of what you have to offer. I'm sure you understand."

"I can arrange that."

"No. I mean *now*, Morgan." The playing around was gone; now Simpson sounded dead serious. Sky's heart raced.

"I don't keep the product here," Mac said. "I'm not stupid."

"So take us to where you do keep it."

"Sure. When you show me that storage facility you keep talking about."

Simpson sighed theatrically. "We seem to be at an impasse. Why are you so interested in the facility anyway? There's no shipment there right now. Isn't that what you wanted?"

Mac was clearly trying to control his temper. "I don't know what you're implying. I thought we had a deal. If you don't like the way I do business, you can walk away."

"I'm not walking away," Simpson replied coldly.

"Then what the hell do you want?"

"Honesty. I want to know why you claim to like rough games but you handled your slave like a precious heirloom. I want to know why you're so curious about the specifics of how I run my business. I want to know what the fuck you're really after. And I want to know where you're keeping the ten kilos of cocaine you claim to possess."

"I don't—" Mac's reply was cut off with a thud and a load groan.

While Sky crouched behind the closet door, his bowels feeling watery and his heart beating so hard it hurt his ribs, he heard what were unmistakably the sounds of a scuffle and somebody being beaten. Something shattered. Mac shouted, and Sky gave a savage smile when an unfamiliar voice swore loudly. But then came a loud electrical crackle and buzz. Mac screamed through a tightened jaw, and the loud thump must have been him falling.

Sky tasted blood and realized he'd bitten his lip.

"Come on," Simpson snarled. "Let's get this show on the road."

Feet shuffling, more thumps, and a muted groan. Then the sound of something heavy being dragged across the floor. The front door swung open with a creak, and a moment later slammed shut.

Silence.

Although he mentally called himself a coward and every bad name he could think of, Sky couldn't make himself move. He was frozen with fear and uncertainty. He waited for what felt like years, but as far as he could tell, he was in the apartment alone. And Mac wasn't going to show up and tell him it was safe to come out.

Sky finally forced his legs and arms to work. He opened the closet door very slowly, half-expecting someone to attack him. Nobody did, and eventually the door was open wide enough to show that the upstairs was empty except for him. He crept down the stairs one by one, jumping at every shadow.

Nobody was downstairs either. The coffee table had been shoved out of place, and a large leather armchair was tipped on its side. Broken glass littered the area near the couch, glittering dangerously. When Sky cautiously moved closer, his breath caught at the sight of a few smears of bright blood on the floor.

He thought that his legs would give out and that he might be sick, but he managed to remain upright, his stomach unhappy but not trying to empty itself.

What should he do?

He could . . . just leave. With Mac gone, nobody might even realize Sky was missing. He could hide his bracelets under his sleeves. He had no money, of course, but he'd seen freemen busking on the streets—playing a guitar or drawing caricatures of tourists in exchange for a few coins. Sky could sing. He could probably earn enough to buy food, maybe even enough for a bus ticket out of town, to somewhere far away, where he could live cheaply. He could find a way to remove the bracelets. A tool of some kind. And with nobody looking for him, he might even remain free. Maybe not permanently, but for a while. And wasn't even a taste of freedom incalculably precious?

But what about Mac?

It occurred to Sky that Simpson and his men might have killed Mac—an idea that hurt far worse than any beating. Sky's feelings for his master were complicated at best, but he definitely cared for Mac and didn't want him harmed.

If Sky walked away, how long before Mac's friends noticed he was gone? Well, he didn't really seem to have any friends. Coworkers? That woman he spoke to on the phone sometimes: Trish. Teague, the man who'd delivered the suitcase. And the men at the parties Mac attended—although Sky suspected that none of them cared about Mac at all. By the time anyone who did care realized Mac was gone, it would be too late.

Hoping that he could maybe call Trish or Teague, Sky searched for Mac's phones but didn't find them. Whenever Mac was downstairs, he kept the phones in his pockets or on a nearby piece of furniture. The laptop was missing too.

Evidently calling for help was out of the question. Even if Sky could borrow someone else's phone, he didn't know what number to call.

The police? Just the thought made Sky shudder. They were more likely to haul him away for being unsupervised than to investigate Mac's disappearance, and if they saw the blood, they might even suspect Sky of harming him. Freemen always seemed more willing to accuse slaves than their own kind.

Avoiding the glass, Sky sat on the couch and tried to think. Simpson had taken Mac somewhere—if Sky was lucky, Mac was still alive. Maybe he'd been driven far away. Maybe they'd gone to that mysterious storage facility they'd spoken about. If so, Sky had no hope of finding them. But Sky did know where Simpson lived.

Let Mac be there, Sky prayed to the freemen's God.

But even if he was there, what could Sky do about it? Knock on the door and demand the return of his master?

Then he remembered the gun.

Moving faster than the doctor would have approved of, he ran upstairs and yanked open Mac's bedside drawer. He felt a tiny bit of relief—no doubt misplaced—when he saw the gun and the cardboard box of cartridges. He picked up the weapon as gingerly as if it were a venomous snake, turning it over in his hand. It wasn't especially heavy, but it felt solid.

He had no idea how to use the thing. Still, a gun could be useful—he could wave it around to threaten people. But he had the suspicion that Simpson and his men weren't easily scared. They might be carrying guns as well, and if so, they undoubtedly knew how to use them.

"What do you do when you want to know something?" he whispered. The answer was obvious: you looked it up online.

The internet provided a wealth of information on weaponry. Sky soon learned that Mac's gun was a Beretta, a nine-millimeter semiautomatic. That meant that as soon as one round was fired, the next round automatically entered the chamber. The iPad's good screen resolution nicely displayed numerous videos of people loading magazines, sliding them into guns, removing the safety, and firing.

Not that difficult.

Sky filled the Beretta's magazine and carefully inserted it into the weapon, then chambered the first round. He didn't bother taking additional ammunition because he doubted he'd have a chance to reload. He took the gun downstairs, where he put on his running shoes, then Mac's leather jacket. Although the jacket was big on Sky, the gun fit perfectly in the inside pocket, staying secure without being visible. He wouldn't have been able to carry it as well in his hoodie.

He paused with his hand on the doorknob.

What am I doing? He would be sent to the mines simply for carrying a gun, and now he was going to trek across the city and point it at freemen in hopes of rescuing a man who might not even be there. Sky would be lucky if they killed him quickly.

And this man he wanted to rescue—the man *owned* him. Had bought him and handed him over to be brutally abused by others. Had demanded the truth from Sky, yet never provided it himself.

But he'd been kind as well. He'd treated Sky like a person, like a *man*, and while he might not have divulged his secrets, he'd kept his promises. He'd lied to Simpson to keep Sky safe.

Mac was a good guy, he'd said—or at least trying to be one. Sky believed him.

That alone might not have been enough to set Sky on such a reckless path. But everything Sky had done since Simpson took Mac away had been Sky's own decision. And if he did undertake what was likely to be a suicide mission, he was doing so solely because he chose to.

For the first time in his life, Sky was fully in control.

He wouldn't waste that opportunity cowering in a corner and sobbing over his fate.

Sky opened the door and left the apartment.

CHAPTER FIFTEEN

Sky didn't have a driver waiting to whisk him away. He didn't even have money for a taxi or a bus. He tried to jog, but that hurt his ribs, especially when the gun banged against them. That left walking as his only option, and even that made his body ache, more so when he had to climb hills. San Francisco was a lovely city for a leisurely stroll, but not at all convenient when a wounded man was attempting to rescue someone and time was of the essence. He walked as fast as he could, but it still took him an hour and a half to cross the city. With every step he chided himself for being a suicidal idiot—and with every step he worried about Mac.

Night had fallen by the time he reached Simpson's house. At least it was easy to find, since it stood kitty-corner from the edge of Lands End. The brown-shingled building looked cozy and inoffensive with its lights glowing through curtained windows. Sky hoped the lights meant Simpson was there—with Mac.

For several minutes, Sky skulked in the park and watched from the darkness under the trees. Despite the long walk, he hadn't formulated a plan. He wasn't experienced at planning anything—a meal, his daily schedule—so how could he be expected to come up with a reasonable method of rescuing someone? Especially when a reasonable method likely didn't exist. He thought about movies and TV shows he'd seen, where the hero rushed in against impossible odds to save the day. But none of those heroes had been terrified slaves.

Hesitating wasn't helpful either.

The best he could do, he decided, was to get inside and see if Mac was there. Maybe find a way to give him the gun and let Mac rescue himself. If he owned the thing, surely he knew how to use it.

Simple, right?

He moved the gun from the inside pocket to an outside one. It reassured him slightly, and with his legs shaking and his guts twisting into knots, he crossed the street, climbed the several steps, and pressed the doorbell. He didn't run away.

The door opened, revealing a very large man Sky didn't recognize. The man was wearing jeans and a tight white T-shirt and looked like someone who spent all his spare time in a gym. "Yes?" he asked, face and voice neutral.

Sky kept his chin up and tried to emulate the expression and tone he'd heard his owners use when dealing with flunkies. "I'm here to talk to Scott Simpson." No *sir* appended to the statement. That felt good.

"Mr. Simpson's busy."

Oh God, let that mean he's here with Mac. "It's urgent. Tell him it's about Morgan Wallace."

The big man frowned. "Wait here." He closed the door in Sky's face.

Sky waited patiently on the little concrete stoop, wishing it were daytime so he could see the ocean once more. Instead he watched an SUV idle impatiently behind a stopped bus, and a car pause in front of the entrance to the motel across the street. The air smelled of salt, eucalyptus, and wood smoke.

The door opened so quickly that Sky jumped. The big man jerked his head. "Come in."

Sky walked into the dragon's mouth. He tried not to think of what had happened to him in this house—and what was likely to happen to him now. When he stepped into the little foyer, Simpson was standing there, wide-eyed. The big man locked the door.

"So he lied about you, too," Simpson said, holding a wineglass in one hand. His bland face was slightly flushed—whether from alcohol, exertion, or anger, Sky couldn't tell. Like the other man, he was dressed very casually in jeans and, in Simpson's case, a black T-shirt.

"Where's my master?" Sky asked.

Simpson smiled. "You came trotting after him like a well-trained puppy. How sweet."

"Where is he?"

For a long, painful moment, Simpson stared at him. Then he gave a small shrug. "Follow me."

With the big man trailing them, they walked into the large room where the party had been held. Sky's heart gave a great shudder when he saw Mac hanging from the same manacles where one of the slaves had been during the party.

Mac's naked body was slumped in the chains. A ball gag filled his mouth, pinkish drool running down his chin. He was bruised and bloody, as if someone had been using him as a punching bag, and small circular burns formed a constellation on his chest and belly. His penis and scrotum were swollen, maybe burned as well.

Sky was immensely relieved to hear Mac's breathing, even if it sounded harsh and painful. Mac didn't open his blackened eyes, and he was clearly in no condition to do anything with the gun. Above the iron bands, his fingers looked mangled and broken.

"Master," Sky said.

Mac lifted his head. As soon as he saw Sky, he began grunting around the gag and struggling against his bonds. He shook his head forcefully, sending droplets of sweat and blood flying.

"Let him go," Sky said to Simpson.

Simpson laughed loudly. "You *are* a good puppy! Sure—I'll let him go. Onto a big ship that will take him far away. He's a little older than my usual stock, but I have customers in Istanbul and Hong Kong with especially exotic tastes."

As Mac continued to struggle, Sky stepped closer to him. "He's not a slave," Sky said to Simpson.

"Not yet. Easily remedied."

Unsure what Simpson meant by that, Sky shook his head. "Let him go and take me instead. I'll be perfectly obedient, I promise. I'll do anything you want." He wasn't certain whether his offer was an honest one, and he knew Simpson wouldn't accept it, but Sky had to make the attempt. Just in case.

"You'll do anything I want anyway," Simpson said. He looked thoughtful. Then he turned to look at Mac. "You've been stoic so far. Good for you—my clients enjoy a slave much more when he's hard to break. But I'm wondering if you might be cooperative if I play with your boy a bit."

Mac's thrashing became more frenzied, causing fresh blood to ooze from his wounds. He was trying hard to say something, muffled consonants joining the sound of rattling chains like a chorus of the damned.

The odd thing was that Sky was no longer frightened. His heart beat steadily, his breath came easily despite his injured ribs, and his head was clear. *I'm strong,* he thought. *I'm in control.* And for these few seconds, even if Simpson didn't know it, Sky was free.

Sky watched Simpson reach up and remove the gag from Mac's mouth. Mac spat a mouthful of bloody phlegm onto the floor and snarled at Simpson. But it was Sky he spoke to, and when he did, his voice was thick with grief. "Why did you come here?"

"To save you," Sky answered, smiling.

Mac looked like he might cry. "Sky, no."

Simpson grinned like a child on Christmas. "You two are fascinating!" He dug two fingers into one of Mac's uglier burns, making Mac hiss. "Want to just spill the beans now and tell me who you really are?"

"Fuck you."

"Not exactly," Simpson replied cheerily. Then he cocked his head at Sky. "How about you, songbird? Tell me who your master is. What does he want from me? Who's he working for? Does he have ten keys of cocaine? Sing nicely and maybe I'll go easy on you."

"I don't know," Sky said with complete honesty. Despite all the frustration he'd experienced over it, maybe it was just as well that Mac had refused to divulge his secrets. This way, Sky couldn't divulge them either.

"Maybe, maybe not," Simpson said. "I'll have fun either way. A two-for-the-price-of-one deal." When he smiled, the corners of his eyes crinkled and he was handsome in a polished sort of way, like a salesman on TV. Still grinning, he punched Mac hard in the balls.

Mac made a terrible low moan.

Sky pulled out the gun and fired.

It wasn't a very good shot. He didn't take time to aim it well, and of course he'd never practiced. The gun had more recoil than he expected, kicking back in his hand. The noise of the shot was deafening.

He was so busy readying the next shot and trying to ignore the ringing in his ears that it took him a second or two to realize he'd hit his target. Simpson had fallen back against the wall beside Mac, his mouth a shocked O, hand gripping his shoulder. Blood gushed between his fingers. The white rugs would be ruined.

"Sky!" Mac yelled, but Sky barely heard him. He raised the weapon again, pointed the muzzle at Simpson, and crooked his right index finger.

Blood spurted crimson on the wall and floor as voices raised in screams. And when Sky tried to breathe and choked on hot fluid instead, he realized some of the blood—and maybe one of the screams—was his own.

He staggered, spun around, and saw the big man pointing a gun at him.

Two shots rang out almost simultaneously. One of them hit Sky in the thigh, sending him crashing to the floor. The Beretta fell from his hand and skittered out of reach. But the big man was down too, and he wasn't moving.

More yelling came from outside the room. Running footsteps. An enormous bang that didn't sound like a handgun. Shots. Mac screaming his name: "Sky! Sky! Sky!" like a song written just for him.

Sky tried to sing back, but he had no air. He tried to turn his head, so at least he could see Mac, but he couldn't move. He wished he wasn't wearing the slave bracelets—he'd have liked to die without them. That was all right, though. He was dying well enough.

CHAPTER SIXTEEN

He lived. That surprised him. Even more shocking, the hospital doctors and nurses treated him kindly, making sure he was as comfortable as possible. For an immeasurable time, he floated on a drug cocktail, too distanced from the world to care about it. He dreamed of his mother and Mac and the Paradiso, but the dreams were insubstantial, dissolving before he made any sense of them.

When a gentle man in purple scrubs finally removed the breathing tube, the first thing Sky croaked was "Mac?"

But nobody would tell him anything. When he became agitated and tried to disconnect himself from all the tubes and machines, the medical personnel drugged him into oblivion.

Later, when he was settling back into himself, he tried to laugh. These freemen were taking such care to put him back together just so other freemen could take him apart again.

A few days afterward he was staring blearily at something on TV when a woman entered his room. Instead of scrubs, she wore a dark suit with a pale blue blouse. She looked to be in her fifties, her graying hair cut in a sensible bob, her skin tanned and slightly leathery. She was tall and lean and moved with brisk authority, but she gave Sky a warm smile.

"Hi," she said. She scooted a chair closer to his bedside and sat. "I'm Trish Loomis." A hint of a southwestern drawl colored her voice.

"Mac's friend," Sky whispered. His throat hurt.

"His boss, actually. But sure, his friend too."

"Please! Is he . . . is he all right?"

She shrugged. "Not quite all right. The fool took a stray bullet in the chest, and from what the docs tell me, he wasn't in great shape even before he got himself shot. But he'll live. He's hooked up to even more gadgets than you, up on the fifth floor." She jerked her chin toward the ceiling. "And he's asking about you."

Sky shuddered so hard it hurt, but the pain was more than counteracted by sweet relief. Mac was alive. He was going to be fine. And he was safe.

With a small smile, Trish cocked her head at him. "When I realized Mac was getting goo-goo over you, I figured it was just your pretty face. Well, I'm allowed to be wrong once a year. Turns out you're a very interesting fellow."

"I don't understand." Plaintive, maybe, but he was done forever with *sir*, *ma'am*, *Master*, and *Mistress*. It wasn't as if a penalty for disrespect would add much to a murder charge.

"You're due a story. It'll be a while before Mac can tell it, so I guess I will." She shifted in her chair, making herself more comfortable, and looked around the room. "I hate hospitals. If we can send people into space, you'd think we'd know how to make a hospital room less dreary. At least Mac has flowers and balloons in his. I'm gonna steal some and bring them down here."

Sky blinked at her. "Balloons?"

"Yes. And let me tell you one thing first. If anyone starts asking what happened at Simpson's house—and I mean *anyone*—you just tell them Agent Webster has given a full statement already."

"Agent Webster?" Sky had a feeling that even without the drugs he'd have no idea what was going on.

"Special Agent Mackenzie Webster. And his statement agrees with what Agents Teague and Delancey said. Mac was being held captive, you were pleading for his release, and Teague, Delancey, and several other agents entered the premises. Teague shot Simpson twice with his agency-issued Beretta nine millimeter, Delancey shot one of Simpson's associates once with *his* Beretta. You and Mac got caught in the crossfire. Forensics says the bullet that hit your leg went through and through and hit Mac. Good thing it lost some momentum inside of you or it would have killed him."

Sky opened his mouth and closed it. When he opened it again, what came out was "But *I* shot—"

"Delancey and Teague shot the perps. Agent Webster was unarmed and in no condition to shoot anyone. And of course, slaves don't handle guns." She grinned.

As the import of what she was saying sunk in, Sky could only gape. He wasn't going to be blamed for shooting freemen. He wasn't going to be sent to the mines or worse. "Why?" he rasped.

She crossed her legs, leaned over a bit to peek through the doorway, and then shook her head. "Mac's a fool, but he's a good man. A good agent when he's not blinded by love. And if you hadn't acted, by now he'd be dead or sitting in chains on a ship bound for China. Instead, we've got one bad guy dead, a second one in pretty sad shape, and a whole lot of them eager to rat out Simpson if it means they get prison instead of slavery." She sighed. "Slavery would be more apt, though." She rummaged in her jacket pocket and pulled out a pack of cigarettes, then seemed to remember where she was. She scowled and tucked them away.

Sky tried to put together the puzzle. Mac was some kind of . . . policeman. Simpson was either dead or permanently out of commission. And Trish and her agency were willing to pretend that Sky had broken no rules.

"What's going to happen to me?" he asked.

"Not sure yet. You're a work in progress. But Mac has threatened to die on me if I don't move mountains, and I do hate to lose an agent."

She was about to say something more, but a nurse entered the room. She spent a few minutes fussing with Sky's tubes and machines, then filled a plastic pitcher from the tap in the bathroom. "Do you want some water, honey?" she asked him.

"Yes, please."

She poured a cupful and stuck in a straw. The head of his bed was already raised, so she simply held the straw in place for him as he sipped. He might have been able to manage it himself, but moving hurt. Besides, the doctor had warned him not to pull out the stitches in his back or jostle his twice-broken ribs.

The nurse beamed. "Very good. Jell-O soon. Later we'll work up to real foods." She set down the cup before fluffing his pillow. "And maybe a sponge bath." Ignoring his blush, she smiled at Trish and left the room.

"They're being so nice to me," Sky said.

"They'd better be. Bureau's paying a fortune to keep you here."

"I'm a slave."

She pried a bit of imaginary dirt from one of her unpainted fingernails, which were cut short and occasionally ragged. "Do you know the story of Hercules?"

"The myth?"

"Uh-huh. Roman. Although he was Greek first, but then weren't they all? He was a great hero."

Sky nodded. He'd heard a bit here and there over the years. Maybe he'd seen something on TV. "He killed the Hydra?"

"Among other things, yes. He engaged in twelve labors. But afterward he went crazy and killed a prince. To atone, he had to be a slave for a year. His mistress made him wear women's clothing and do women's work." She smiled. "I guess that was supposed to be extra punishment. But she eventually fell in love with him and set him free."

"That could happen in myths. Slaves being set free." Sky met her gaze without flinching.

"It could. But Hercules was a lot of things. Did slavery make him less of a hero?"

Sky closed his eyes. Just a few minutes of talking and he was exhausted. Or maybe it was Trish who exhausted him. She seemed to speak mostly in riddles. Sky preferred Mac's approach: just refuse to talk about things you can't say.

He opened his eyes. "I'm Hercules?"

"A hero. And you deserve to be treated respectfully. Tell me, Sky. Why did you do it?"

"I couldn't think of another way to rescue him."

"Why bother after what he put you through?"

A framed print of the Golden Gate Bridge hung on one wall. It was opposite the window and had faded a bit. Sky remembered Mac promising to walk over the bridge with him someday. They'd never gotten around to it.

"I couldn't have lived with myself if I'd just left him to die," Sky finally said. "I know going to Simpson's house was . . . I knew it wouldn't end well. But it was my choice."

Although he doubted his explanation made sense, she nodded as if she understood. Then she rose and walked to the window. From where Sky lay, he couldn't see anything but a large brick building. Maybe there was a better view if you stood closer.

"Simpson and his colleagues were engaged in illegal slave trade," she said without turning around. "They kidnapped free people here—young people mostly—slapped bracelets on their arms and stuck chips in their bodies, counterfeited their stud lines and database entries, and then bundled them overseas. Sold them to people who wanted extra spirit in their slaves. And the business went both ways, because Simpson had counterparts elsewhere who did the same. Largely in Europe. They sent those people here."

"That's terrible," said Sky, meaning it. All slavery was terrible, as far as he was concerned.

"Yes. People's sons and daughters and husbands and wives would just disappear. I can't imagine what it's like to be taken from your family like that, never to see them again." She turned to Sky. "Is it like breaking off a piece of yourself?"

He swallowed thickly. "Yes."

She nodded and moved briskly back to the chair, but didn't sit. "Once a slave leaves the country illegally, tracking is nearly impossible. All the people Simpson kidnapped are likely lost forever." She frowned. "Just as your mother is likely lost forever."

Nobody before Trish had ever made Sky feel so mentally unsteady. Yet she didn't frighten him, and for some reason he trusted her. "Like my mother," he whispered.

"I'm sorry, Sky. We tried. We'll *keep* trying. But she's pretty much fallen off the face of the Earth, and I'm not optimistic. We're fairly certain she was illegally exported."

"Why would you try to find her?"

"Because Mac asked me to. And when he bats those big brown eyes at me, I can't refuse."

Sky suspected Trish could refuse anything she wanted to, and he imagined she often did. "Thank you for looking," he said. He'd never held any hope of seeing his mother again, not since the day he was sold. But it was nice to know Mac had wanted to look.

His head still overflowed with questions. "What was Mac doing with Simpson?"

Trish sat back down and leaned forward. "We were pretty sure what Simpson was up to, but pretty sure isn't good enough to get someone convicted. We needed proof."

"We?"

She smiled, dug in a pocket for her wallet, and flipped it open. A gold-colored badge gleamed, and above that, a card containing Trish's photo and name, along with large blue letters: FBI. After waiting long enough for Sky to get a good look, she closed the wallet and tucked it away.

"He was pretending to be a drug dealer," Sky said.

"Yep. The idea was that Mac would become buddies with Simpson and make a deal to exchange coke for a fresh-off-the-boat illegal slave. Then we'd have enough to nail Simpson and shut down his business. But then there's the question: how to make friends? Well, we knew about Simpson's hobbies. So I picked Mac because I knew he's experienced in BDSM." She chuckled. "Mostly from the other end, I take it, but whatever floats your boat."

"And I was—"

"His golden ticket into Simpson's world. A handsome slave who's a little out of the ordinary. Unfortunately, you turned out to be *too* extraordinary, and Mac lost his head. Fucked up the mission. Almost got himself killed."

Sky was thankful that she was telling him so much, speaking to him as if he were a freeman. And it didn't bother him that he'd been used as bait—or a prop—since he'd long suspected that was the case. If he'd been instrumental in helping people avoid slavery, so much the better, but now he understood the difficult position Mac had been in. Maybe Mac had meant it when he said he was falling in love with Sky. Trish seemed to think so. But sweet heavens, where did that leave Sky? Especially now that the FBI didn't need him anymore.

Trish waited patiently, perhaps understanding his turmoil. She went for her cigarettes again, but this time stopped before they were completely out of her pocket. She took her lighter out instead and rubbed her thumb against the polished chrome.

"You said I saved him," Sky said finally. "But I didn't. I just got shot."

"Let me ask you something, Sky. When Simpson kidnapped Mac, what were your options?"

He remembered the sickening combination of fear, indecision, and urgency. "I could have run away."

She nodded and pocketed the lighter. "If you'd chosen that option, what would have happened to Mac?"

He shook his head; he didn't know.

"Well, I'll tell you. We had no idea Mac was meeting Simpson that day. The idiot should have told us, but he didn't. Too busy worrying about you, he says. We had no idea he was missing until he skipped the usual early evening check-in. That was over two hours after he was kidnapped. Teague went to the loft then, saw the broken glass, discovered you and Mac gone. He figured you were with him and used your chip to track you."

It hadn't occurred to Sky that anyone but Mac would be able to track him that way, but of course the FBI could. They owned him. Sky's head hurt. He cast a longing glance at the cup of water. Trish noticed and walked over to hold the cup as he drank. When it was empty, she remained at his bedside.

"If you'd done a runner, we'd have found you all right, but without Mac. And when we would have finally found out from you where Mac was, the wasted time would have made us too late."

Mac naked and chained in the hold of a ship, in pain, terrified. The half cup of water threatened to make a sudden reappearance, but with effort Sky managed to keep it down. "You tracked me to Simpson's instead."

"Yes. Teague and Delancey saw you waiting outside the front door and called for backup. The other agents arrived just in time to hear gunshots. And Mac wasn't mortally wounded, thanks to our perps being a little too busy bleeding at the time." Her grin was downright evil.

For a few moments, he thought about what she'd said. "I could have just stayed put in the closet like Mac told me to. Then when Teague showed up I could have told him what happened. You knew where Simpson lived, right?"

"Sure. And if that had happened, Mac probably wouldn't have ended up sailing for Asia. But one of two things would have happened. Our agents try to negotiate with Simpson, who's not about to cop a deal knowing he's heading for the mines, so Mac dies. Or our agents storm the castle, and since Simpson and his pet goon aren't preoccupied with you at the time, Mac dies. Maybe some of our agents too."

"I don't—"

"In any case, it doesn't matter. You walked all the way across the city—with cracked ribs—and voluntarily walked into the hands of a bad man. You did this knowing the outcome for you would be disastrous at best, but you did it anyway." She shrugged. "If that's not heroic, I don't know what is."

Although he was unconvinced, Sky decided to drop the issue. He was exhausted.

Trish poured more water from the pitcher and held the cup for him. She seemed to be practiced at it; he wondered if she had children. Maybe she used to care for them like this when they were ill.

"You look done in," she said when he was through drinking. "I'll let you get some rest. Mac should be well enough to come see you soon—or he'll bully the nurses into letting him come anyway."

Although Sky wasn't sure what he'd say to Mac, he badly wanted to go to him. Anything to help erase the image of the last time he'd seen him, bleeding and panicked. "He's really going to be all right?"

"More or less. Some scars. You'll have some too."

Sky didn't care about that. He'd almost welcome them as souvenirs of his little brush with freedom. "Did they die? The men I sh—"

"The man Delancey shot—the big fellow?—he was probably dead before he hit the ground. His brains made quite a splatter on one of Simpson's expensive rugs." She looked pleased about that.

Maybe Sky should have felt something about killing the man, but he didn't. No joy, but no sadness or regret or guilt either. "And Simpson?"

"Survived. Those kinds of men are like cockroaches. We rounded up his coconspirators, and they're happy to testify against him in exchange for a plea deal. And the good news, if you want to think of it like that, is once Simpson's trial is over, he'll be shipped to the mines. He'll probably even survive for a few months."

"Oh," said Sky, who couldn't take delight in anyone being sent to the mines. Not even Simpson. Sky wondered whether Simpson, as he labored away miserably, would think about the lives he had ruined and the pain he had caused. None of his suffering would help any of his victims. Trapped in the hell he'd made for them, they'd never even know his fate.

"How do you feel about Mac?" Trish asked, startling him with the non sequitur.

Rule one, he told himself. "I . . . I'm not sure."

"Understandable. He is a good man, though. You should know that. He blames himself for everything that happened to you. He always will."

Sky frowned. "I don't blame him." And that was true. In a way, Mac hadn't been much freer to make choices than Sky was.

"You might think about telling him that," she said. "I'll let you rest. I have paperwork to do. Lots and lots of paperwork."

He was asleep before she was out the door.

Sky had never been in a hospital before. They were strange places—odd smells, confusing noises, weird foods. People came into the room at unpredictable intervals and poked at him in various ways. They asked embarrassing questions and monitored the most intimate details of his bodily functions. The television seemed to magically receive only talk shows, ancient sitcoms, and children's programs.

After a few more days of recuperation, Sky was allowed out of bed as far as the bathroom, but only with a walker and close supervision. His leg throbbed constantly, his wounds itched, and he couldn't sleep well. At least the boredom lifted slightly when Trish stopped by again. It was a briefer visit, but she brought his iPad in a nice leather case, which would allow him to read and play games. She also brought a bright bouquet of sunflowers and purple statice, which made him grin.

Late one evening—after the mealtime bustle in the corridors had long since quieted but the nurse hadn't yet arrived to help Sky to the bathroom—the door slowly opened. Sky expected to see the sleepy-looking nurse who worked the night shift. Instead a wheelchair rolled in, pushed by a round woman in yellow scrubs. Mac was sitting in the chair, smiling tentatively.

He was dressed in a hospital johnny identical to Sky's, a blue hospital blanket over his legs, and brown slippers. His stubble had grown into a full-fledged beard, dark against pale skin, and without any gel or other product, his hair looked wild. All his fingers were splinted.

Mac looked over his shoulder at the nurse. "Give us a few minutes, will you?"

"Just a few," she replied sternly. "And don't you dare get out of that chair."

"Could you push me closer?"

She maneuvered Mac to the bedside and then walked away, her shoes squeaking on the vinyl floor. She closed the door as she left.

Mac and Sky stared at each other.

Finally, Mac sighed. "That was the stupidest thing I've ever seen. What the *hell*, Sky?"

Sky kept his gaze steadily on Mac's eyes and didn't answer.

"You know what I was thinking while I was hanging there, being tortured by those fuckers? *At least Sky's safe.* Then you come strolling in there like it was Starbucks and you wanted a half-caff latte. 'Let him go.' Did you really think Simpson was going to unchain me and just send us on our merry way?"

"No."

"Then why—" Mac stopped, scrunched up his eyes briefly, then shook his head. "I know you're not stupid. So why?"

"Nobody made me," said Sky. "I chose to."

Mac's silence seemed to stretch forever. "Freedom of choice, even if you know it'll get you screwed in the end. Okay."

And Sky smiled at him—just a little—because Mac understood.

Smiling back, Mac asked, "How long had you known about the gun?"

"A long time."

"And how'd you know how to use it?"

"The internet."

Mac started to laugh, but it must have hurt, because he winced and hunched his shoulders. "Ow. Dammit. God, Sky, how do you feel? Trish said you took a bullet in your lung and one in the leg."

"I'm getting better. It itches."

"Yeah. Mine too. Least you don't have to deal with these." He held up the splints. "I can't even take a piss by myself. I'm fucking useless." He sounded as if he was referring to more than his injured hands.

"I don't blame you," Sky said. "Not for anything."

For a moment, Mac worked his jaw. "You should."

"Would I be better off if you'd left me in that cage in the warehouse and bought someone else?"

"You wouldn't have been shot."

Sky shrugged, which hurt a little. "Maybe not. But I wouldn't have had a chance to . . . do all the good things either. And eventually something bad would have happened to me, maybe even worse than being shot. Something still might. Slaves don't get happy endings."

Mac's eyes glinted and he leaned in closer, even though doing so clearly caused him pain. "I promised you a good, safe outcome. I'm sure as hell not backing away from that now."

"But I don't belong to you, do I? I'm . . . what? Government property?"

Mac ducked his head. "Sky," he said miserably.

Although it made his chest and leg ache, Sky scooted on the bed a little so he could put a hand on Mac's blanket-covered knee. "I'm glad you're alive," Sky said quietly.

Then Mac raised his head, his eyes glistening. "Are they treating you well?"

"Like royalty."

"But you don't get any visitors."

"You. And Trish. Have you had any?"

"Trish," Mac replied. "Teague. A few other people from the Bureau. Some reporters tried to see me, but I'm going to let Trish handle that, I think."

Sky could feel the warmth of Mac's body even through the thick blanket. He remembered how good it had felt to press against that body in bed, how soothing he'd found Mac's quiet snores. And then he remembered the nightmares Mac had frequently suffered. "Are you sleeping okay?" Sky asked.

"Not really. Damn hospital. Now I dream about you. Someone's hurting you, and I can't stop them."

"I don't want to haunt you."

Mac looked away.

"What will you do now?" Sky asked, his hand still on Mac.

"Dunno. I'll be on medical leave for a while. Maybe I'll take some vacation time too. Got a bunch saved up. They'll need me to testify when the case hits court, but that might not be for a year or more." He looked down at Sky's hand, and with head still bowed, he said, "Sky?"

"Yes?"

"If I could pull a few strings—or get Trish to pull them for me—would you want to stay with me for a while? Given a choice, I mean."

Sky's heart made a funny little leap. Stupid heart. "I'd want that."

Mac gave him a wide, genuine smile. "Me too."

The door opened abruptly and the nurse in yellow came squeaking in. If she was surprised to see Sky touching Mac, she didn't show it. "Time's up," she said as if she were scolding a naughty child. "We don't want to overdo it."

"We're just talking," Mac complained.

"And that's enough for today."

With an enormous sigh—and another wince—Mac carefully placed his splinted hand atop Sky's. "I'll talk to Trish about those strings."

"All right. Sleep well, Mac. No bad dreams."

Long after Mac had been wheeled away, Sky remained awake in the room's dim light, feeling the weight of the bracelets on his wrists.

CHAPTER SEVENTEEN

If Sky had been released from the hospital first, he didn't know where he would have gone. But he developed an infection and then a fistula in his chest wound, and the doctors ended up dragging him back into surgery. That led to additional recovery time—even more uncomfortable than the first—and very limited visits from Mac, who had to wear a mask when he entered Sky's room. A bout of pneumonia stretched Sky's hospital stay to almost a month, and Mac ended up getting discharged first, his fingers still healing but now somewhat operational with the splints gone. During his brief times with Sky, Mac seemed agitated, but he wouldn't explain why. "Details," was all he would say.

At long last, Sky healed to the doctors' satisfaction. He felt weak, but it was mostly from spending so much time cooped up. Despite the slight limp that the doctors said might be permanent, he walked pretty well. He hoped to gradually work his way up to exercising again. He really missed running.

Mac came to pick him up from the hospital. He was in exceptionally high spirits, grinning from ear to ear and joking with the orderly who wheeled Sky to the waiting car. Sky was a little aggravated that the wheelchair was hospital policy.

This car wasn't a limo or even a town car. It was simply a taxi with advertisements on the side and a backseat that smelled like onions. Mac must have already given the driver his address, because as soon as they were seated and the back doors closed, the cab pulled away from the curb.

Sky made it up the stairs and down the hall to the apartment by himself. He was pleased with that. As he entered the apartment, he looked around. His books were shelved neatly not far from the couch, and a bouquet of fresh flowers sat in a vase on the breakfast bar. Something in the kitchen gave off the heady aroma of wine and spices and tomatoes.

Mac must have noticed him scenting the air. "It's a stew. Mostly premade, I'm afraid. The fingers aren't up to much chopping yet. But I added a couple things. I bet you're eager for some decent food after the hospital slop."

Actually, Sky hadn't minded the hospital food. It wasn't nearly as good as Mac's cooking, of course, but it was better than what he'd usually been given in the past. "Thank you," he said.

"I baked some bread too. Well, the machine did. And I got some really nice asparagus at the Ferry Building farmers' market." Mac paced restlessly, his hair already a mess from his nervous fingers. Sky didn't know why he was so keyed up, and he didn't ask.

It was a typical San Francisco afternoon, the fog settling on the city like a shawl on an old woman's shoulders, softening the light coming in through the windows. It would be a good evening to settle in with a book and a pot of tea, maybe with some jazz playing quietly on the stereo.

"Nicer than the hospital, huh?" Mac said. "The lease ends at the end of the month, though. I need to start looking for a new place. Probably not in the city; everything's out of my price range."

"You told me once you'd like a place with a little garden."

Mac smiled. "Yeah. But on the coast. Up in Mendocino maybe, or down south of Monterey."

"It would be nice to live near the ocean." Sky tried not to sound wistful, but he didn't know how long he'd get to stay with Mac, or what the FBI had planned for him next. Surely they'd sell him, but to whom? He shivered whenever he remembered that bleak warehouse.

Mac stopped pacing and walked close to him. "I want to show you something."

Obediently, Sky followed him across the large space to the far corner and into the playroom. All the equipment was gone, and the shelves and hooks were bare. Frowning in confusion, he turned to Mac.

"I had them take everything away," Mac said.

"Why?"

"Don't want to take it with me. Don't need it. Not that I'd mind you using some stuff on me again, but I'd want us to pick it out together."

Sky had a quick mental image of shopping with Mac at a store that sold whips, paddles, and chains—and the shocked looks of store employees when they realized it was the slave who was doing the choosing. "I might not mind that," he said.

Mac gave him a small smile, his mind clearly elsewhere. He ran a finger over a bare shelf as if testing for dust, then ran a hand through his hair. "I tried to buy you," he blurted.

"You did buy me."

"No, no. I mean from the Bureau. I tried even before the shit went down with Simpson. You're expensive. But I have some savings and a retirement account, and I was hoping I could work something out. I was bugging Trish about it."

As Mac spoke, Sky went very still. What if Mac *was* truly his master? Sky would be secure, he was confident of that. Mac would treat him well. Mac would love him. But Sky couldn't love a man who owned him. Or maybe he could, but he'd never know whether the feeling was honest. His heart couldn't be free if the rest of him was a slave.

"Did you buy me?" Sky asked carefully.

"No." Moving somewhat stiffly, Mac walked to one of the drawers and opened it. For a split second, Sky thought he was going to pull out a gun. Perhaps he was going to shoot the rogue slave as he might put down a rabid dog. But what Mac actually retrieved was a red-handled bolt cutter.

"Hold out your wrists," Mac said.

"Why?"

"Jesus you're stubborn. *Please* hold out your wrists."

With considerable trepidation, Sky did. Then he stopped breathing as Mac worked one blade of the cutter under the bracelet on Sky's right wrist. A quick movement of Mac's arms—accompanied by a grunt—and the bracelet fell to the floor with a jangle. It lay in a snaking heap, gold and silver glinting.

"M-Mac?"

Instead of answering, Mac cut off the other bracelet.

Sky looked around for the replacements, figuring the FBI would want the expensive ones back. He'd probably be back to stainless steel. If he was lucky. Some slaves just wore dull iron.

Mac placed the bolt cutter on a shelf, paused a moment, and turned back to Sky. "You're free," he said.

Sky laughed harshly. "That's not possible."

But Mac wasn't smiling. "Sometimes Trish can do the impossible."

"But—" Sky's legs felt weak, and he grabbed a shelf for support. He shook his head. "No. No, you can't—"

"Trish can. It took some effort, but she said she owed you one."

It was too much. Sky sank to the floor, feeling as if he were in a dream. His ears were ringing. Maybe it *was* a dream. A hallucination. Maybe he was dying on Simpson's floor or under the surgeon's knife.

Mac sat opposite him, knee to knee. "Your chip's gone. Trish had them dig it out when they operated on you the last time. She was pretty happy about it—said it saved you a surgery and the Bureau some expense. The doctors weren't real thrilled because it's illegal, but she said the government planned to put in a new experimental chip later, and it was all very hush-hush top secret." He gave a small grin. "Trish is a hell of a liar."

"No chip."

"Nope. You walk out that door right now, and you're free. No bracelets to mark you as a slave, no way to track you. But hang on." He rose, opened a different drawer, and returned with a thick padded envelope. After sitting again, he dumped the contents onto Sky's lap.

"Freedom's great, but it'll only get you so far. You need papers to officially exist as a freeman. Lucky thing the Bureau's really good at creating an identity."

"Identity," repeated Sky, surprised he could manage even that much.

"The wallet has a driver's license, social security card, a couple of credit cards. And those documents? Birth certificate, high school diploma, passport. Trish even got you an associate degree in, uh, communications, I think. You have a whole new life there, Sky.

And a new name because we figured some people might know who Sky Blue is. Was."

"Who am I?"

Mac gestured at the wallet, and Sky opened it. Sure enough, there was a California driver's license with his photo and the name Sky Walsh. Sky blinked a few times, but the license was still there. "Walsh?" he croaked.

"Um, yeah." Another raking with his fingers and Mac's hair was now a snarled mess. "That's another thing. And it wasn't my idea. She didn't even tell me about it until after she did it."

Sky couldn't keep up with all the shocks. He was numb. "Did what?"

"Did a DNA test on you—and then contacted Jonny Walsh. She . . . Shit, Sky. I'd be royally pissed at her if she hadn't come through so spectacularly on the rest of this. She says she kind of felt Walsh out, got a feel for how he might react. Did you know he donates to abolitionist groups?"

His throat too dry for words, Sky just shook his head.

"Well, the FBI knows," Mac said with a wry chuckle. "Anyway, after Trish talked to him, he had himself tested too. There's something like a ninety-nine point nine-nine percent chance he's your father."

That bit of information, at least, didn't surprise Sky. The physical resemblance was clear. He even sounded like Walsh, especially when he sang, which is why Sky had avoided performing any of Walsh's songs. "What did he say?" Sky asked, unsure whether he wanted to know.

"Well, he asked Trish to give you his name. Inside . . ." Mac stopped and cleared his throat. "Inside that wallet is an open-ended plane ticket to LA. He'd like you to consider visiting him. His phone number's in there too. And a check for two hundred grand, made out to you."

That was just too much. Sky stood, allowing the wallet and the folder full of papers to tumble to the floor. He stalked a few feet away and then back, meeting Mac, who was now standing. "Slaves can't be freed," Sky said firmly.

"As far as the law is concerned, a slave named Sky Blue died in San Francisco from the lingering effects of gunshot wounds.

And a free man named Sky Walsh was born thirty-two years ago in LA, got his degree in communications at a community college, and has a solid job history, mainly in restaurants. He has a good credit score and money in his social security account. He— Well, I can't remember the whole biography, but it's in with those papers."

"Trish can do this?" Sky wanted to believe, but it all seemed so unlikely, a fantasy spun from unicorn breath and fairy dust.

"FBI, remember? We're good at sneaky shit. She made up Morgan Wallace, drug dealer and sadist, right?" He settled his hands very gently on Sky's shoulders. "You're *free*, Sky. You have a whole world of choices now. And opportunities." Tears gathered in the corners of Mac's eyes and tracked down his cheeks, but he was smiling.

"I don't . . . I don't . . ." A world of choices and Sky couldn't even choose the right words. He impatiently dashed tears away with the heels of his hands.

"Stay with me. Please?" Mac implored. "At least for a little while. I know you hate me, but God, I love you. I haven't said that to anyone since Mom died. Stay with me until you get your bearings at least. You're not even completely healed yet."

Amid all the emotional turbulence, a layer of ice began to form over Sky's heart. "Why should I hate you?" he asked.

"What I let those people do to you. What I did to you myself."

"I understand why you did all that. You were in a hard spot. If I'd known why you were doing it, I might even have volunteered."

Mac shook his head angrily. "Volunteered to be raped and beaten?"

"I've been raped and beaten before. At least this time maybe some good came of it." The calculation of pain versus pleasure escaped him, but he was certain that a few days of misery on his part was more than balanced by lifetimes of freedom for the people Simpson would no longer be able to enslave.

"Maybe so," Mac said, stepping back and crossing his arms over his chest, his hands on his shoulders. Whether it was self-protection or self-comfort, Sky wasn't sure. "But I fucked up and got you shot. You almost died."

The coating of ice filled his chest until all Sky felt inside was rigid cold. "*I* got myself shot." He pounded his chest with his palm. "I did.

I picked up your gun, I walked across the city, I rang that doorbell and went inside Simpson's house. I shot those men. Slave or freeman, I'm not a helpless puppet who gets thrown into danger." He knew the next sentence was cruel, but he said it anyway. "I'm not your sister."

Mac's head jerked back as if he'd been struck. He worked his jaw silently, and for a terrible moment, Sky thought Mac's tears might bloom into open sobs. Sweet heavens, he couldn't face that.

Sky knelt, scooped up the wallet and documents, and stuffed them into the padded envelope. He was still wearing his shoes and jacket, so he didn't even pause as he made his way to the front door. Mac touched his arm just before Sky walked out.

"Please don't." Mac's eyes were pleading.

Sky just gritted his teeth and shook his head.

Mac's shoulders—usually so square and straight—slumped. "You have clothing here. Books. At least let me pack your things for you."

"No." Sky had two hundred thousand dollars. That would buy a lot of clothes and books. He needed to leave right now. But before he walked out the door, he tucked the envelope under his arm, took a half step closer, and cradled Mac's face. Sky kissed him, long and hard and deep, then broke away before the ice could melt.

This time Mac didn't try to stop him.

But as Sky walked down the long hallway, Mac called out. "Sky?"

Sky turned back. Mac looked terrible—messy hair, puffy bloodshot eyes, kiss-swollen lips, lines of grief etched deeply into his face. Sky wanted to tie him down and paddle him, help to leach out Mac's pain through his sweat, his tears, his come. He wanted to hold him and tell him everything would be all right. But Sky didn't move and didn't say anything.

Mac gave a tiny nod. "If you need anything—maybe just a friend?—I'll always be there for you. Trish's card is in that envelope, and she can tell you how to reach me. Anytime. Please."

"Thank you," Sky whispered, just loud enough for Mac to hear. "I don't hate you. I never have. Be safe, Mac."

With a watery smile, Mac nodded again. "Be happy, Sky."

Sky turned around and walked away.

He wandered the city for a time, the envelope clutched tightly in his hand. He had thought everything would look different now that he was free, but it didn't. Same shivering tourists, same gray water and chugging ferries, same buildings clinging to steep hills. Eventually his recent injuries caught up with him, and he realized he didn't have even a penny in cash. So he found a bank, presented his check and ID, and opened an account. The bank employees called him *sir* and *Mr. Walsh* and brought him tea, and were patient with him even though he had clearly never done this before. He wondered what they thought his story might be, what explanations they assumed for a man his age who was so unknowledgeable. He tried to push away despairing doubt that he'd ever fit in among freemen.

With most of his money safe in the bank and his wallet stuffed with cash and debit and credit cards, he went to the Apple store. He bought himself a phone, not because he planned to make or receive calls but because it was so portable and could be used to surf the internet and to read books. And because, he admitted to himself, freemen carried phones. At a nearby Walgreens, he purchased basic toiletries and a zippered bag to store them, and from the Old Navy store, jeans, a couple of shirts, and some underwear and socks. Looking to the future, he picked up a pair of sweatpants for when he started running again.

He checked into a nice hotel. He'd seen people go through this process—freemen who'd rented him for a night—and he managed tolerably well. The handsome clerk smiled and upgraded him to a corner room with tall curved windows and sleek modern furniture. Sky ordered a steak and baked potato from room service, ate it all, and then with his clothes still on, fell onto the bed and into a deep sleep.

He woke up with the morning sun streaming through the windows, then made his groggy way into the bathroom, where he peed for a long time. As he took a shower and the hot water sluiced over him, he mused over his own foolishness: his first day as a freeman, and he chose to sleep for nearly fifteen hours straight. But then he looked down at the fresh scars puckering his chest and leg, and he forgave himself. Everything about him was so new and raw.

He was ravenous, but choosing a restaurant was harder than he'd anticipated. He'd never done it before, and San Francisco had so many options. In the end, he wandered into a retro-style diner, where a tired-looking lady served him pancakes with sausage and home fries. He had peach pie for dessert—à la mode.

He walked around slowly for a while, eventually finding himself back at his favorite haunt, the Ferry Building. Although he had plenty of money to buy the tempting foods offered there, he was still full from breakfast, so instead he bought a novel from the bookstore. He sat on a bench outside, facing the bay and reading about an ex-con who became employed by a god. Sometimes he set the book down to watch the boats or to smile as the gulls squabbled over discarded bits of food. Sometimes he just sat and marveled at how light his bracelet-free wrists felt.

Sky had no plans, no idea of what to do with the rest of his life. He didn't know whether he would contact Jonny Walsh, either by phone or in person. He didn't know whether he would stay in San Francisco for a while or travel elsewhere. But then, he didn't need to decide right away. He had enough money to last a long time and no reason to rush. What had Mac said to him the previous day? A world of choices and opportunities lay before him. And nobody to control him but himself.

He watched as two men leaned back against the railing. One, short and tubby, had his arm around his partner's waist. The partner was also short but thinner, his sparse hair blowing in the breeze. He was holding a phone at arm's length, trying to get a photo of them as a couple, but they were laughing too hard to keep the phone steady.

Smiling, Sky approached them. "Would you like me to take your picture?"

"That'd be great," said the thinner one, handing over the phone. He and his partner posed for several shots.

"You guys look really happy," Sky said when he gave the phone back. "Are you on vacation?"

"It's our honeymoon," they replied, almost in unison. Then they laughed and, their joy infectious, Sky laughed too.

"Congratulations. I hope you have a long, happy life together."

He was still smiling after they walked away hand-in-hand. Sky sat back on the bench next to his book and took his phone out of the inside pocket of his jacket. After several minutes of staring at the blank screen, he reached for his wallet. It had accumulated quite a few items over the past day, so it took him a moment to find what he was looking for. But there it was: a white card emblazoned with an official-looking seal and, in large blue letters, Federal Bureau of Investigation. Underneath Trish's name and title and above a printed list of numbers, someone had scrawled the word "cell" followed by a phone number.

Sky ran his thumb over the screen of the phone, but didn't activate it.

"You should get a case for that thing."

Not startled, not even surprised, Sky looked up at Mac. "I haven't decided on one yet."

Mac nodded. "There are a lot of options." He gestured at the empty side of the bench. "May I?"

"Sure."

Mac's hair was tamed with gel, his carefully cultivated stubble just right. He was wearing a burgundy sweater under a new leather jacket, his old one ruined when Sky was shot. "I like that book," he said, pointing to the novel on Sky's other side. "I haven't read it in a long time, though."

"You can borrow it when I'm done."

"Yeah?" Mac's voice was suddenly hoarse.

"Did you track me here?"

"Can't. Chip's gone, remember?"

"Then how?"

"Give me some credit," Mac said with a small grin. "I *am* an FBI agent, after all. And I know how much you like this place, so I just . . . hoped."

Sky realized he'd been hoping too, but was so unused to the emotion he hadn't even recognized it. He smiled back. "A few minutes ago, I took some pictures of two men on their honeymoon."

"Yeah? That was nice of you."

"No big deal. I like taking pictures." He paused. "I bet I could take a photography class," he added thoughtfully.

"That's a good idea. I've always wondered about all that stuff with lenses and apertures and whatnot."

"You could take it with me."

Mac scooted a little closer on the bench. "I'd like that."

They were silent for several minutes. A ferry chugged to the pier, and a long line of people disembarked, then a new group walked on board. Sky had never been on a boat before. Maybe later in the day he'd take a ride to Sausalito. Or . . . He turned to Mac. "Do you have plans tomorrow?"

"Not yet."

"What if we walk across the Bay Bridge and take a ferry back?"

"But you're still not—" Mac shut his mouth with an audible pop.

"You were going to tell me I'm still not healed, weren't you?"

"Yeah."

It was Sky's turn to scoot a bit. Now their thighs touched. "But you stopped yourself," Sky pointed out.

"You're a grown man and smarter than I am. You can judge whether you're in good enough shape or not."

"I'm . . . not so sure." The words were difficult, but Sky said them anyway. "I'm not used to making decisions. I think it's like a muscle that needs exercising. I need to get into shape. And I can't . . . I don't know the shape of my own heart yet."

"I just recently learned mine, and I've been free all my life. Give it time."

That made sense. And Sky had all the time in the world now, didn't he? "I don't know what love feels like. I don't even know if I'm capable of it—"

"Not that slave gene bullshit!" Mac interrupted.

"No, not that. I just wonder whether someone who's never been loved can love someone else."

"But you *are* loved, remember?"

Sky thought about that. "You love me."

"I do."

"Even though I'm— I used to be a slave? And even though you know—"

"I love you, Sky. I want to rent a little bungalow by the ocean and cook for you, and I want to listen to you sing when you're happy. And when I'm feeling stressed I want you to chain me up and spank me, and when I'm *not* feeling stressed I want you to make love to me. I want to get in fights with you because we're both damned stubborn. I want to watch you continue finding out who you are because, man, you're going to discover you're fucking amazing."

A man untied the ferry from its moorings, and it pulled away from the dock. An elderly black slave pushed a broom around the plaza, sweeping up wrappers and cigarette butts. He looked content enough, whistling to himself as he collected the trash, but Sky knew that slaves were good at hiding their sorrow.

"What if I discover I want to join the abolition movement?" Sky asked Mac.

Mac thought a moment before answering. "That would be your decision. I might want to join too. But I'd worry about the consequences, especially for you. I'd probably share those worries with you." He crinkled his eyes. "That's what partners do, I think. Doesn't mean I'd be trying to control you."

Sky nodded, his choice almost made. It felt good to decide. "I can't promise you anything now, Mac. It's too soon. But I can tell you that I'd much rather be with you than without you." He grinned. "Rule one."

"You don't have to follow those rules anymore, remember?"

"I think they're good rules in general for two men in a relationship. As long as we both follow them."

Mac made a choked little noise that wasn't quite a sob, and he let his head fall onto Sky's shoulder. After tucking away the phone and Trish's card, Sky took hold of Mac's hand, entwining their fingers. And as they both gazed out at the shifting waters, Sky began to hum.

Explore more of the *Belonging 'Verse*:
riptidepublishing.com/titles/universe/belonging-verse

Dear Reader,

Thank you for reading Kim Fielding's *Staged*!

We know your time is precious and you have many, many entertainment options, so it means a lot that you've chosen to spend your time reading. We really hope you enjoyed it.

We'd be honored if you'd consider posting a review—good or bad—on sites like **Amazon, Barnes & Noble, Kobo, Goodreads, Twitter, Facebook, Tumblr,** and your blog or website. We'd also be honored if you told your friends and family about this book. Word of mouth is a book's lifeblood!

For more information on upcoming releases, author interviews, blog tours, contests, giveaways, and more, please sign up for our weekly, spam-free newsletter and visit us around the web:

Newsletter: tinyurl.com/RiptideSignup
Twitter: twitter.com/RiptideBooks
Facebook: facebook.com/RiptidePublishing
Goodreads: tinyurl.com/RiptideOnGoodreads
Tumblr: riptidepublishing.tumblr.com

Thank you so much for Reading the Rainbow!

AnglerFishPress.com

AN IMPRINT OF RIPTIDE PUBLISHING.

ACKNOWLEDGMENTS

After reading the first two books in the Belonging 'verse, *Anchored* and *Counterpunch*, I was visited by a great big plot bunny. That bunny was a blond, blue-eyed singer who once came in second on *My Slave's Got Talent*, and I couldn't shake him. I ended up emailing Rachel Haimowitz, who wrote *Anchored*, and asking her if I could attempt a novel in her universe. She very graciously agreed, for which I am thankful. And when the manuscript was complete, she also agreed to publish it. I am so happy that I got the opportunity to tell Sky's story, and that his story found a home.

I'd also like to thank the rest of the wonderful people at Riptide Publishing. They welcomed me enthusiastically from the beginning, making me feel right at home.

As always, I am indebted to Karen Witzke, whose editing skills are superlative yet still surpassed by her strengths as a friend.

I am appreciative of my husband and daughters for many things. When I escape the family home for a few days in San Francisco or elsewhere—in the name of research—they complain only a little bit.

Finally, I wish to thank my readers, who patiently follow me on journeys to all sorts of unexpected places—even when those places are dark. I hope even the scary parts are worth it in the end.

ALSO BY
KIM FIELDING

ABOUT
THE AUTHOR

Kim Fielding is the bestselling author of numerous m/m romance novels, novellas, and short stories. Like Kim herself, her work is eclectic, spanning genres such as contemporary, fantasy, paranormal, and historical. Her stories are set in alternate worlds, in fifteenth-century Bosnia, in modern-day Oregon. Her heroes are hipster architect werewolves, housekeepers, maimed giants, and conflicted graduate students. They're usually flawed, they often encounter terrible obstacles, but they always find love.

After having migrated back and forth across the western two-thirds of the United States, Kim calls the boring part of California home. She lives there with her husband, her two daughters, and her day job as a university professor, but escapes as often as possible via car, train, plane, or boat. This may explain why her characters often seem to be in transit as well. She dreams of traveling and writing full-time.

Website: kfieldingwrites.com

Enjoy more stories like
Staged
at RiptidePublishing.com!

Earn Bonus Bucks!

Earn 1 Bonus Buck for each dollar you spend. Find out how at RiptidePublishing.com/news/bonus-bucks.

Win Free Ebooks for a Year!

Pre-order coming soon titles directly through our site and you'll receive one entry into a drawing for a chance to win free books for a year! Get the details at RiptidePublishing.com/contests.

AN IMPRINT OF RIPTIDE PUBLISHING.